MAN UNDER
the
MOUNTAIN

MAN UNDER
the
MOUNTAIN

A WEST VIRGINIA HOMECOMING

LESLIE W. DALTON, JR.

Ordering Information:

For orders and inquiries, please contact:
1-888-404-1388
www.goldtouchpress.com
book.orders@goldtouchpress.com

Printed in the United States of America

DEDICATION

My "bride" of 70 years deserves far more than a simple acknowledgment given here. On our first date, and most after that, was to her favorite establishment—for a five cent Dairy Queen, that to this date, is still the only reward she wants.

CHAPTER ONE

Dᴀᴠɪᴅ Cᴀʙᴏᴛ, ᴀ ꜱᴜᴘᴇʀʙʟʏ qualified physician and surgeon, was discontentedly serving his time as a draftee in the Army Medical Corp. He and several other draftee doctors were responsible for still another set of draftees, the front-line soldiers. The assemblage of doctors, nurses, corpsmen, cooks, ambulance drivers, helicopter pilots and others were embraced in a new concept, a Military Advanced Surgical Hospital (MASH), in U.S. Army acronym lingo. In previous wars minimally trained fellow draftees were assigned the task of providing enough first aid—medic or corpsman—to get the wounded troops out of combat to a secondary patch-up facility and then, if they survived, to a hospital where treatment could finally begin.

The Korean Conflict[1] brought the MASH unit to the front lines so that the wounded could receive the finest

---

[1]   The Korean War, sometimes called the Korean Conflict, provides the beginning dialogue, and subsequent events, for this story. Over 40,000 Americans died in that "police action." It was not a "popular" war, the first of many including the current conflicts. Robert Taft, a popular senator from Ohio at that

immediate-care available and even provided the impetus for future trauma centers in hospitals. The presence of MASH facilities reduced the time lost in the initial delivery of superior medical care of the wounded by being next to the action.

Dr. Cabot was one of the MASH surgeons whose skilled hands had saved many who would not have survived the 1918 'War to end all wars' and the one that followed some 18 years later. How many of the 521,715 deaths in those two wars could have been saved by the existence of MASH? No one knows but such questions plagued Dr. Cabot and fed

---

time, epitomized the opinion that Korea was an unnecessary war begun by President Truman without the approval of the electorate. The same can be said for the Vietnam war and multiple other wars including the 1798-1800 Franco-American War, the 1801-1805; 1815 Barbary Wars, the war of 1812 against Great Britain, the 1836 War of Texas Independence and 1846-1848 Mexican-American, the 1861-1865 war between the States, the 1898 Spanish-American War, 1914-1918 World War I, 1939-1945 World War II, 1950-1953 the Korean War, 1960-1975 the Vietnam war and the 1961 Bay of Pigs failed invasion of Cuba orchestrated by the CIA, 1983 Grenada Intervention, 1989 Invasion of Panama, 1990-1991 Persian Gulf War; United States and Coalition Forces vs. Iraq, 1995-1996; Intervention in Bosnia and Herzegovina United States as part of NATO acted peacekeepers in former Yugoslavia, 2001 Invasion of Afghanistan; United States and Coalition Forces vs the Taliban regime in Afghanistan to fight terrorism and the 2003 Invasion of Iraq United States and Coalition Forces vs. Iraq still in progress. The sad fact is that of the 241 years since our War of Independence, less than 100 have been without some kind of military conflict, and only recently have the front-line troops not been, in part or completely, draftees.

his reluctance of being a party to another war. His angst at being in Korea was palpable; but his love for his profession, and his concerns for the many young men of many nations for whom he cared, was limitless. He was a physician with a heart.

Now the war was winding down. Daily rumors from the peace talks were rampant causing a constant state of anxiety. Finally, the end came: July 27, 1953. On the same day a miracle occurred. He received an unbelievable opportunistic letter from his father.

THE LETTER

July 15, 1953

My Dear David:

Your mother and I are thrilled with the prospects of your returning to a sensible use of your medical talents and training. That war in Korea has driven a wedge into the fabric of our country. Many of us were conservatively opposed to entering into another war at a time when we were just beginning the healing process from the greatest of all wars. We had thought when our boys returned from around the world in 1945 that we were through with war. Well, on to more cheerful news. In our last Correspondence, you stated that you were uncertain as to what you would like to do once you returned stateside. You could, of course, begin the slow process of building a practice of your own or joining me. There

> *is another opportunity that has presented itself to allow you to make up the three years spent in the army. A very dear friend and classmate of mine passed away last week. His death leaves behind a successful and satisfying solo practice that requires only a physician to continue. I understand that a very competent RN is holding the practice together until a replacement can be found. Stan was one year behind me at Harvard Medical. Our paths crossed several times as we rotated through the program. I assure you that you will find his practice in more than satisfactory array, reflective of a conscience, a physician who cares about his patients. While in Boston*

Capt. Cabot peeled the first page of the two pages contained in the envelope, slid the first page under the second, and continued to read:

> *he developed a very loyal and generous following where finances have never been a concern.*
>
> *I have checked with my lawyer and he will gladly look into the estate and arrange for a purchase if you are interested in taking over Stan's practice. Let me know your wishes.*
>
> *The weather here has been typical Boston with the feeling of fall in the air. I hope the weather there is a bit more tolerable now that you have moved out of those horrible MASH tents that*

you have called home for the past two years. We look forward to your arrival home and Godspeed.

Affectionately, Father

Two short pages presenting such an extraordinary opportunity! He would be a fool not to accept. He wasted no time over-thinking the possibilities and rushed to the Orderly Room to arrange for a telegram. It read: PLEASE PROCEED WITH PURCHASE OF MEDICAL PRACTICE RE DR. FIELDS BOSTON POST HASTE STOP I WILL HANDLE DETAILS UPON MY ARRIVAL HOME STOP.

CHAPTER TWO

BOSTON, MASSACHUSETTS TWO WEEKS earlier:

Dr. Alexander Cabot slowly eased the phone back in its cradle. He had just been informed of the death of his longtime friend and medical school classmate, Stanford Fields, MD. Both had received outstanding educations placing them at the top of the lists for jobs but while Alexander had chosen to stay in Boston to practice, his good friend yielded to an unbelievable offer via a headhunter representing a very wealthy West Virginia coal mine operator. Alexander sat at his cluttered desk in his rather small den and unconsciously fiddled with the papers on his desk. His hand fell on the last letter from his son, David. He picked up the letter and reread it. The letter had been written at a time when his son was feeling particularly sympathetic towards the downtrodden and weak and had written an exceptionally good essay on the plight of the underprivileged. Was it possible that David had developed a sense of unselfish compassion to go along with his top-notch medical training? The son's letters for the past year had included poignant narratives of the horror experienced by the civilians caught up in the Korean "police action" and how he was spending more and more time with them outside his military medical practice.

"Maybe, just maybe, my David is not really suited to a high pressure, big-city practice," thought the father. "Only one way to find out; I'll write him and submit the possibility to him."

So, he did.

Dr. Alexander Cabot pulled out an old, beat-up Remington typewriter and inserted a five-by-eight sheet of writing paper into the carriage. He began to type:

July 15, 1953

My Dear David:

> *Your mother and I are thrilled with the prospects of your returning to a sensible use of your medical talents and training. That war in Korea has driven a wedge into the fabric of our country. Many of us were conservatively opposed to entering into another war at a time when we were just beginning the healing process from the greatest of all wars. We had thought when our boys returned from around the world in 1945 that we were through with war. Well, on to more cheerful news. In our last correspondence you stated that you were uncertain as to what you would like to do once you returned stateside. You could, of course, begin the slow process of building a practice of your own or joining me. There is another opportunity that has presented itself to allow you to make up the three years spent in the army. A very dear friend and classmate of mine passed away last week. His*

> *death leaves behind a successful and satisfying solo practice that requires only a physician to continue. I understand that a very competent RN is holding the practice together until a replacement can be found. Stan was one year behind me at Harvard Medical. Our paths crossed several times as we rotated through the program. I assure you that you will find his practice in more than satisfactory array, reflective of a conscience, physician who cares for his patients. While in Boston*

Dr. Cabot rolled the first page out of the carriage, inserted a second identical half sheet into the carriage and continued to write:

> *Knob, West Virginia he has been quite content. He told me on several occasions, that he could not have made a better choice as to a place to really enjoy the practice of medicine. He told me that the mountain people there brought him into their families early on in his work and would have it no other way than to be certain of his welfare and comfort. They are mostly poor and uneducated people, principally supported by the coal mines, railroad or timber. He found their faith in God and Country to be refreshing. He also enjoyed their frankness in all matters as it pertained to logic. They believe the law is intended to fit only special roles and that certain rights are not fitted to the laws of Man if they are not covered in the Bible.*

> *Stan has been more than a physician; he had become the all-things advisor and expert for townsfolk of Boston Knob, West Virginia. He even obtained a notary license as an aid.*

Again Dr. Cabot reached the bottom of the page, rolled page two out of the typewriter, and placed it face down on the desk. He then inserted a third page into the old machine, and continued to peck away.

The phone rang.

Dr. Alexander Cabot promptly answered without delay as he always did. A voice on the phone announced that he had a home-bound patient in distress. Searching his desktop for something on which to write, he grabbed the second page of the letter to David that he had placed face down on his desk whereupon he jotted an address, folded it, placed it in his pocket and left the house hurriedly on his mission. That emergency managed, he returned home and his letter-writing with page two still in his pocket and page three—incomplete—in his typewriter. He continued to write:

> *He has developed a very loyal and generous following where finances have never been a concern.*
>
> *I have checked with my lawyer and he will gladly look into the estate and arrange for a purchase if you are interested in taking over Stan's practice. Let me know your wishes.*
>
> *The weather here has been typical Boston with the feeling of fall in the air. I hope the weather there is a bit more tolerable now that you have*

moved out of those horrible MASH tents that you have called home for the past two years.

We look forward to your arrival home and Godspeed.

Affectionately,
Father

The letter was complete. He pulled the third page from the typewriter and placed it on top of the first page that he had set aside before going to the hospital. He folded them, placed them in an envelope, sealed it, addressed it, and put it on top of a stack of other letters to be mailed. The second page was still in his coat pocket.

CHAPTER THREE

THE LINK BETWEEN DR. Alexander Cabot, his son Dr. David Cabot and Dr. Stanford Fields of Boston Knob, West Virginia, was that they were all graduated from Harvard University. Dr. David Cabot was very proud of this heritage to the point that he was sometimes a real pain-in-the-butt snob. His diction was exaggerated Ivy League that probably had become even more pronounced during his stint in the social poverty of the MASH unit in Korea.

Yet, under that classical veneer, was a sensitive man who would cry when faced with a medical problem beyond all possibility of a solution. At times he was lulled into the unreal belief that his Harvard degree granted him powers that defied failure. When failure did occur, as it surely must, he took the responsibility upon himself and did not fully consider that some things are out of the control of human skills. This trait had been sorely tested during the past months but the end was drawing near. Truce talks that began in July 1951 appeared to be finally coming to fruition but the fighting continued until July 27, 1953, when the negotiations at last bore fruit and the conflict ended in a cease-fire agreement. It was time for Dr. Cabot to go home.

The Mobile Army Surgical Hospital or 'MASH' in military abbreviation jargon, was awaiting orders regarding the redeployment of the personnel and facilities from their current location 'somewhere' in Korea close to the action that was ended as the result of the armistice just completed. The hospital portion of the MASH unit was gone. Only the quarters and dining facilities were still intact. Dr. Cabot and a Medical Service Officer (MSO) remained along with a skeleton crew of non-coms and enlisted support personnel. Dr. Cabot was bored beyond belief when a young sergeant approached him with a coffee pot in the mess tent.

"Could'je handle another cup of this battery acid?" he inquired.

"No thank you, Sergeant, but if you are as bored as I am I could do with a bit of congeniality," Doctor replied.

"Sure'nuf, Ahm at your disposal. What do you want to talk about? How about my love life? That's an excitin' topic. Or maybe I could regale you with my military exploits as an Army Food Specialist MOS 95 somethin' or other. My wooden spoon handle is fully notched as a result of the causalities in mah kitchen. By the way; Ah know your name. Mine is Tom Duggan."

Doctor laughingly responded, "I sense a bit of the 'Old South' in your diction there, am I correct?"

"Ah reckon ah'm only partly guilty since ah'm from Rocky Gap, Virginia. Ah consider myself southern without the 'Ol South' hang-ups on who is God's chosen. You see ah have been called a 'rebel' not because of where ahm from but for what I believe and practice. Ya' see I am a genu'wine conscientious objector and when I was drafted ah told'm to give me something to do that didn't require a gun. They did and here ah am."

Doctor Cabot was immediately taken to this young man for his forthrightness.

"You must have at least partially adhered to army regulations for most of your military time based on your rank. How long have you served?"

"Two years. Yeah, ah've been lucky, but you see, ahm kinda' sneaky, ah tend to my own business and ah don't hang out with people who I don't feel measure up to my standards."

"Your standards?"

"Yes sir, my standards. Take you for example. I know who you are. You are serious, honest, faithful to your profession, and if you don't mind my saying so, a bit of a snob. Now hold on before you bust me to a buck private for insubordination. I mean that in a good way. Aloofness is just one way of self-preservation in situations we find ourselves in a military hierarchy. The easy approach is to go with the flow and sometime to compromise our morals and skills. You, Sir, are a tower of responsibility and competence in your profession. I hear all of the tales about the shenanigans that go on here even in surgery and you never were a part of it although the rest of the officers called you a snob. I see it as restraint. Are we gonn'a be friends now? Can I tell you my deep dark secrets and know you will retain confidentially forever?"

Doctor Cabot laughed, extended his hand to Sargent and declared, "Yes, indeed, we are compatriots forever, or at least until we get out of this miserable place. You say you like to 'beat the system'. Entertain me with an example."

"Okay. Try this one. When I was in basic training the obstacle course was a plaything for me because what they were doing was what we did for play back home. Mah task then was to figure out a way to get around the whole stupid routine but still come out ahead. The course was laid out in a big 'U' with start and finish points about the length of a football field apart. The first time ah ran the whole thing ah discovered that the very beginning and end both crossed a creek. At the beginning was a rope swing over the creek. At the end was another rope stretched across the creek that we had to hand-walk across. We had to swing across the creek as the very first obstacle and most of the city boys would not drop off at the high end of the outward swing but would hold on too late and fall somewhere short and then climb up the bank and continue on. On mah second try ah intentionally dropped into the creek and walked along the stream until I came to the other crossover at the end. Every time I ran the obstacle course after that I would drop off short of the first bank, climb down to the creek bank and wait for the rest of the squad to hand-walk toward me on the rope where I would be waitin' for them. I though nobody had figured it out until the final day when an old-World War II veteran, serving out his last days before retirement, was waiting for me when I climbed up the bank. He offered me his hand and pulled me to my feet and declared, "Ah been'awatchin' you, boy an' all ah gotta'say is, if'n we'd had more boys lahk yew fah'n fer the south w'ed a'won that war."

Doctor expressed his appreciation at such ingenuity with laughter followed by a question. "An age-old rule of never volunteering must have caused you to 'be volunteered' many times, am I correct?"

"Non, j'ai toujours fait du bénévolat." Tom answered in passable French.

Doctor responded. "Ah, vous parlez Francais?"

"In your words, 'yes, indeed'. I had two ways of beatin' the system. First off, when I indicated my interest in cooking they gave me a direct appointment as an 'apprentice' cook and shipped me directly to Korea where I was assigned to a United Nations dining hall workin' for a French Chef. There I learned to cook and to speak French. Likewise, there I found out that the dislike for the French was so widespread that if I volunteered and spoke French I was ignored. Second, I always volunteered for the odd jobs or the ones that other GIs shunned. For example, early on when I had KP, I would offer to sharpen knives. Another job I would volunteer for, that nobody else wanted to do, was janitorial at Post Headquarters. Very few of the people at headquarters were regular army and they mostly ignored me if I seemed busy, so I would carry a broom and dustpan around all day in an air-conditioned building while all my 'equals' were scrubbing garbage cans or washing dishes. On top of that, if the officers had donuts they would offer some to me."

The sound of a helicopter approaching broke into their conversation. They both attended its approach with different interests: Tom curiosity, Doctor as a ride home. It landed and the whoop, whoop of its rotors slowly faded into silence. They could see the pilot going into the orderly room carrying what looked like mail. Shortly after, the pilot came into the mess tent, flung a haphazard salute in Capt. Cabot's direction and called out, "Garcon, some victuals, se vous whatever," as he approached Tom. He then turned to Capt. Cabot and said, "Ol' Tom here is my favorite army French chef. He can turn SOS into a truffle soufflé. Are you Cabot? You got a telegram in the mail pouch. Oh, by the way, get your gear together; I'm your ride home."

Capt. Cabot rushed to the orderly room where the clerk sat waiting with the telegram in his hand. He handed it over to the Capt. who anxiously ripped open the official envelope and began to read. As he read his face went from anxiety to incredulous to something like fear as he shouted, "Dear god in heaven above please tell me this is a mistake! Sargent, read this and tell me what it says!"

The young soldier took the telegram and read it. He then looked up and declared, "Capt., looks to me like the population of the Mountain State of West Virginia has just increased by one."

CHAPTER FOUR

THE FLIGHT FROM KOREA to the only airport near Boston Knob was Bluefield, West Virginia/ Virginia; long and tiring, but certainly not boring. The first leg of his trip was from the chaos, via helicopter, of the dismantling of his MASH hospital and the deployment of its patient-load and staff. The MASH helicopter was also carrying two seriously injured marines to a stateside medical evacuation center where David hoped to hitch a quick ride to his new home. He had little to offer the wounded pair since they were strapped in pods mounted on the skids of the helicopter while he sat next to the pilot. Nonetheless, he felt that he was paying his fare to the airbase where he would likely find a slot on one of the two large planes used for medical evacuation. As a doctor, he was welcome on any of the large air-ambulances since medical personnel were in short supply for transport duty.

While waiting at the MATS Operational Center in Tokyo, he had exhausted the reading material that he had quickly assembled while packing back at the MASH unit. Alternately pacing and squirming in an uncomfortable chair, he watched the clock crawl forward. He stood up and then again plopped into the chair, glanced over to a side table where the only reading matter was a journal with a picture of a C-47, just like the aircraft he had flown in from Seoul. He would read anything to stop the image of his new home from dominating his thoughts. He picked up the magazine and flipped through the pages. He came upon an article on the aircraft used in the MATS service and found it rather interesting. The first plane that caught his attention was the C-47 that was featured on the cover. It occurred to him that the second leg of his trip from Seoul to Tokyo was on a C-47. The interior of that C-47 had been configured for a medical evacuation flight. In this 'police action' and WW-2, C-47s served dual purposes on many missions. Supplies would be flown to a combat area and as soon as the aircraft was unloaded, litters would be installed to help evacuate the large number of wounded personnel on the return flight.

After what seemed like weeks, Capt. Cabot was assigned to accompany severely wounded troops being airlifted to Hawaii on a C-118A Liftmaster modified for aeromedical evacuation. The 29th DC-6 was ordered by the Air Force, adapted as the Presidential aircraft and designated the VC-118, and named it 'The Independence' after President Harry Truman's hometown, Independence, Missouri.

Dr. David Cabot had flown in from Cincinnati to Bluefield via Charleston on a Piedmont DC-3, which was the civilian version of the C-47 that had carried him from Seoul to Tokyo. This C-47, however, bore no resemblance to the military version. He was deeply ensconced in plush leather seats and served a Coke in the classic glass bottle. He couldn't resist looking at the bottom of the bottle to check its home place since all bottles at that time were glass and bore the city and state of its origination. This one was from Roswell, New Mexico. Too bad he had no one to go distance with; he would win for sure.[2] The airline seats, unlike the military canvas ones, reclined almost into a bed. He was not interested in reclining as his gaze flitted from sight to sight below. It was on as clear a day as he had ever seen.

The pilot announced the descent into Charleston and almost immediately the sun disappeared as the plane dug into a cloud of dirty haze. The senses were further assaulted by a smell strong enough to turn one's stomach. David's eyes began to burn.

He motioned to the steward and asked, "What is that filthy mess?"

The steward responded, "Don't worry about it. It's just Charleston."

---

[2]   When I was in the air force we would all gather around the Coca Cola machine at break time and compare the cities shown on the bottom of the bottles. 'Going Distance' was sort of a 'pool' whereby the farthest bottle would win the pool. At that time Coke bottles were not generic as they are today. Since all bottles were reused, they would often travel with the purchaser to be returned far from their original home.

19

The DC-3 plowed on through the nasty cloud and approached the runway. David watched for the ground below. When he could finally see it, he was frightened to see the side of a mountain rapidly rushing toward them. The thoughts of crashing churned in his head when suddenly, at the edge of the mountain, the plane smoothly glided onto the runway.

Charleston, West Virginia mountainous airport.

The only passenger deplaning at Charleston was a small wiry man carrying a violin case and a small suitcase. He held himself with unease and walked with a slight slump. He caught David's gaze his way and specifically greeted him with a friendly smile and said, "Hi, my name is Bob Byrd, and ah'm runnin' for the senate. Vote for me if you can." [3]

---

[3]   Robert Byrd, a member of the Democratic Party, served as a U.S. Representative from 1953 until 1959 and as a U.S. Senator from

David thought to himself; "Good luck, Little Fellow. If you are elected you won't last one term."

They were on the ground just minutes before the door was closed and the plane began to taxi towards the end of the runway. David saw that indeed the runway did end abruptly on the edge of the mountains. The plane accelerated down the runway and lifted off towards the south. Out the window to the east it became clear where the haze was coming from. Large smoke stacks were relentlessly spewing massive columns of unabated black smoke into the air. The plane continued to climb through the dense haze and suddenly broke into a brilliant clear blue sky.

David had experienced the worst smog that he had ever seen.

The airplane seemed to follow the valleys gaining altitude only to cross a ridge. The view below was a mass of color. It was early October and the colors were truly awe-inspiring. The pilot announced over the intercom, "They're saying that this is the best year ever for color." Yet, the color could not offset the unbelievable scarring that had been left behind by the process of "strip mining." One could see the

---

1959 to 2010. He was the longest-serving Senator in United States history. In addition, he was, at the time of his death, the longest-serving member in the history of the Congress. He became one of the Senate's most powerful members, serving as secretary of the Senate,

Democratic Caucus from 1967 to 1971 and—after defeating his longtime colleague, Ted Kennedy—as Senate Majority Whip from 1971 to 1977. Serving three different tenures as Chairman of the United States Senate Committee on Appropriations enabled Byrd to steer a great deal of federal money toward projects in West Virginia.

sorry remains of the lovely Appalachian Mountains where the tops had been pushed into the valleys in an endless scene of environmental murder. He would learn later that the 'correct' regional pronunciation of the regional mountain chain was 'ah-pu-**latch**-chun' NOT Ah-pu-**lay**-chun.

Strip mining destruction of lovely mountains.

The pilot on the flight from Charleston to Bluefield was as verbal as a tour guide. He kept a running discourse on the sights below. He pointed out the rudimentary beginnings of the West Virginia Turnpike that would run from Charleston to Princeton. He explained the large patch of black covering the side of one mountain and the smoke billowing from it. He opined that it was an 'eternal flame' honoring the mining industry's rape of the Mountain State. In reality, it was a slag heap, or debris, from mining that even a heavy snow would not extinguish.

Finally, the pilot announced the approach to the Mercer County Airport that had been built by pushing smaller hills into a valley, (similar to Charleston but with far lesser dramatic results), between them to make a single runway.

The DC-3 approached the airport from the northeast. One look to the south into Virginia revealed that those beautiful mountains had escaped the destruction done to their sister mountains to the north. "That," he thought "must be what West Virginia once looked like."

As the plane descended it followed the East River Mountains southwestward directly over the cities of Bluefield, West Virginia, and Virginia, then north again for a landing from the northwest. Small villages and farms, in the valleys and on the ridges, rushed past. One Irish green farm, with a large white silo and a herd of snow-white cattle lazing about, caught his eye and then was gone as the plane touched down on the runway.

CHAPTER FIVE

THE PLANE SLOWED AND turned towards the small brick terminal. David caught a glimpse of a well-dressed redhead standing at the gate so lovely that she practically took his breath away. His eyes remained fixed on her even after the plane had come to a complete stop and the door was opened for its single passenger to deplane. The steward stepped back to David and informed him that, "We are here, Capt."

Snapping out of his fog David looked again at the lovely redhead and said to himself, "Oh, what a heavenly body. Could that gorgeous vision be waiting for me? Improbable since I am not expected. Yet, I can dream."

Dr. Cabot stepped away from the plane and paused at the foot of the steps. He placed his military hat in its proper position and tried to brush away the wrinkles accumulated in his uniform before picking up his bag that an agent had placed next to him. Then he walked uncertainly toward the door that displayed a greeting sign that said 'Welcome to Bluefield, West Virginia, Nature's Air-Conditioned City'. The temperature in Bluefield seldom reached 90 degrees and when it did, the city served free lemonade.

As he meandered to the gate his 'dream' approached him with an extended gloved hand and simply declared, "You are

Dr. Cabot. Ah'm Jenny Lou Gullion. Folks around here caw'll me Jenn. Ah'm your welcomin' committee and also your office nurse if you want to continue the arrangement ah had with Dr. Fields. Are you hungry? Ah have an early supper ordered for us at Frankie's but ah can cancel that if you don't want to go. Do you like chicken cacciatore? Mama Ferranti makes the best in the world. You can even have wine with it if you join the club."

David hoped he did not look as confused as he felt. He was at a loss for words both from her introduction and her striking beauty.

He finally stammered, "O…O Oh, y…y… yes I will most certainly keep the arrangement" and, to himself, "thank you, heaven, for such an angel."

He stood silently in sort of a fog. Jenn said, "You with me?"

"Oh sorry," David almost shouted. "Supper would be nice. How did you know who I was?" Jenn retorted, "Well, ah don't know. Could be 'cause you're the only passenger gettin' off the plane in a uniform of the United States Army, or it could be my super observational powers. What a dumb question. Let's go," she snapped.

CHAPTER SIX

JENN DROVE THE CAR with graceful familiarity. He was to find out later that the Packard Clipper she was driving came with the new practice. Soon they were winding down the mountainside towards US highway 52 that would take Dr. Cabot to his new practice. The road flattened and straightened somewhat and he could see an attractive example of a new craze sweeping the nation. The Skyway Drive-In Theater sat in the juncture of the Airport Road and Route 52.

Jenn turned right onto 52 at the community of Brushfork. Route 52 was no better than the Airport Road. The concrete, poured in 1937, was showing signs of disrepair with broken pavement and unkempt, potholed, shoulders. The road was barely wide enough to be called two-lane and wound upward between two wooded mountains to the community of Bluewell where the road leveled out again. Along the road in Bluewell appeared a large, decrepit greenhouse, Lynn's Drive, In, and a hodge-podge of rinky-dink fruit stands with a wild abundance of fresh produce housed behind chicken wire. Centered between two of the markets was a boxy red brick building bearing an elegant sign reading "La Saluda Club."

Jenn guided the car off of the concrete pavement onto a gravel and dirt parking lot full of deep holes filled with water from a recent, or maybe not so recent, rain. She parked the car so that neither she nor Dr. Cabot would have to dismount into a puddle. Looking about, David saw that others had parked their cars at odd angles, also, so that no parking scheme, except avoidance of mud holes, was obvious. As David stood from the car he noticed that all of the other businesses had similar parking lots. Not a square inch of parking pavement was to be seen. Carefully weaving his way around the puddles towards the restaurant, David was reminded of the time in Korea when he watched the rescue of a small boy from a minefield.

Jenn led the way to the canopy bearing the name La Saluda Club to a door displaying a small sign informing the potential visitor that entry was reserved for 'members only'. To the right was another door through which anyone could get a beer and a hamburger at 'Frankie's Restaurant'. Dr. Cabot approached the door apprehensively. Jenn practically barked, "Well go on in! His spirits were enormously lifted and he practically shouted, "My heavens what a delightful place." The inside of Frankie's was taken up by a long counter that turned 90 degrees to extend most of the way to the south wall and took up all of the north wall. The south wall contained wooden booths. The space behind the counters was an array of coolers containing just about every beer label available. There were no signs of hard liquor. To the immediate right of the entry stood a magazine rack containing nothing but funny (comic) books.[4] Next to that were a single pinball machine and a large, very colorful, jukebox. A small tow-headed lad was perusing the funny

---

[4]   Reading material was practically non-existent in my early life. Delp School in Bluewell had no library. Books were not provided by the state but 'funny books' were plentiful and were

---

books and offered the new entrants no more than a quick glance. A very blond attractive woman stepped through a set of curtains from the kitchen, smiling broadly.

"Hey, Jenn" exclaimed Mary, Frank's sister. "Where you been? Who's your friend? I bet he's the new doctor, right? Frankie, come out and meet'a the new doctor. He look'a like he a good one. Sit down, Doctor. You, too, Jenn. Are you hungry? We got'a your supper ready just'a like you say."

From a curtained door behind the counter, a very small smiling man emerged.

"Hey, Jenn", he likewise shouted in a thick Italian accent. "I see you drive'a the Packard; you do'a somethin' special? Why you have'a the big car?"

"She has the new doctor with her," Mary explained, "and they're hungry. You ready to eat?" Mary asked again.

Frank excitedly proclaimed, "You will like Mama's cookin'. You like somethin' to drink Doc?" Frank asked.

"I would love a brandy—a good brandy," David blurted out, "but all I see is beer."

With an exaggerated gesture, Frank smugly commanded, "Follow me," which David did. Frank led them through the curtains behind the counter into a very large room taken

---

a source of barter. Frankie's had the only rack of funny books in the area and they were always up to date.

Frankie was to provide another valuable service to me during World War 2. I suffered frequent attacks of asthma and was undernourished to the extent that I developed rickets. The treating doctor suggested no treatment but did suggest that to provide nourishment during an actual attack, when keeping food down was a problem, that I be given 7-up. Mama took this as being specific. Sugary drinks were hard to get then. Frankie came to the rescue by giving me his entire allotment of 7-up.

up mostly by a hardwood dance floor surrounded by tables with white linen covers, mounded napkins, and properly placed dinner-ware.

"In here is the La Saluda Club," Frankie said. "In here I give you brandy after you sign your membership card."

David was later to learn that West Virginia, along with most Southern States, was 'dry' and that only 3.2 beer was available outside State-run ABC stores. He was also to learn that this restriction on alcohol contributed to the colorful moonshinin' business throughout the Virginia's, Kentucky, North Carolina, and other states with restricted liquor sales.

Frank dug into a drawer behind a matre de pedestal and came out with a printed card declaring the holder to be a member of a private club. He then disappeared through the curtains and soon reappeared with a bottle held high in one hand and stemmed brandy snifters in the other. The bottle in Frankie's left hand bore a label with a large 84 centered below the word STOCK.

David conjured up an image of pure rotgut that an Italian-West Virginia-hillbilly would likely call brandy. He steeled his stomach to receive a liquid somewhat akin to kerosene but was pleasantly surprised to experience the most delightful warmth of delicious and most excellent liquor.

"My," exclaimed David. "I do believe this fine nectar to be among the best I have ever tasted. Surely, it's French. Let me see the label."

David's surprise grew, even more, when he saw that the brandy was of Italian vintage bottled in 1932 in Trieste.

"I am being served a 26-year-old brandy in a backwoods café in West Virginia," David marveled to himself. "Not only that, it's good brandy!"

Frank asked: "You like it? It was made by my family friends, the Stocks. The old man, Lionello Stock, was my father's friend, and made the best wines in Italy until The War. This bottle is from a shipment of 12 cases sent to me when I opened my restaurant here."

"Mr. Ferranti," David said. "You have now won yourself a new member of the La Saluda Club. Place my name on a case of that fine brandy, and I shall be a regular." They followed Frank to a table where they sat and sipped the brandy.

Dr. Cabot, still a bit unsure of himself, finally said, "Well, I must say, this is a most pleasant surprise. White table cloths and napkins, real silverware and cut-class water pitcher. The lighting is perfect for a dinner for two."

Jenn responded vehemently, "Don't get any ideas, soldier. It's this or Lynn's Drive-in and I really don't like eating in a car parked beside a carload of teenagers." David, somewhat nonplused spoke more sharply than he intended, replied, "Forgive me, dear lady. I was just making a comment on the ambiance. No intentions implied. Do I sense a bit of hostility?"

Jenn retorted tearfully. "Now that you mention it, yes. You big city snobs think you can buy anything and anybody. You don't know anything about us and yet you move in here with your money and fancy college degrees takin' the place of sweet and kind Dr. Fields. You can't replace him. Nobody can replace him."

Doctor stared at her with stunned silence. He was at a total loss for words or actions.

"Well, don't just sit there and look at me with that dumb look. I meant what ah said. You bought this set-up at an auction and won. You were then, as now, ignorant as a newborn baby as to what you have here. You bought me like a cow!"

"Wait just a dam… confound minute," David practically shouted. "In reality, as it happens, I did not buy anything, most particularity you. My father and Dr. Fields were classmates and very good friends over the years. Dr. Fields, according to Father, had confided in him that if I was available upon completion of medical school he would like for me to join him in practice. This led father to write me about this, ah…set-up, suggesting that I might consider it. I made a commitment and I will honor it. I have no intention of forcing you or anyone else to continue with me. You are free to leave but I must say, I would be a first-class fool to let you go. Selfishly speaking, what would I do? I have never had a sole practice in my entire life; I am among strange…. unique people, that will probably be more skittish of me than you appear to be. Lord knows, I am petrified of this transition. I am more frightened of being here that I ever was in Korea. A little tolerance would be welcome!"

Jenn, sobbing almost uncontrollably, responded, "A'hm sorry. Ah've been a real bitch. Oh, ah shouldn't use that word but it's true."

David moved to her side to console her. She made no effort to move away from him. He quietly appealed to her, "Forgive me if I appear insensitive. It's not my intention. You have lost a dear friend and you fear for your future. Please give me the opportunity to show you that I am a sensitive physician…person… in spite of perceived social baggage that I may carry. I, too, am still grieving. I spent two years trying to prove my worth as a surgeon in a military advanced army hospital but I failed miserably. We went from battle to battle, trying to pick up the pieces of broken humanity but we all failed. I failed, in spite of my fancy degrees and schools. I don't want to fail here. I need you." Jenn leaned into David and wept uncontrollably.

CHAPTER SEVEN

THE MOUNTAIN RIDE FROM Bluefield down to the coalfields was both magnificent and ugly. The community of Bluewell was on level road with very little wooded area but that changed with an upward slope into progressively higher hills and deeper valleys. The road traversed the mountainsides first to the left and then to the right. To the left side of the car, one could view the colors of the treetops and to the right, looking upward, to the trunks. Occasionally, the near trees gave way to reveal the glory of the rugged color-covered mountains.

Around one bend an apparition of stone filled the whole of the view over the left fender of the car.

"My Heavens," exclaimed David. "What is that magnificent formation?"

"That's Pinnacle Rock," responded Jenn.

"Pull over, if you don't mind," asked David. "I would really like a closer look."

The parking lot would probably hold 200 cars but theirs was the only one there. The lot was delineated from the footpaths by endurable stonewalls punctuated here and there by stone steps and walkways. The main walkway led upward to an impressive stone building with arched openings. Inside were modern toilet facilities and large wooden tables and benches. A rear deck of stone looked out over the valleys and mountains to the south. To the east of the building loomed the namesake of the park.

Jenn launched into a travel log description of the park with a note of pride in her voice. "Just over the hill yonder is what's left of the Town of Bramwell built by the rich outsiders who own the coal mines. They would'nt dare stoop to live among the po' white trash miners. It has been said that Bramwell has had the highest ratio of millionaires over the years than any other city in the country. The park was built by the WPA, you rich folks probably don't know what that was, back in the depression. Ah'm told that there is a lake over the hill yonder with good fishin' if you care about things like that."

CHAPTER EIGHT

Boston Knob, West Virginia consisted of a row of mostly two-story buildings lining one side of Route 52. On the other side of the highway, two train tracks and a coal-blackened river ran parallel to the town and road. The town, the tracks, and the river were in a deep valley created by rugged mountains on both sides so tall and steep that it was doubtful to Dr. Cabot that the sun showed its presence more than a short time around noon each day.

Other roads likewise followed valleys, known locally as 'hollers', and creeks as they headed into the hills from the main road. As the Packard had carried him along the highway Dr. Cabot had noticed huge structures mounted high upon the mountains with long covered chutes descending downward to a large building sitting over multiple train tracks. Jenn told him that they were tipples where slate was handpicked from the coal and then washed and sized before being loaded on long strings of rail cars that would carry the "black gold" to markets around the world. Men standing beside conveyer belts spent their days sorting through the coal. Theirs's was the better job. Beneath them, in the deep pits, other men blasted the coal or loaded it onto the special trains to be hauled to the shafts or drift mouth.

Others set timbers to hold up the roof that followed the route of the coal seam.

"This one has been here for a long time and there's over a hundred men workin' in that miserable heap," volunteered Jenn.

A coal Tipple where coal is processed directly
from the mine for shipment.

Jenn guided the Packard smoothly along the narrow street in the evening shade of the buildings when suddenly she swept the car into a side street and then again onto an incline parallel to the main drag just abandoned. On one side of the inclining street stood substantial houses with steep steps leading to large porches; on the other side of the street were similar houses but with porches on level with the street some with catwalks bridging the gap between the house and street. There were no sidewalks.

"I must say," mused David aloud. "These are not poor-folk homes."

"Spoken like a true snob," retorted Jenn. "Not everybody here is poor white trash."

Dr. Cabot was abashed. "Well, I am certain that every community must have its professional element, and I find it revolting that you refer to your poor as trash."

To which Jenn replied, "Why don't you just shut up so as not to dig yourself deeper down?"

Eventually, the street leveled somewhat as the car approached a cove grudgingly given up by the dominating hills. The road curved into the cove through a pair of native stone columns. A narrow cobble-stone drive led to a massive stone and beam house, nestled within a forest of giant trees. The architecture closely followed the Tudor style brought over by the British during the colonel days. This was not the humble abode David was expecting. It was short of a mansion but not much. Unlike the mansions of his upbringing, this one stood out by the amount of natural beauty gracing the grounds and the organic nature of the architecture that caused the house to be a part of the surrounding environment.

It was difficult for Dr. Cabot to remain calm as the enormity of his 'inheritance' became apparent. He unintentionally gushed as he inquired of Jenn.

"What is the history of this magnificent edifice," he asked almost in a whisper.

Jenn responded indifferently. "Been here since the beginning of Dr. Field's practice. This area didn't have a doctor and couldn't get one so old man Jenkins who was as rich as Solomon, makin' his money from coal, sent a team of Pinkerton men up north to find the best doctor they could find. Part of the offerin' for a doctor to come here was a house, land, and a complete medical set-up with protected money set aside in a trust to keep the clinic up-to-date for ten years. Whoever took the deal had to stay for ten years and then the whole shebang would be his plumb free. On top of that, at the end of the ten years if the doctor stayed, was another trust fund that pretty much supported the clinic for about a hundred years, according to the First National Bank that held the trust. Jenkins owned all of the land around here including the place where a civil war house burnt down. He hired an architect to design a cottage to fit on the foundation of the old house and that's what you see here. Jenkins lost everything in the Great Depression, but this house was protected because it was in a trust. You like it so far? Wait n'til you see the inside cause you haven't seen anything yet."

CHAPTER NINE

T HE FRONT DOOR OF the house banged open and rushing towards him was a slender man with a head topped with the brightest red hair that David had ever seen. He was an attractive youngster with freckles to match the hair. His smile was as bright as his hair and freckles.

"Howdy. You Doc Cabot?" he gushed.

"I am. And who might you be?" responded David.

"Ah'm Jim Corborn; I wuz Doc Field's all 'roun handy man. Ah us't to work at Woodlawn[5] diggin' graves but Doc

---

[5] Woodlawn Cemetery was an anomaly in Bluewell. We had two very large cemeteries one for Whites and one for Blacks. Both were extraordinarily "plush" and well-kept and both served as local playgrounds. Both had paved roads meandering up and down the hillsides making them ideal for bike riding. Woodlawn had a very large three-foot-deep reflection pool that was suitable for swimming albeit not allowed. The Black Cemetery, on the other hand, had no such arrangement with us. Our favorite game there was night-time hiddy-go-seek. One of the challenges –or fears–was not to step on graves. Once, while running to hide, I stepped on a month-old grave where the earth under the sod had settled leaving the sod as an unsupported

Fields said ah wuz too smart for that and give me a job with 'im. Hits a good job and I git a place to live and all ah kin eat. Never had to worry none 'bout gittin' sick neither. Ah do ever'thang from fixin' tars on his car to makin' sure nobody needs nothin' ever'whar else. I guess ah work for you now that he's dead'n gone."

"Woodlawn. You mentioned Woodlawn. What is that?" queried the Doctor.

"Hit's a cem'tary. A rel'tive of mine runs hit. Hit has paved roads a'goin all through hit and all the kids ride thar bikes in thar. Theys a great big reflection pool that we ain't supos'ta swim in but we do anyhow."

Doctor Cabot was to learn later that Jim epitomized a real family of men who made up an important portion of the non-mine labor force in the area. The dialect,[6] indigenous of much of the white population of southern West Virginia at that time, was nearly impossible to understand.

"And why would you assume that I will need your services, my good man?" David inquired.

"Only natchrul" said Jim. "No one else'll do it less'n you plan to do hit chur'self. Course you could git one of

---

dome. I stepped on the dome and my weight drove me up to my knees into the grave. I froze there with one foot, literally, in the grave as scared as I have ever been in my life. I couldn't yell or even whisper, I couldn't move; I was sure the devil had me by the foot and that I was on my way to hell.

[6]   Southern American English as a regional dialect can be divided into various sub-dialects, the most phonologically advanced (i.e., the most innovative) one being southern Appalachian English. Here I use Ah to represent the southern pronouncement of the long "I" /ɑː/ instead of the general American diphthong /æ/. (See Wikipedia for a detailed discussion on this topic.)

them laid off coal miners that don't know how to do nothin' less'en hits minin' coal. Anyhow, most'uv'em air near dead from the black lung and tabac'ie. An 'sides that, they all want union pay. Come on in and met th' rest'a'Th folks. Annie Colburn was Dr. Field'es housekeeper an' cook. She'll take gud ker of yew if'n yew decide to keep'er on. She makes the best chickin' un dump'lins yew ever tasted. Her bis'kits beat any yew ever had. She's kinda' bossie but Dr. Fields put up with'er causin' she don' need no bossin'. She jes knows what needs adoin' and she does hit gud. Twix the two of'us yew don't be need'n to worry 'bout any'thang aron' cus we git to'hit a'fore you even know hit needs uh'doin'."

David scratched his head in puzzlement as he wondered what Jim had said. "I believe he is telling me I have another employee that comes with my new practice" he thought to himself.

"Well, Mr. Colburn, is it? Why don't we take a tour of the kitchen and meet this culinary genius that you hold in such great esteem" David responded.

"Wh'cha say?" Jim asked.

"Let's go meet Annie," David simplified.

"Sure. Yew'll l'ahker."

Jim led the way into a large foyer that provided access to the rest of the house through massive beamed doorways. Most every opening was supported by post and beam construction whether needed or not. To the right was a massive great room with a double balcony, part serving as a massive library, taking up one whole wall. The side walls were probably 12 feet high and supported by scissor trusses reaching heights of 24 feet or more. The trusses were constructed of hand-hewn timbers joined together with cast iron connector plates about one-quarter inch thick, and secured with bolts. Wood was the only material visible in the room.

"Wh'cha look'n at is uh'house of nothi' but wood that come off'un this place rit'cher" volunteered Jim. "They h'ain't narry a piece'a store bought wall coverin' in the whole dang house. Th' floors air all oak an' the walls air either walnut or heart pine panel'un. The ceil'uns air three anch pine, an all the post un' beams air oak. They's even'down some cherry wood mixed in."

Jim continued to narrate the tour as they walked to the end of the foyer to a large sunroom that seemed to serve as a central point. Above the windows directly in front of him was a long balcony/sitting room ending at a door and the other to the head of the steps leading from a point near to where he was standing. A wide hall ran parallel to the steps and led to what appeared to be an eat-in kitchen and joined by a large dining room.

A turn to the left in the sunroom led to three closed doors of lesser proportions than all of the other construction.

David inquired. "Where do those doors go?"

"One goes to the clinic and the other two go to suites, one on this floor and the other upstairs," interjected Jenn. "The clinic is attached to the house but has separate entrances for patients, deliveries and such. Nobody comes through here to the clinic except those of us people who belong in the house."

"Hum?" thought Doctor. "What does 'except those of us people who belong in the house' mean or imply?"

CHAPTER TEN

A VOICE CALLED OUT. "ANYBODY home?"

Jenn excitedly said. "That's my brother, Bill. Wonder what he's doin" here? We're in here. Back in the sunroom; come on back," she called out.

Bill bounded down the hall and engulfed his 'little sister', who had followed him into the world by about ten minutes, in a bear hug. He always had declared that she was the slow one in the family.

"Hey, skinny, how you doin'? Busy bossin' our new doctor around? He inquired.

David retorted. "Call it bossing if you like, but I think I am in for a treat having her as a boss."

"Well now, Sis, you have done gone and pulled the wool over the doctor's eyes. You don't fool me none. It's your beauty that has caught the doctor's attention."

David turned every color of red in the rainbow and sputtered, "Her merits have nothing to do with looks. I mean…. she…." he wisely broke into silence.

Bill laughed heartily and hugged both David and Jenn with an arm around each and declared. "That's okay. I love her and so will you one day."

David hastened to change the subject by asking, "William, I recall in an earlier conversation with someone that you have had architectural training. Perhaps you can recall the style of this house?"

Bill smiled broadly as he welcomed the opportunity to display his educational prowess. "This house is an excellent example of Tudor revival architecture although I don't think the architect knew that when he designed it. The design was mainly to take advantage of locally available building materials. I'm sure you have noticed the wide range of woods used. They all came off the place. Historically this is a unique house sometimes called 'Free English Renaissance' loosely modeled after the more domestic styles which were cozier and quainter. It was associated with the Arts and Crafts Movement. I know the architect by the way. It was Mr. R.A. Sheaffe of Bluefield who was actually the first local to practice architect in the area. He designed the 'Oaks" for a judge, one of the first very fine houses built on Oakhurst Avenue in Bluefield. It is claimed that it is the largest Four-Square house in West Virginia, 8,000 square feet. A doctor later acquired the house."

"My word," said David. "Your explanation reminds me of a young corpsman in Korea who asked me a question that I was reluctant to answer for fear that I would misdirect him. I told him to go asked the commanding officer who was known as somewhat of a 'know-it-all'. He looked at me sincerely and replied, "I don't want to know that much about it."

The tour moved on to the kitchen accessible by an extension of the sunroom that opened into another magnificent, wood-paneled, high-ceilinged room very similar to the parlor. A large table sat in a space that was obviously a dining area surrounded by a hodge-podge of chairs ranging from Windsor, early American to even wooden barrels. The tabletop was made from a single piece of maple with matching pedestals. All cabinetry was a mixture of walnut and maple.

They entered the kitchen to the halloos of a woman who could be thirty or sixty.[7] She wore a flowery dress down to her ankles. Over that was an apron large enough to serve as a surgical gown. Her broad smile revealed a healthy set of teeth of which spoke to her self-image.

"Come on in. Ah'm uh, bakin' bread for tomair'e. Since nobody much'es been roun' I ain't been doin' no bakin'. Fresh hot coffee's on th' stove. Hep yer'self. Cream's in the ah'ce box an' sugar's on th' table oar thar. Now do'n you warry none cause ah'll take good keer of yew jus' lah'k ah done for poor ol' Doc Fields a'for he up and died. Wha'ca lahke to eat? I kin fix al'mos anythang if'n you jes tell me what it is yo're awantin'."

---

[7] Annie was created as a split persona one being my Mother, the other an archetypical hillbilly woman. Mama never slowed down and was a source of community energy that was always doing something for someone. She has been gone now since 1997 and it's probably a good thing for me because if she saw me describing her as toothless and talking hillbilly I would get the first spankings of my life! She was full of metaphoric expressions such as "Never be seen on a galloping horse, Hollow in the butt cleaning and too much sugar for a cent." She had one for every occasion. Mama was a nut for ridding the house of trash. When I entered the Air Force in 1952, I hid a collection of phonograph records and comic books as far back in the attic as I could at a ceiling Hight of less than one foot. On returning home for a visit I found the items gone. Upon inquiring as to their whereabouts, she informed me she thought they were just trash and that she had thrown them out.

David had an instant fondness for this unassuming woman. He decided right then and there that she was to be a continued member of his extended family. In the meantime, Jenn had poured coffee in cups with saucers that David recognized as Havilland's Amaryllis that he had seen at homes of Boston Old Money. This was not Montgomery Ward merchandise. He gingerly took the cup and saucer from Jenn.

"Well, take it," she snapped. "And, don't get used to bein' served coffee by me. It's not a part of my job description. Annie keeps a fresh pot going most of the time and you can help yourself."

Annie piped up. "Now Jenn, that ain' no way to be a'talkin' to the doctor. Now you tell him yer sorry an' git him a piece of that chock'lt cake out'n the ah'ce box."

Strangely Jenn did as she was told almost meekly. Could it be that Annie ruled more than the kitchen around the house?

CHAPTER ELEVEN

THE VERY FIRST THING that David decided he needed to do was to parse the dialect.[8] He had never in his life experienced such mangled usage of the King's English, but yet, marveled at its rhythmic beauty. While he found the language harsh to the ear he also found it full of basic color. In trying to find an algorithm, he decided that comparing the dialect to a painting worked best. If the dialect were a painting the artist would have been Monet. The dialectical painting was full of overlapping strokes and voids requiring the eye to fill in the details. The colors were not true to the actual word but yet the substitute offered more of an artistic fulfillment than the actual. The end result was a canvas filled with broad, bright-hazy images, breaking all of the rules of color mix, but still leading the viewer to grasp the intent of the painter. Mountaineer impressionism: a unique art form lived on the ridge, up the holler, or in town. Education, too, was a determinant of grammar and dialect. The differential was evident even in those having a high

---

8

school education. The one constant was the long "I" /ɑ:/ instead of the general American diphthong /æ/.

Latching onto an opportunity to delve deeper into the regional dialect, Doctor prodded Jim to continue talking by asking, "Where did you go to school, Jim?"

"Ah /ɑ:/ went ta Delph School up in Bluewell."

"Who was your teacher? Was she well educated?"

"Well educated?" Jim inquired with surprise. "Well, heck yes; she was a teacher wa'nt she? Her name was Miss Jam'son. She drove'uh real fancy car cus her paw was a big x'tive in the Bram'ul Bank uh'fur hit went broke ah hear'd. He did okay cuz he did'nd own none of hit. He owned a hotel and after the depress'un let up he went to work fer a bank in Blue'fil an. That's when she wuz air teach'ur. We lah'ked her 'cause she give us pres'uhns. If'n we did'n miss no skul for one week she give us a ten-cent prize. Course, we had to have come to skul on mundi with clean clothes, havin' taken a bath an' air har combed uh'for we got anythang. If, n we did that fer a whole month, she give us a twenny five cent prize. Course they wuz only twelve of us in'a whole room. One tiem Mz Jam'son gave us a Chirs'mus party and guess what we had?"

"Let me see", pondered Doctor. "A surfeit of ice cream; lots of ice cream?"

"Naw" chortled Jim. "Strawberries! Strawberries for Chris'mus! Kin yew believe hit?"

Two of the more articulate folks were to play a major role in David's new world. The first was Jenn, the gorgeous young woman so stunningly beautiful that David lost his ability to articulate in his typical Bostonian suaveness. This magnificent red-head, in the most pleasing way, made it quite clear from the outset that she, and no one else, not even the Doctor, was in full control of the Boston Knob Medical Clinic. The second was the tall male carbon copy of the gorgeous redheaded nurse-in-charge at the clinic who was becoming his close friend and confidant. William had already proven his meddle by dealing with all of the legal matters regarding Dr. Fields's estate. Of course, there was little to do since Dr. Fields had meticulously arranged the disposition of his estate before his demise. Some way there were no funds required from Dr. Cabot. This seemed strange but he didn't contest it. He was not going to, as the locals would say, look a gift horse in the mouth. He had asked William what that meant and got the following explanation: "When a person buys a horse it makes no difference what the seller says about it, there is a routine to be followed, kinda' like kickin' the tires on a car before buyin' it, that reveals genu'wine facts. A horse's teeth, along with the condition of its hooves can be a good indicator of its age, health and bone condition. "Oh," said David. "I will take heed of those truths when I buy my next horse."

Bill said laughingly, "Now who's being a smart mouth?"

Annie was another enigma introduced into his new life. She too held a senior position in the 'clan' that he had inherited along with the doubles and Jim.

CHAPTER TWELVE

THE DOOR IN THE middle of the three emanating from the suntoom lead to an amazing suite of rooms obviously designed for a man. The curtains, the bedspread, and the chair covers were of a striped brown and tan rugged fabric that no woman would have chosen for herself or her house. The room was spacious with one corner serving as a miniature office centered on an antique roll-top desk of massive proportions. The top was up, and a new supply of pencils and paper were neatly arranged on the writing surface. Stacked to the side were several medical charts with a tag spelling out that these were the patients to be seen on his first days' work.

Next to the charts was a stack of X-rays corresponding to the names on the individual charts with a note written in precise cursive, "These are the only nonsmokers I could find without going deep into the files. Please don't think I am being bossy. I know that most of your work over the past three years was totally different from what you are mostly going to see here."

There was a total of eight X-rays and attached to each one in cursive was the notation 'non-smoker'. Also, with the film was a medical book opened to a section titled 'Black Lung Disease'.

Doctor flipped on the X-ray box sitting on the desk, and glanced at the X-rays. He was relieved to find that he could make a diagnosis from every one of them since the common elements of each were low set diaphragms and hyper lucent lung fields that were also common findings in emphysema, and other obstructive pulmonary diseases. He was grateful for the filtering Nurse had done, hence making his first visits on a new job a bit easier. Additionally, she had scheduled about one hour for each patient allowing him to carry out a full evaluation and history without being rushed. He appreciated her apology immensely and would remember to thank her for her consideration of his new environment.

He rose from the desk and took another look at the room having not spotted a bathroom when he first entered. He swept the room visually again and still could find only one door in the room and that was the entry door. There were double doors opening onto an outside deck but no bathroom door. Surely, he thought, a room of such bounty would contain its own bathroom of equal luxury. As he scanned the room again he noticed that most of one wall had no furniture placed against it. He approached it and began to search for cracks that would indicate a door and low and behold he found one. He pushed inward near the crack and a floor-to-ceiling door opened. He had found the bathroom and much more. In the large room were closets, a dressing room complete with a full mirror and modern plumbing fixtures including a shower and a separate bathtub. Behind another door was a small but complete kitchenette. It was obvious this was not what was available when the house was built. This was an update. This caused him to recollect the main kitchen. It too had been updated with all new appliances and equipment. As he took it all in he was overcome by the efforts of "his people" to make him welcome and comfortable. He reminded himself to find out who made the revisions and where the funds came from.

Feeling the need to move about Doctor drifted downstairs where he found Annie working in the kitchen.

In a clumsy effort at camaraderie, Doctor blurted out, "Don't you ever rest?"

Annie laughed and with the ease of a mother to a child responded. "Never. Ah've got a family ta'feed. Come on'n. Want some tea er som'n?"

"Tea would be nice."

"Cream'n sugar?"

"Just sugar, please."

Annie placed a teapot on the new electric stove offering the comment. "Ah'm havin' trouble with this here new-fangled stove. They done gone an' taken'out all'uh the gud kit'shun thangs and put in this mod'urn junk that takes a mine engineer to op'rate."

David broke into genuine laughter. "How long have you worked here, Miss Annie" Doctor inquired.

"Long tah'm. I come here to he'p when the lady of the house tuk sick. They wuz a ol' black man pertendin' to cook then. When he up and died uh the black lung hit was only nat'curl that I tuk over."

"A black man? Are there many here in the State?"

"Not many. Most moved up here for work. Some to escape the KKK. That bunch of no-gud white trash have got plum'outa' han' some places. We hav'em aroun' here but they don'n bother the black folks none. I think the leader here is a self 'pointed preacher who thank's he's better'n most. Last year the KKK burn't a cross'un whupped two white girls cause the preacher said they wus women-of-the-well. That kind'a mis'chuf 's what they do here. Silly foolish stuff."

Annie quickly glanced at the doctor and put her hand over her mouth. "Goodness, Ah've done gone an got out'a line. Please excuse me, Doctor, Ah should'a kept my mouth sh'et bout thangs lik'at. Ah wuz plum'outa order."

"Never you mind. I admire people who speak out against social maleficence," Doctor assured her.

CHAPTER THIRTEEN

'HIS PEOPLE': THIS WAS the first time he considered such a personal relationship with the population he was destined to serve as their primary care physician. Coal was the lifeblood of southern West Virginia and had been for maybe 100 years or more. The Coalfields were active before the two 'Great Wars' and had grown primarily because of them. His People were immigrants from Poland, Hungary, Italy, and Greece; they came in large numbers from Ireland and from the Post-Civil War South.

They might have been diverse but they had one terrible commonality: Black Lung. Doctor Cabot mentally reviewed his studies of pulmonary diseases. He knew that Black Lung was not a new disease. Ever since humans first started mining coal thousands of years ago back in the Bronze Age, those who worked in the mines breathed in the black dust that, over time, destroyed their lungs. He knew also that the widespread and excessive practice of smoking tobacco was mimicking the black lung, both becoming epidemic, and both included in the diagnosis of chronic bronchitis and/or emphysema. Neither was likely to subside in the near future because King Coal was the absolute economic life blood of West Virginia.

This large circa 1948 sign shown in the photo above, stood at the intersection where Federal Street ends at Princeton Avenue at the juncture of Federal Routes 52 and 460 and State Route 21, all primary roads in and out of Bluefield. Route 52 was the major road to and through the West Virginia Billion Dollar Coal Fields.

The insidious black-lung disease was an evil byproduct of coal mining. Miners breathed coal dust every day and it was accepted as a part of their job. Large dust particles settle in the tracheobronchial tree, the passage way from the mouth to the interior of the lung, causing mucus that can be coughed up efficiently at the outset, but worsens with continued dust or smoke aggravation. Smaller particles, on the other hand, are another issue, causing emphysema and its devastating consequences on the quality of life.

CHAPTER FOURTEEN

THE MORNING WAS YOUNG and Doctor Cabot had not had breakfast. He arose from the clutter of his new desk in his new office which looked to be ages older and no way measured up to the quality of his new home. He correctly assumed that this was intentional on the part of those involved in the remodeling of the complex. However, it had all of the appurtenances of a well-managed medical office. He moseyed up the steps to the kitchen and found Annie casually working around doing whatever she usually did. As he entered the room he felt a presence behind him. He turned to see a happy-faced mongrel looking up at him.

"Git, Bo, you sorry, gud fer nuthin' houn' dawg," she yelled. The dog ignored her and continued to favor the Doctor who uncharacteristically bent and scratched the dog's ears. From that day forward, for reasons only known to the dog, Doctor had become Bo's forever buddy and companion. Bo learned the Doctor's routine and followed it as his own.

Annie announced, "Yew'r brek'fes air ready. Set'ch'self-down and ah'll brang hit to yew. How do'ye wan'cher aigs fixed?" she asked as she set a steaming cup of coffee in a saucer before him.

"Over easy if you please, ma'am," He responded.

The coffee was excellent and before the eggs were served, he requested a refill.

"Tell me, Miss Annie. Is it true that menfolk around here pour their coffee into their saucer to cool it and drink?" Dr. Cabot asked.

"Some of the old men did, but that habit's dyin' out." She answered as she placed a large plate of hot biscuits on the table followed by a platter of three eggs and country bacon. Already on the table was a plethora of, obviously, homemade jams, jellies, and other condiments.

"May I inquire as to where you live and about a family?" He asked as he sampled a small bite of everything on his plate along with a biscuit or two slathered generously with wild strawberry preserves and home-churned butter.

"Ah ain't uh'shamed to taw'k bout my fambly. I live in'a house here on'th place with my husbun' and my retard' dot'er. My husbun' is near daid with'th black lung that jus about ever man aroun' here has. Yew'll meet him t'day since he's down to see you in yer office.""Thank you for telling me that. I'll want to learn all about your family. They sound nice," as he pushed away from the table and commented. "You cannot feed me in this fashion on a regular basis," he proclaimed. "I will swell up like a balloon before you can say Jack Robinson. How is that for my use of the local vernacular?"

"Believe me, yew'll work hit off jes kep'n up. Hit ain't easy tend'in to the folk up here."

"I'll do my best," he said earnestly.

"Miss Annie?" He said cautiously. "About your daughter? You said she was retarded? Would I offend you if I ask you to be more specific?"

"Heck no. Hit ain't nothin' ta'be 'shamed'uv. Ah'v hear'd a lot'sa talk about hit from lots of people. I went over'ta Bluefield to a healin' preacher one tahm to see if'n he could cure my baby gurl. Hit was my cousin, Bobbie's, ah'dee. She wuz a nurse, well, not really, she jus' worked in a hospital. She's a reel strong-will' gal. One tahm back when Bluefield switched Fed'ral and Bland streets tu'one way, she kept git'n in tru'bl cause she wod'nd pay no nev'r mind to the one way sahns. If'n she went the rahgt way she had'da stop at two stop laht's, one a'goin' uphill. So, instead, she went the wrong way on Bland Street, a'gin traffic so'ns not to have to go through the laht's. Th' same po'leec'mun stopped her ever' day and she jus' kept'on a'goin' the wrong way. Whur'wuz ah? Ah wandered off'n mah way. Oh, Th'heal'in preacher. That thar preacher man did'n do nothin' but go 'roun col'ectin money in a bushel basket and, you know what? He filled'um plumb up and had to empt'um a'for goin' back fer more. He said hit was the work'uf th'devil and said that he saw in one of his learn'n books that the Martin Luther, ah thank he wuz a preacher of some sort too, said a kid lah'k my littl'in air soulless mass'us of flesh 'ssessed by the devil, and orta be suff'cated. Now ain't that thu'berries?"

"Speki'n of Bobbie, her and Lula tuk their boys up to that big hospital up North to see a doctor who was supposed to be a expert with kids with probl'ms. I don't know wahy cuz, Sonny didn't have enythang a'wrong with him except'n as'mee. Course, he cud'nt read wur'th a hoot, yeah, none to gud, if'n at'all. I guess though, if'n yor an expert, hit's yor job to fahn som'thang wrong that nobody's seen a'for. He said Sonny had that dis'lex'uh. Bobbie's boy, too, as ah re-clet. "Well," Annie concluded. "Yew better git'ta work. Yew gon'na be buzy today an ah hav'ta give this here house at least a holler in the butt clean'un. Yew git now. We both have work ta'do."

David, pretending compliance, meekly replied "Yes ma'am," and trundled towards the clinic door with his new-found friend, tail wagging furiously, trundling along behind.

CHAPTER FIFTEEN

Doctor WENT FROM THE kitchen by the 'front way' meaning he used the steps from the sunroom hallway. He paused in the sunroom to see a clear day with storm clouds building up to the north. Jim was busy working in the yard doing what, Doctor could not detect.

He arrived at his office that was situated next to a flight of stairs going directly to the kitchen instead of the sunroom which he supposed was to give him an exit from the clinic without being seen. Hanging on a hook to the right of the door was a blindingly white lab coat. He assumed it was for him and he knew for sure when it fit him perfectly. He turned to his desk and was surprised to observe the charts and films had preceded him thereupon. His curiosity was piqued as to who had made the transfer. His face flushed with the thought that Jenn had been in his bedroom but he dismissed the thought as being insignificant since she appeared to have the run-of-the-house by somebody's authority. Curious.

He had gotten situated in his chair only briefly before Jenn knocked and entered the room.

"Good mornin" she said expressionless. "People are waitin'. Ah have scheduled only black lung patients today," repeating what she had written the night before.

"What's Bo doin' in here. You want me to take him out?"

Bo acknowledged his name by thumping his tail on the floor.

"No, leave him alone. He isn't bothering me," David said.

"I have some walk-ins comin' just in case you finish up in less time than ah have scheduled for the black lung people. Ah'm sure I misjudged on the time given; you are an accomplished physician but I didn't want to rush you in anyway. I will get better at scheduling as we get use to each other. We can set up a scheduling book to fit your wants or I can do them and you can change them anytime you want."

"Nurse Gullion … Jenn … as clinic director … 'Boss' as your brother William calls it … I certainly cannot surpass your abilities to manage the practice. Really, I am a klutz in matters of organization. So, please, don't let me interfere. Tell me how I fit into your management style, okay?"

Jenn manages a tiny smile and did an abrupt about-face and said in parting, "Okay, your first patient is in room one. Oh, you should know if you don't already. The girl up front, the receptionist, Shirley is her name, has been here a long time. She's good at her job and knows everybody by their first names. She can be a big help to you if you need anything and I am not around."

The patient information needed for his visit with the doctor was in a wall-mounted box just large enough to hold a standard file folder stuffed with clinical notes and X-rays. Dr. Cabot collected the file, stood at the door to "room one", took a deep breath, and then entered. Sitting forlornly in a chair was a medium height youngish man who could not have weighed more than 110 pounds. He wore a blue work shirt underneath a pair of oversized bib overalls that made him appear even smaller. He clutched an old misshapen Fedora firmly in both hands as if it might attempt escape.

"Mr. Spradlin?" Doctor inquired.

"At's mah name al'rat."

"How are you feeling today?"

"Tol'r'bol, thanks."

"Breathing okay today?"

"Hit h'ain't no worse, h'ain't no better. I got'th black lung, Doc. Hit don't change none."

"Mmmm. Let's have a look."

Doctor Cabot took another look at the chart in his hands. It became painfully obvious that Dr. Fields had not updated his knowledge of current medical practices. Currently, in most medical settings, the basic evaluation of lung diseases skimmed over the implications of one disease or another totally different one as being pertinent. Not one of the records of the patients scheduled today mentioned co-occurring diseases thought now to be associated with black lung with diabetes being a major one; pulmonary hypertension resulting in heart failure being another. Kidney disease and blindness were often considered but diagnosis was primitive at best. He knew that glucose levels depended on urine tests, showing only an increase of blood sugar. Heart attacks were common in 50- 60 year olds because there was no known treatment.

"Well", he said under his breath. "Maybe Dr. Fields knew more than I thought he did. Sometimes when one is fighting a losing battle, facts become meaningless, so why bring them up?"

After the pause for reverie, he began his evaluation including those areas excluded by Dr. Fields, or perhaps in spite of Dr. Fields. Then a second revelation struck him; maybe, just maybe, nurse Jenn is more astute than he had anticipated?

CHAPTER SIXTEEN

DAVID LEARNED JUST HOW in control the gorgeous redhead was to be when the phone rang on Friday afternoon at 4:00 and she began to issue do-it-or-else orders to the new doctor.

"They're callin' from the camp up on the ridge that there's been an accident up on Buzzard's Roost," announced Jenn. She pronounced "accident" with the emphasis on the final syllable: ax-uh-DENT.

David looked at her with a questioning expression expecting more information. Instead, he received a rather impatient command.

"I'd go with you but there's too much to do here. Well, don't just stand there; get ready to go while I get your bag. And don't let that dog go with you."

"Why will I need my bag? Won't the ambulance take the injured party to the hospital?" inquired the doctor.

"Of course not, even if he wasn't trapped under a fallen tree," retorted Jenn. "And besides they won't take him at the hospital until you tell'em to. A Company Doctor has to make the referral and right now you're the closest thing to a Company Doctor we have. So, get goin'. Go south down 52 'til you come to a dirt road going west to the sawmill.

You'll come to a creek with a wood bridge over it. Go left up that road and you'll find the sawmill. They'll meet you there. Go!"

Dr. Cabot did as ordered. The excitement emitted by the redhead beauty sent him scurrying to the parking area where there was the Packard and a jeep station wagon. Giving no thought to local terrain and road types and conditions, the Doctor slid into the Packard ignoring the sturdy jeep parked alongside.

All-day rains had made even the best of the mountain roads difficult to travel. He easily found the turnoff from Route 52 as well as the wood bridge heading up to the logging camp. But here things definitely fell apart. It had started to rain again as he turned left at the bridge and instantly discovered the road to be a pair of muddy ruts cut deep by trucks laden with mine props. The rain became a torrent and the thunder and lightning transcended into nightmare proportions. The Packard gave a valiant effort but the road was destined to win. Finally, the car bogged down and would go no further.

The situation bore down on Dr. Cabot to the extent that he was emotionally returned to a harrowing experience during his service during the Korean War. He and his driver, Sargent Walton, were trying to reach an isolated group of wounded British soldiers trapped by enemy mortar fire. The weather precluded evacuation by helicopter.

The lightning and thunder were fierce and continuous, causing David to become agitated and more withdrawn from reality. His movements became erratic as he screamed and pushed the car door open and tumbled into the mud.

"Get out, Sargent, they're killing us. Crawl to those rocks, follow me, we can make it. No, you can't be hit.

I need you. Get up. Get up. Stop it, damn you. Stop it. Stop it."

"Git up doc. You're ok. Hit's me. Stop fighten' me doc. You ain't hurt," someone was saying.

"What? Where? Who are you? Where is your uniform, Sargent? Who are you? I have to get up to the ridge. There are people injured. Help me up. I've got to go. Where is my trauma kit? Get it for me. Why am I covered in mud?" David inquired out of his confusion.

A man was trying to lift David out of the mud onto the rain-soaked grass beside the mud-ensconced Packard. David continued to fight as he slowly became aware of the situation. "Thank you. I think I'm recovering now. Who are you? I thought you were my Sargent from Korea. I was obviously dreaming."

"Ah'm one of the Hicks boys. Yew ain't never met me but ah know who you air. Yew okay now? Yew need me to go with yew? Ahm here't'tell you they's been a axe'dint up on the ridge. Yew want I should go with yew?" Inquired his benefactor.

"No" replied David. "I believe I am sufficiently recovered to proceed on my own. Just point me in the right direction."

David decided that his only alternative was to proceed on foot. He walked about fifty feet in the roadbed when he realized it would probably be better to walk alongside the road where the leaves and grass afforded a more stable surface. He had walked about a half a mile when he encountered what looked like a road leading into the woods and he decided that this probably led to the logging camp. He was now wet and cold but he slogged on. He had walked what seemed like miles when he spotted a pickup truck sitting in the middle of the road. He called out but got no answer. He looked inside the truck and saw a pile of clothing in the floor. He opened the door and discovered a pair of very dirty but dry coveralls, a military-issue field jacket, and a pair of goulashes. There was also a sweat-stained hat that looked inviting since he had left the clinic without one. He pulled off his jacket, and tie, and donned his new wardrobe including the hat placed jauntily on his head. Now, more appropriately attired, he struck out up the road thinking that he would soon find the camp. He was in for quite a surprise.

CHAPTER SEVENTEEN

Now warmed by the borrowed clothing he found himself actually enjoying the walk through the bright fall colors of the heavily wooded area. The rain had stopped and the thickness of the trees had protected the blanket of bright leaves covering the forest floor so that they rustled as he pushed his feet through them. The ambiance was so pleasant that he imagined the aroma of fine cooking brushing his nostrils. Soon he realized that the wafting olfactory delight was not his imagination but rather quite real. He decided it was bread; definitely bread. He headed towards the smell but was started by a voice.

"Stop rat th'ar and pu'cha hands whar I kin see'em," pronounced a voice from nowhere. "Ah swar I'll shoot'cha if'n yew don't."

Dr. Cabot quickly complied but answered the voice by declaring who he was and why he was there. "My good fellow", he said, "I'm Dr. David Cabot from town looking for an injured man up on the ridge."

"Yew ain't no Doctor. Yew'r a dadblamed gov'ment man. Ah ain't no fool. If'n yew'r a doc whar's yer bag? Sides, no self respectin' Doc's gonna be caught dressed in duds like yew'r a' wearin'." He announced with certainty.

"Hey, Bootjack," He called out. "Ah got me an intruder claiming to be air new doctor."

A second man emerged from the direction of the cooking smell and slowly studied David.

"He's right, June Boy. He is air new doc. I seen him the day he come to town. What'cha doin' dressed like at?" he asked David. "At hat looks like the one belong'ta Daddy. Whar'chu git at' hat?"

David's thoughts illogically flickered to the popular song "Where did you get that hat" but he realized joviality was not in order at the moment.

"I found it along with the rest of these … uh … duds, in a rather disreputable vehicle that I believe you folks refer to as a pick-um truck. Down the path," he responded.

"They air Daddy's. But whar's he? Did'n'chu see him down the path?" asked the one called Clarence.

Before David could answer, a third man broke through the underbrush and enthusiastically greeted the doctor. "Hey Doc! Good to see yew. Hit was me what tol' them to call you 'bout the tree fallin' on June. He's ok so you don't need to worry none. Come in'ta the camp and have a snort to warm you up. I ges we can trust you as one of us to not spread the word aroun' as to what we be doin' here. Name's Riley; That'n's Clarence, he's June Boy and I'm Chance," said the old man pointing a bony finger towards his 'boys'.

David followed behind the one called 'Paw' expecting to see a cabin of some sort. What he finally saw was so unexpected that he involuntarily explained, "My heavens, I've lived with one of those for almost two years in a MASH tent in Korea!" recalling the still his tent mate's operated.

It was a moonshine still. The apparatus was nestled deep inside a large cavity left where the roots of a fallen red oak tree had been. Saplings were suspended between the outside rim of the hole and the roots resulting in a dome roof. Covering all of this were several tattered tarps that had probably been salvaged from some mine operation. The still was centrally located on a well-packed dirt floor. Makeshift stools constructed with greenwood frames and thatched seats were strategically placed around the still. A firebox was fashioned from flat stones readily available from the small spring-fed stream running close by. A sluice, made of split hollow logs, zigzagged downwards from a rudimentary dike and carried the spring water through the still house and dumped it further down the hill where it found itself back into the stream. A long section of copper tubing, beginning at the top of the still contraption and extending to the sluice, ran submerged in the cold water for a length of about eight feet, and terminated into a half gallon Mason jar. This ingenious design negated the need for a coil above the still body.

Paw invited the doctor into the still house and instructed him to "pull up a cheer (chair)."

David complied and sat down on one of the homemade stools close to the friendly fire glowing in the rough stone firebox. Paw dug into a gunnysack and came out with two bunged-up tin cups that he proceeded to fill partway from the dripping copper tube.

"Yew boys git'ch yer own, These air for the doc and me," instructed Paw, passing the clear warm brew to David. "Hit may be a mite raw comin' straight from the tube like this but it'll warm up your innards"

David took a tentative sip and found the product to be surprisingly mild. Just as he was preparing to take a second apprising sip, the world around him turned into a hornet's nest.

"Federal officers; up with your hands," shouted the first man in, brandishing an enormous double-barreled shotgun. Others followed shouting various commands suggesting arrest was underway. One lifted a booted foot into the air and kicked the still into a pile of rubble. Steam spewed from the fire where the mixture from the cooking pot had spilled. Paw and David were immediately cornered but June Boy and his brother had managed to make their way into the woods to avoid arrest.

David was stunned but not into silence. "How dare you," he cried. "I'll have you know that I am a respected physician! How dare you! How dare you!"

"And I'm President Truman," responded one of the agents. "Shut'cha mouth and keep your hands up."

David, along with Paw, was unceremoniously loaded into the back of a rugged vehicle with huge tires and hauled to the Mercer County Jail in Princeton, West Virginia where he was incarcerated like a common criminal.

Dr. Cabot had exhausted his lamentations of being in jail. No one seemed to care that he was a Harvard Medical School Graduate and that the Cabot's were amongst the first families of Boston.

"Pa, what possessed you to engage in the manufacture of illicit whiskey… uh… Pa…uh…by the way, what is your name again? I can't go on calling you Pa," exclaimed David.

"Hey, I ain't possessed. I'm a God-fearin' church-going man an' nobody's going to accuse me of havin' the devil in me, an' my name is Chance Riley. I wuz a'goin to tell you that early on. Don'cha listen when folks talk to ye?"

"No, no" David quickly backtracked. "My inquiry had to do with your choice of profession. No reference to your religiosity was intended."

"What in tarnation does that mean? I never know what yew air a'talkin' about."

"Why do you make moonshine?"

"So's I kin put food on the table. Why else do people do thangs tha'make money? They's not a'nuff jobs in minin' since all them newfangl'd machines wuz brung in an' they ain't 'nuf timber to har all of us and they ain't nothin' else reg'lar nuf to feed a dog much les'un a fam'ly and they ain't no shortage of buyers. We kin sell ever drap we kin make, jus' like at. Hit ain't nuthin' wrong with makin' it. Hit ain't none of the gov'ment's biz'nus but they done went an butted inna air lives in pert nur ever' way yew kin emagin'. "

Chance fell silent. David watched the old man with a sense of understanding. He, too, had had his life 'butted into' by a government dedicated to political expediency and corporate greed. He had been plucked from a potential medical practice in Boston to be unceremoniously dropped into a primitive hospital in the middle of a war (police action?) to attend to young men who were being slaughtered in the righteous fight against communism. His resentment of that incursion upon his life would never be abated; he would always carry that resentment within. David found himself wanting to know more about this gentleman who wished no more than to lead a simple life protected by the mountains around him.

"Chance," asked Dr. Cabot gently. "Tell me why you feel so strongly about your occupation. Is it something you grew up with similar as I with medicine?"

"I ges you cud say that" answered Chance. "My grandpaw was the first man ah re'member runnin' a still up these hollers. He did it much different than us today. He tol' me that back in 'em days they wuz called blockaders 'stead of moonshiners. He said that the name come from when the early set'lers started, they wuz called free-traders who wuz fightin' for rights against being taxed by the King of England. We ain't no diff'rent today. All we want is to be left alone. We ain't got nothin' agin nobody. We leave other folks alone, why can't they leave us alone? We always bin law abidin', church goin' people who jist want to be left alone without the inner'ference of outsiders. Well, Ah'm jist foolin' myself. Ah know why. They want air coal. We don't git none of the money fur the coal. Hit all goes outside to rich folks. Look up air at Bram'el. More millionaires up air than any place in the world. All we do is dig the coal and git air'selves kilt with nobody giv'n a gol'durn if'n we live'er die. Well here's one feller that ain't going ta die down thar in them dirty pits."

"Tell me how you make your whisky," prodded David.

Before Chance could respond the cell door was opened. Dr. Cabot looked up and his jaw dropped in amazement. Standing in the door, next to a uniformed law officer, was Jenn's double; brother William.

71

CHAPTER EIGHTEEN

"WELL, THIS IS A fine way to establish your name in the neighborhood," said the young man with a bit of a twinkle in his eye. Dr. Cabot recalled his brief earlier encounter at the home-place. Home-place: For the first time in his life the concept of a 'place to call home' with family around resonated as more than a place to just live. He summoned up his best glare and responded to William. "It was absurd and totally uncalled for to treat a man of my station like a common criminal. And who do you think you are to assume such familiarity?" asked David with his nose high in the air.

"I'm your lawyer, I suppose." Bill appraised the doctor for several seconds and finally laughingly said, "Yep, you are definitely attired in appurtenances of a proper Bostonian."

David had forgotten what he was wearing. He looked down at the dirty clothes and glanced back up with a look of disdain on his face that finally morphed into one of amusement. "Under the circumstances I am indeed pleased to accept your offer as my attorney. Perhaps we can better complete our discussion outside of this…this… uh…cell? If the local constabulary has no objections might we be on our way?"

"You can thank Sheriff Hare here for your release. If it was up to the feds you would be on your way to Charleston to face a federal judge for moonshinin'. You're still not out of the woods on that account. Let's get out of here."

"At the moment, William, all else is inconsequential. What I need is a bath and some decent clothing, plus I am near starvation since I have not eaten one bite since being seized by that bunch of federal hoodlums. Where might I acquire something suitable to wear that does not smell of wood smoke and sweat?" pleaded David.

"We can get all of that in Bluefield." said William. "I know the folks at the West Virginian Hotel and any one of them will gladly give you a place to clean up while I go across the street and get you something to wear. You wear about a forty long don't you?"

"My dear boy," David haughtily retorted. "I have no idea of my size since I have always had my suits fitted by the best tailors. Are you suggesting that I obtain a suit off of the rack?"

"Oh, you'll be fine. The store I sometimes use will send a tailor along, and that's saying a lot since we have shops here with top brand clothing. You can't do any better." William informed a befuddled David.

They departed the jail through the front door. David was not impressed by the City of Princeton. It was like thousands of other county seats all over the country. But after an unimpressive ride of ten miles he was not prepared for the City of Bluefield.

They had been traveling across ridges and down into valleys for several minutes when the road sunk down between two tree-covered mountains. On the left side of the road situated on a piece of rarely seen flat-land, sat a gigantic, bright red building with the name 'Hillbilly Barn' emblazoned across its front.

"My, my," exclaimed David. "Isn't that the most vivid reflection of the area? Hillbilly Barn where fiddlin' and'a kickin' is alive and well in them thar hills of West Virginia."

Suddenly, Bill swerved across the oncoming lane and skidded to a stop in the dancehall parking lot. He turned angrily to the doctor and firmly declared. "Okay now! I've had a belly full of your sanctimonious holier than thou, upper-crust rich Yankee bull malarkey. For your information, the Hillbilly Barn is just a name in no way reflectin' the type of music played there. The best representation of the quality of music served up there is the bands of Duke Ellington, Glenn Miller, Woody Herman, Sonny Brown, Tommy and Jimmy Dorsey, Robny Goodman, even Spike Jones and his City Slickers, as well as many others. Furthermore, there may be some country-western music performances there, but not Hillbilly! And for your further information, we don't hold well to bein' called Hillbillies by self-righteous outsiders. Maybe if you work hard and learn some humility you might just earn the title of Hillbilly as an honor of being a valued resident of these glorious mountains. And while ah'm on the topic of music, a least four times a year we have performances from such respected groups as the New York City Ballet and the Metropolitan Opera right here in this hick town. My nephew actually played a supporting role in La Traviata when the Met was here a couple of years ago. He sang and even danced the waltz, would you believe that?"

The ensuing silence was deafening.

Dr. Cabot's thoughts went back to the luncheon with Jenn and thought to himself, "This is the second time since I have been here that I have been 'chewed out' over an observation someone considered offensive. Perhaps mountain folk are a bit paranoid or could it be just the one family?"

Bill slowly put the car in gear and returned to the highway where they gradually emerged from the darkness of the deep valley onto the side of one of the mountains. David could see a steep drop off to his right. To his amazement, a wide valley opened up and was filled with train tracks covered with long strings of open gondolas filled with coal.

David, seeking to break the silence and to show Bill he understood his outburst said, "My heavens what a spectacular display. I assume that is all coal."

Bill, taking the cue softly replied, "Yep, and you're lookin' at a slow day. More coal goes through here than just about anywhere in the world. It's why Bluefield is one of the best shopping towns this side of New York. Wait til' you see what can be bought here. Then you won't feel so bad about being isolated here in West Virginia. The wholesale market is so well established that if you want to get one particular refrigerator, I forgot which one, in New York City, it has to be ordered through Bluefield Supply Company.

"Leslie, my sister Lula's husband, has a little grocery and feed store in Bluewell and all of his family can go into just about any wholesale house, and there was a bunch of them, and buy with cash, at a discount, just about anything possible. Bluefield has five movie theaters with first-run movies going on all the time. Let me see if I can list them: the Colonel, the Granada, the State, the Rialto that usually show movies like the "Outlaw" that the others would not, and the Lee in Bluefield, Virginia. The West Virginian Hotel is 12 stories tall and has a very nice dining room. My favorite place, though, is Kresges where they have an automatic doughnut machine. I really like to watch the machine spit out the dough from the spout into the hot fat and push it halfway around before a thing comes up and turns it over and then picks it up and dumps it into the sugar. I used to leave art lessons in the Coal and Coke building just across the street on my way to the Consolidated Bus Terminal. You'll see the buses with the slogan: "Serving West Virginia's Billion Dollar Coal Fields' on the side. I'd stop in and buy a fist full. They're still only a nickel uh-piece and taste just heavenly. Doughnuts are absolutely no good unless they are right out of the fat."

"There are two hospitals here in town and you will no doubt be invited to join them both.

"As your lawyer, I'd advise you to be on staff at both. The bigger of the two has branches in Welch and Richlands which gives you a good network of coverage. Another reason to join the big one is that they put on a very nice staff party and dinner at Christmas every year. There're two architectural firms here and Lula's boy worked for both of them. If you look across the tracks you can see the college sittin' up there on the mountain side. You can enter that building on the fourth floor on one side and exit it from the first on the other side. You'd never guess that to be a Negro college, would you? Well, yes you would; who would put a white college on a hillside like that. Besides, that side of the tracks is where the colored folks live and you want to be sure to keep them over there so the best place to put their college is on the colored side of the tracks; and yes, that comment was tainted with sarcasm. BC is a fine college and the white folks are beginning to recognize it and are beginning to attend classes there. The composer or I guess you would say songwriter, who wrote *Sweet Georgia Brown,* Maceo

Pinkard, was born here in Bluefield and graduated from what was then the Bluefield Colored Institute. *Sweet Georgia Brown* became the theme song of the Harlem Globetrotters basketball team. Another great song of his you will probably remember is a song you still hear today: *Them Their Eyes* was recorded by Bing Crosby and Jenn Holiday and the bands of Louis Armstrong, Robny Goodman and Duke Ellington and others I can't recall."

Finally, Bill lapsed into an unexplained, almost embarrassed silence. After Bill's long rambling soliloquy, David realized, for the first time, that this young man was decidedly worthy of his friendship.

William, or Bill to his long-standing dismay, was an educated man. He studied architecture and finished a law degree from The University of Virginia. His education was a result of the GI Bill that provided many a World War II veteran the opportunity to attend college. The government had paid for his architectural degree and he worked as an architect for the Charlottesville, Va. firm of Booker, Heywood and Lorentz in order to complete his law degree. The architectural degree was a long-time dream and the law degree was so that he could go back home and serve his people. More realistically he needed a profession that would provide some degree of income reliability in view of the failing economy in his beloved West Virginia Mountain Home.

Dr. Cabot was to develop a strong and lasting friendship with Bill, first by refusing to call him "Bill", and secondly through many long discussions from politics to religion. Music was to become a strong bonding agent since both enjoyed the classics. The term 'classic', however, definitely bore different translations for each of the two.

Leslie W. Dalton, Jr.

Fully loaded coal cars fill the Bluefield Yards waiting to be shipped to sources such as electric power plants around the World. Today the yards are sadly empty along with a city being cleared of historic buildings.

CHAPTER NINETEEN

Dᴀᴠɪᴅ ᴡᴀѕ ғᴀɪʀʟʏ ᴀᴄᴄᴏᴍᴘʟɪѕʜᴇᴅ on the violin. He fancied himself to be far better than he really was and could be a bit overbearing in discussions centered on stringed instruments. Bill, on the other hand, was a mountain virtuoso with a fair ability on a number of instruments including the fiddle, banjo, Dobro, and a brushing familiarity with just about any component found in a folk, country, or Bluegrass band. As more of a joke than anything else, Bill invited David to "sit in" at one of the music sessions.

"Why don't you bring your violin and join us one night in one of our practice sessions?" Bill invited.

David was ecstatic. Although he doubted the ability of the local musicians, if you could even call them that, he was sure that he could take this bunch of yokels and turn them into a presentable chamber group. Most of his sheet music was still in storage so the selection would be limited to a few of his favorites that he kept in a loose-leaf binder along with his record collection. He came upon a violin arrangement of Beethoven's Ode to Joy and pulled it from the folder. He also had a well-worn 78 RPM recording that he had played along with many times during his tour of duty in Korea -- much to the dismay of his colleagues who were forced to share his austere living quarters.

"This," he said to himself, "Should be simple enough for the uninitiated locals." A couple of weeks after he had delivered the music to Bill, Jenn asked if he was free for Sunday dinner followed by a music session with Bill and his band of musicians.

"Yes," he enthusiastically responded. "I have been looking forward to this for some time. Tell me when and where and I shall be there."

The following Sunday, after a delicious meal of roast beef, twice-baked potatoes, black-eyed peas, cornbread, and peach cobbler, the band gathered in the parlor for music. David was somewhat aghast when he saw the instruments being pulled from their cases: A banjo, guitar, bass violin, fiddle, and mandolin and, "what is that peculiar device?" he almost said aloud.

He got his answer without asking the question.

"Dr. Cabot, you probably recognize all of the instruments except that guitar-looking thing with the shiny plate underneath the strings. That's a Dobro and Walter's a master on it. It's played with a slide so that every note is infinite, kind'a like the violin. Are you ready to lead us into a little Classical Mountain Music? We have been rehearsing Ode to Joy so that we could at least start somewhere on an equal footing with you. Just speak up if we do anything wrong. We'll depend on your direction."

"Fine," David said. "I'll direct you first so that you can feel the gentleness and solitude of this particular piece. Remember, this is a song of love; your instruments must whisper with the gentleness of a butterfly's touch and color. This is not foot-stompin' ho-down but the essence of sweetness that evokes tears of joy. Now… let's start; one, two three, all together with feeling."

The music started with all of the instruments quietly supporting David's better-than-average violin solo through the entire piece. Once David brushed the bow to fade away for the ending as written, the others did not follow suit. David was first annoyed that these hicks would dare to interpret Beethoven on these crude hillbilly instruments, but something caught his emotions along the way. The guitar and mandolin had each played a run, followed by the five-string banjo, after which the Dobro took the lead. Bill then turned to David and indicated that he was to take his turn on the violin. But David did not respond. The mournful sound of the Dobro gliding through the sadness of the music itself brought visible tears to David's eyes. He could only stare at the players with a look of puzzlement on his face. He had experienced this feeling in the great concert halls of the big cities but how could this small band of hillbillies cause those emotions to rise, on a Dobro for heaven's sake! It was as if Beethoven's Ode to Joy was written for the Dobro! David sat motionless for several seconds and quietly whispered, "A-men."

CHAPTER TWENTY

Dr. Cabot was often called to traumatic and medical events caused by the excessive use of alcohol. It was a scourge of the mountains, particularly in those of Irish descent. The Italians, for the most part, were not abusers of hard liquor, or even beer, since their culture of wine-use mitigated the continuous guzzling of beer in quantities enough for inebriation. He found Annie to be an expert on the behavior of drunks and alcoholics. She said she was well acquainted with both and summed up her view, "They's a diff'runce between a out'raht drunk an' uh man uh'dict'ed," she opined.

That bit of wisdom lay dormant until one wintery day a heavy snowstorm shut down the community. Doctor, Annie, and Jim were at loose ends there in a home with little to do so they sat around the large kitchen table drinking coffee and chattering contentedly on matters of no particular concerns, generally nonspecific and generating periods of long silence.

Jim broke the silence. "Doctor Dave, wuz th' war hard fer yew? Whut ah mean, yew wus'nt a sol'jur lahk all them others so hit had'a been diff'runt, rah't? M'ah 'spur'unce has taught me that ever' thang we do learns us some'thn new. H'ain't that right for yew too, even in'a war, right?"

"Jim, you are a wise man. You are correct in your observation about 'learning from our experiences'. But it is also true that we are destined to often relive old experiences in a new situation or environment, thus only changing the characters. Don't you find that true, Annie? I recall a conversation we had one day some time ago when we were discussing alcoholism. You differentiated between a 'drunk' and an 'alcoholic'; that observation has led me to numerous reflections on how to deal with the abuse of liquor. While in Korea, addressing your question about the effects of war on me, Jim, I observed a focus…no; fascination is the word; not focus…on obtaining some form of alcohol at every rank level, possibly attributed to boredom or anxiety. Rank was often the differentiator as who could drink hard liquor, or beer and indeed, who could drink at all, considering the stupidity of a policy that a young man could be demanded to give his life for, more often than not, politic expediency and still be too young for a 3.2 beer or glass of wine with his meal.

"Every installation with roots for any period of time had an officer's club with a bar. The enlisted grunts could sometimes get beer at the service clubs or by going to the invariable 'gin mills' always, historically, popping up around a military encampment to exploit the troops. Therefore, it appeared to me that alcohol was engrained in the military way of life and likewise in our everyday life. Thus, anytime we encounter stress, fear, anxiety, loneliness…"

Doctor lapsed into silence. His mind was regressing to a time coinciding with the announcement of the Korean Armistice when a rumor was circulated that the MASH units were to be sent to Indochina where another war involving the United States was brewing.[9] The fear felt by those whose lives would have been inexorability impacted forever, led to a couple of suicides and promises to defect to North Korea or China by others, if the transfer was implemented. Fortunately, it was a rumor, nothing more.

"Wake up Doctor," Jim was saying. "Wha'ch mean 'don keep me here', you want to leave us?"

---

[9]   In May, 1950 President Truman approved $10 million in military assistance for anti-communist efforts in Indochina. This was the emerging iceberg of U.S. military personnel assignments as Naval, Army and Air Force attaches. Following soon after, September 1950, President Truman sent 'Military Assistance Advisors' to Vietnam to help the French who were getting a royal whipping by the Viet Minh. The President claimed they were not sent as combat troops, but to supervise the use of $10 million worth of U.S. military equipment to support the French in their failing efforts. Following the outbreak of the Korean War, Truman announced "acceleration" in the furnishing of unspecified military assistance to the forces of France and the Associated States in Indochina and sent 123 non-combat troops to help with supplies to fight against the communist Viet Minh and authorized another $150 million in French support.

General McArthur, in 1952 got in the mix when he loaned twelve Fairchild C-119 aircraft, to be flown by French crews, to "facilitate" their war at Dien Bien Phu. In 1954 additional transport aircraft flown by CIA pilots posing as French and being maintained by the USAF were added to the conflict. In 1954 President Eisenhower quelled a major intervention by the U.S. but later in 1955 following 1954 Viet Minh defeat of the French at the battle of Dien Bien Phu and coinciding with the end of the Korean War, deployed the Military Assistance Advisory Group to train the Army of the Republic of Vietnam. From there it escalated into another war with draftees on the front lines.

"No, no. Please excuse my lapsing into the past. I was thinking of our present activities in Vietnam and what a disaster it could have been for me, and you, too, Jim. What is your status with the draft board, Jim?"

Annie quickly jumped in, apparently in protection of Jim, "That h'ain't of no concern. Who wants som'thun ta'eat?"

Both Jim and Doctor responded in the affirmative and food became the immediate focus.

Shortly Jim said, "Doctor Dave, yew di'nt answer my question. Jis what did yew learn in tha army that hep's yew today?"

"Sorry for my relapse, Jim. My past fears-induced reverie momentarily placed me under a state akin to hypnosis."

"Wh'cha say?" Jim queried.

"Never mind. I'll finally get around to answering your question about what I learned in the army. First, I learned that no one wins a war. Second, I learned the war really begins when it ends."

"Dang, Doc, that don't make no sense a'tall. Hit shor'nuf is over when all the boys come home, don'hit?"

Annie injected a thought into the dialogue with the observation, "Jim, ah'm a'thinkin that the doctor is talkin' about what the war did ta'those who did the fight'en, ain'ch doctor?"

"Indeed I am, Miss Annie. We were discussing alcoholism earlier and I am sure you have also noted the link between those in dangerous professions and the abuse of alcoholic drinks. I saw it in their eyes in Korea and I see it in their eyes here. In Korea, many times soldiers of all ranks, ages and levels of education were brought to the hospital because their psyche could no longer tolerate the fright, the mayhem, the noise; everything. What spirit they brought with them was broken, sometimes unrepairable. Sometimes controlled by numbing the psyche with drink or drugs."

"Wat'sa psyche?" Jim puzzled.

"The psyche is the totality of the human mind and soul. It abides within the 'whole-human' in harmony with the world around him so that he can peacefully provide for himself, his family and community through the boundless gifts provided by the good earth. Man, though, through greed and lust for power, has for many centuries attempted to systematically destroy man by crushing his soul through wars that have exceeded nature in its destruction of natural resources and humanity. So far they have failed but they keep trying. Hitler……"

"Hey, Doc. Ah know a gud story 'bout Hitler. Yew waz' a'talkin' 'bout drafti'n men inna army-? Well, my gran'pa tol me about a man up tha road a'piece that di'nt pay no 'tentsun to his draft papers that come in the mail. So, one day th' Feds come after him an' ast him wahy he did'nt com to jine the army when he got his notice. "Wha'cha need me fer," he as't'm? "Tu'hep us git Hitler", they tol him over. Wahl, ya'll don't need no army ta take keer of jes'one man, the thang to do is ta wait fer him to come out'n on the porch fer his mornin' pee and shoot the rascal." [10]

Annie exploded. "Jim, they's a lady an'uh Doctor at this here table. Don't yew be a'usin filthy language with us!"

---

[10] There is no symbol or mark to indicate a voice rise in pitch that usually accompanies a question when that rise occurs not as an isolated question but as an assumption of understanding of a given phrase. I used a question mark preceded by a dash to indicate that trait in the dialog often experienced in the local speech prosody.

"Miss Annie," Doctor pleaded. "I get his point and it is well taken. But, Jim, she is right about the presence of a lady."

"Well, they's never a mistake in behavin' right." Annie opined. "Reminds me of a story my cousin's husband tol us about misbehavin'. He was born an' raised in Indi'un Valley, Virginia whur so many of the folks aroun' Bluewell come from. He tells the story of a weddin' they had up there a long tahm ago and a man wus a'playin' an ol' banja and a'drink'n way too much bootleg liquor, showin' nary uh'bit of goud sense. He decided he awanted a dance with the bride over the groom's objection-? Well, them two fool drunks got int'a a fight and the banja player swung at the groom but missed and hit the bride and kilt'er. He, the banja player, tuck off a'runnin' and landed just down the road near here an' went'ta workin' in the mines. Sev'ral months later, the shurf uv Floyd counti', he wuz a uncle of th'bride, showed up and shot that fool banja player dead right thar in his sleep. He drug him out and put him in his po'leece car and tuck him back to Indian Valley whur somebody finally buried'm outside the family cem'tary."

'Hey, Aunt Annie," Jim called out. "Yew air u'tellin' me not to do bad thangs? Tell me if what me and Sonny did back a'ways wuz bad. We wuz a'sittin' on a flat rock up'above the road jes a lil bit down from whar Mr. Miller had his garage, yew know the place. Hit's whar Mr. Surface put in his firs' fruit stan' in Bluewell-? Well, whil'st we war a'sitten' thar a car come a'tearin' down 52 a'headin' t'ward Pinn'cle rock so fast it'd make yer head swim. All of a sud'nt hit stopped smak'dab down below us and hid two five gall'un cans in the ditch, then tuk off down the road agin. Jus' about then a state po'leec car came a'runnin' with his si'reen a blarin' down the road. He went on past us ah recon' goin' on after the car that lef' the cans. Me and Sonny waited a mite to be a'sure that nobody wuz roun' and we went down and got those cans and tuck them up ina' woods and hid them proper. We knowed all along what they wuz. We did'n even check ta' see. We went straight to see a man we knowed down on Lortin's Lick and tol him we would tell him whar the cans wuz if'n he'd give us fifty cent uh'piece. Now we seen a crime and we reported a crime. Wus'nt that the right thang ta'do?"

Annie sighed, shook her head and said, "Now don't that beat all?"

Doctor turned as if to look at the snow with a big smile on his face. After a short pause he said, "looks like the snow is letting up."

CHAPTER TWENTY-ONE

David had been exposed to the Episcopal Church in his early years and had little contact with organized religion since then. As far as he could tell the only reason his family attended the church that they did was because it was "the" place to go. During his stint in Korea, he had occasional conversations with the Catholic Priest at the MASH Unit but other than that his exposure to faith-based activities was limited for a man of his intellect and background. It was with disdain that he was inundated with invitations to visit the many congregations found up and down the many 'hollers' in his new hometown.

As the pressure to attend church increased he was surprised to receive one of his father's infrequent letters with a strange request.

> My Dear David:
>
> We are well and I hope this letter finds you likewise. We are busy as usual with the mundane activities of the big city. We attended the opera last Friday evening and ran into your cousin, Melvin, who, as you

might recall, is an editor for the Globe. He has been toying with an idea of a special feature on religions of America and suggested that you might be in a unique situation to contribute some material on the mountain folk. Let me know what your inclinations might be.

Your mother is calling me to dinner and I will sign off for now. Let me hear soon.

Love, Father.

David's first reaction was "never in a thousand years," but upon reflection he considered the possible intellectual challenge to be worthy of his abilities. On several occasions he and William had approached the topic of faith-based activities and he recalled that the conversations proved to be stimulating, at least to a degree. They had never really gone into any depth on the topic of religion; maybe now would be a good time. Several days later the opportunity for discussion presented itself when William dropped by just as Dr. Cabot had finished with his last patient for the day.

Bill and Jenn were engaged in some sibling banter as David entered the breakroom of the clinic.

"Let me ask the two of you a question," David ventured. "How would one go about assessing the religious bent of the mountain folk around here?"

"Go to their church," the doubles responded in unison.

"An obvious answer but not so easily executed," argued David a bit testily. "Don't you think I haven't already considered that possibility? However, I cannot just insinuate myself into their midst without some sort of proper prelude.

Of course, many of them have been inviting me to attend their services but I just don't feel comfortable by showing up without some sort of fanfare."

Jenn, sensing a long-winded exchange not to her liking, excused herself pleading charts to organize and glided out of the room under David's surreptitious glance, leaving the two men to their discussion.

"Tell you what," Bill said. "Buy me a couple'a hotdogs and I'll set up a plan for you."

"My man, you have yourself a deal. Shall we go up to Frankie's?"

"No, not this time. What I really want is from Alex's in Bluefield. You haven't had a hotdog until you have tasted one of his. Alex is Greek and he opened a three stool one booth restaurant across from the post office when I was just a little feller. He has always managed to feed anyone who came in no matter that he only has seats for seven people. My uncle, GC, ate lunch there every day of his working life. Every Saturday my cousin, Joe, and me would go to the Granada to see a western and would eat two hotdogs and an RC cola before. There might be better hotdogs, but I don't know where. The secret seems to be in the meat sauce. Well, I call it meat sauce but it really is no more than a meat flavored hot sauce that soaks into the bun. He doesn't ask what you want on it. You get it his way loaded with onions."

"William," declared David. "Don't you ever have a short answer to a simple question?"

"There's no such thing as a simple question," Bill retorted. "Let's take your car. My pick-up doesn't ride as nice."

CHAPTER TWENTY-TWO

THE TIME FOR THE Sunday visit to a local church rolled around and Bill had decided that the wise choice for the first excursion into the Appalachian religious culture would best be served at the Bluewell Union Church where no division of beliefs (overtly) separated the membership. Membership was probably not the appropriate referent for the mixture of pew-sitters turning to see this new person entering the front door.

All eyes focused on Dr. Cabot until one parishioner exclaimed, "Well I be dogged if'n it ain't the new doctor from down the road in Boston Knob!" With that declaration, all of the pews emptied simultaneously as everyone dashed into the aisles to welcome the newcomer.

The pandemonium was broken when an older dignified gentleman dressed in a severe black suit entered the door and approached the handmade pulpit and sat down in one of the two chairs provided for the leaders of the service. Bill whispered into Cabot's ear that the gentleman was the preacher who was the president of Bluefield College and also, on a rotational basis, served three churches around the area.

The service started with announcements followed by a protracted prayer offered by a white-headed gentleman of advanced years whose speech was affected by severe stuttering. On he went with the dysrhythmia tromping through Cabot's organized mind that longed for an end to the mounting appeal for the blessings of the Lord on everything possible in the minds of this humble gathering. Dr. Cabot was probably not the only one heaving a sigh of relief when an "A-A-A-A-A men" finally reverberated through the rafters of the small building.

With no introduction a quartet made up of two young girls, a young boy, and an older gentleman moved next to a well-scarred upright piano where a stylishly-dressed young woman had begun to hammer out a jazzy version of "Take My Hand, Precious Lord." Following the introductory rift, the quartet's smooth harmony encircled the congregation reflecting a surprising influence of good musical training. While they were singing a couple of men passed through the congregation with collection plates after which the song finished, and the pastor took his place behind the pulpit, bowed his head and exclaimed, "Grace be to you, and peace, from God our Father, and from the Lord Jesus Christ, Amen." This preamble followed the reading of the Gospel and causing David to take pause because the pastor had used a phrase common in liturgical churches.

David, more attentive now, fixed his focus on a rather large man in black who presented total dignity in all respects as he stood beside the lectern preparing to deliver his sermon. He lifted the book to where it was almost touching his nose and the coke-bottom glasses thereon. He began to speak.

"Paul, writing to Titus, is part of the New Testament of which most of us are familiar. Titus, as you recall, was one of the church leaders whom Paul was instructing in the duties of the church as he anticipated the end of his ministry. Paul writes in Titus, chapter three, verses four through eight:"

> *But after that the kindness and love of God our Savior toward man appeared, not by works of righteousness which we have done, but according to his mercy he saved us, by the washing of regeneration, and renewing of the Holy Ghost; Which he shed on us abundantly through Jesus Christ, our Savior; That being justified by his grace, we should be made heirs according to the hope of eternal life. This is a faithful saying, and these things I will that thou affirm constantly, that they which have believed in God might be careful to maintain good works. These things are good and profitable unto men. (KJV Titus, 3, Vs 4-8)*

Barely whispering, but still with emphasis he looked up from his Bible and said, "Oh, what a powerful message embodied in these words."

He looked first to the congregation and then to the heavens to which he raised his voice to a near shout: "That being justified by His gra-a-a-ce, (long pause) we should be made heirs according to the hope of eternal life! Not by works of righteousness which we have done, but according to his mercy he sa-A-A-ved us!"

Dr. Cabot angrily thought to himself, 'Oh shucks. Here it comes. He's going to saAAve us with some old-fashion-honest-to-goodness-hellfire-brimstone-Jesus-saves-preachin'!

David was steeling himself to bear such an affront to his moral beliefs almost to the point of deliberately getting up and leaving the church. However, the next words took him totally by surprise.

"In 1517 Martin Luther preached a sermon about grace that planted the seed of discontent within the church of the day. That sermon was copied down and printed as a pamphlet that has been credited as being the beginning of the Reformation that led to our protestant beliefs whether they be Lutheran, Methodist, Presbyterian or, yes, even Baptist! Luther took Paul's words to Titus to mean that no amount of human virtue or righteousness, replaces the GRACE of God."

For the first time, Dr. Cabot suddenly became curious about the man in the pulpit. He leaned over to William and asked, "Who in that remarkable man?"

To which Bill jotted down on a scrap of paper found in the book rack in the seat in front of him, "Dr. J. Taylor Stinson, past President of Bluefield College."

Confused, David responded in kind "I thought that was a Negro college?"

On the same scrap of paper Bill wrote, "That's Bluefield State in Bluefield, West Virginia. His is a two-year Baptist College in Bluefield, Virginia."

David muttered, "Confusing."

The preacher continued. "Luther introduced his 95 theses, or proclamations, or perhaps we should call them his interpretations of the Words of the Holy Scriptures, or more specifically, the behavior of those entrusted with the task of preaching the Gospel. Luther declared that our Lord Jesus Christ willed the entire life of believers 'to one of repentance'. Luther denounced the practices of the church of the time that placed the priest between God and man and, indeed, even allowed the selling of indulgences."

The preacher paused at length, took off his glasses, and walked a short distance from the lectern. Pinching the bridge of his nose with his head down he continued.

"Now.... an indulgence was a way of buying an exemption for punishment, they called it penance, from the church for minor sins. Purchasers were mostly those who feared that if one of their sins went unconfessed, extra time in purgatory would be required. According to the history books all of this happened because the Crusaders risked dying without the benefit of a priest's doing the final rites, so, they gained automatic forgiveness for fighting to free Jerusalem from other faiths. Church leaders preached that good works earned salvation, and making Jerusalem Christian was 'good works' so therefore, paying money to support good works was the same as doing good works."

Preacher put his glasses back on and began flipping through his Bible finally settling on a page he began to read.

"In Paul's Letter to Titus, chapter three, verses five through seven, He speaks against the practice of 'good works' serving as salvation. He says,

> *Not by works of righteousness which we have done, but according to his mercy he saved us, by the washing of regeneration, and renewing of the Holy Ghost; Which he shed on us abundantly through Jesus Christ our Savior; That being justified by his grace, we should be made heirs according to the hope of eternal life. (KJV Titus Vs 5-7)*

He took off his glasses and continued to speak softly.

"These words tell us that only God is the source of salvation, free of good deeds, assured by the gift of his only

Son and cleansed by God and His grace. Then, why do we continue to demand good works? From this very pulpit, I am told, a man setting himself as a preacher told you, 'if you love me give me a dollar. God loves a giver.' He was telling you, in the very face of the scriptures, that by giving him money you will receive God's grace. What blasphemy!"

"No Church, Synod, Convention, diocese….no organization…. can put a demand or price on the grace of God. No priest, preacher, bishop, deacon, can take the role of providing you the grace of God. No one can sell you what you already have."

Dr. Stenson placed his glasses on the lectern before him and looked to the congregation through the visible dimness of severe cataracts. He paused for long seconds and finally spoke in a volume so soft he could barely be heard:

"Jesus IS the Word and the Word IS God that, through him and by Grace alone we are saved……AMEN"

The sermon wound down as the clock approached twelve noon. David relaxed in anticipation of a benediction and a rapid exit when Dr. Stenson announced: "Turn to hymn number 198 in your hymnal and as we sing those beautiful words, if you have not welcomed the gift of Grace you are invited to come forward and accept Christ as your personal savior."

The piano began quietly at the beat of a dirge. The congregation began to sing: *Just as I am*….

Just as the last of the first verse line faded away, the preacher began to speak in a most pleading voice: "Jesus is bidding you to come forth. The Lamb of God is offering you salvation. Truly his blood was shed for you. The road to his presence is right next to you and leads to the altar of God. All you need do is take that road as we sing the next verse."

Just as I am, ….

Again, the preacher interjected his extemporaneous plea: "Doubt and conflict can be washed away by the blood of Jesus if you just come forward and accept his plea. Don't put your salvation aside for another day. Accept Him now. Be washed of your sins in baptism. Come forward and receive his Grace!"

Just as I am, …

"Jesus is welcoming you with open arms; yes, yes, his open arms offer you his power of grace to cleanse your soul and troubled mind. Come forward now and accept his WORDS OF PROMISE!"

As the next verse began David saw people moving toward him but Bill shooed them away. He made a mental note to ask William what that was all about.

Just as I am, ……….. I come!

"Thank Goodness that's over" thought David but his thankfulness was premature. The Preacher pulled a one-more-time on him as he practically shouted, "LET'S REPEAT THE LAST VERSE AS WE OFFER THE GRACE OF GOD AND THE LOVE OF JESUS TO SINNERS ONE MORE TIME."

Finally, it was over and David and Bill made a hasty exit trying hard to avoid well-wishers. They successfully dispersed to the front yard of the church and William stopped Dr. Cabot by pointing toward the back of the church into a flat area of ground between the church and the back of Sunny South Market over on New Route 52 and said, "See that flat spot right there? I've got a story to tell you about that so don't let me forget to tell it to you some time."

With that they returned to the car and rode away to David's mixed thoughts of chagrin, downright disgust, and genuine curiosity filling his mind. He questioned William about what was going on when he blocked the church members away, during what he had learned was the invitation, to which Bill replied, "They intended to save your soul."

To David the invitation was an oxymoron to the sermon offered by Dr. Stenson. His sermon was educated, well delivered, thoughtful and as worthy of delivery as a homily in any Liturgical Church anywhere. Why then did the deliverer of such a sermon pull a pulpit Dr. Jekyll/ Mr. Hyde? The preacher went against his own litany of 'Grace being free' and put a very specific condition upon receiving it.

CHAPTER TWENTY-THREE

D<small>R. CABOT STAYED BUSY</small> in his practice with days turning into weeks and weeks into months with nothing but routine to fill his mind. Well, that wasn't totally true. His proximity to Jenn was a constant distraction. She went about her business oblivious to her beauty's effects on people around her.

David approached her many times intending to invite her out for a nice meal and a movie but always reversed his actions because of their working relationship. In no way did he want to give Jenn the impression that his interests were anything more than friendship...or professional. So, he arranged a clinic party were all of his professional relations where invited. That meant Bill, Jenn, and himself. He mentioned the plan to William who suggested that he bring a date that would help solve the imbalance but David felt that this would make it appear that Jenn was along as a date for himself. So, being the dignified coward, he was, he canceled the whole plan.

Dr. Cabot was cognizant of the dangers of the mines but the true impact on the lives of his patients was soon to be abruptly thrust into his real world. In random conversations with those around him he had learned that since January

21, 1886, 2394 miners had lost their lives in West Virginia in the coal mine industry with all but about 21 of those a result of violent methane gas explosions. He was anxiously aware of the potential for a mine accident; the question was not 'if' but 'when'.

He knew he would most likely be called to assist in his role as physician and surgeon. True to expectation, that call came at about 2:00 AM, on a cold, wet, miserable, moonless night. He did not think to ask the name of the person on the phone since the shock of the possible number of deaths had practically frozen his ability to move or think. There were 134 men working approximately 400 feet underground in a giant mine extending from an elevator shaft on the Virginia side to a drift mouth on the West Virginia side about three miles away.

Dr. Cabot's MASH experience had not fully prepared him to face the trauma of violent injury and death in a situation where the family was at the scene before others. The Korean War had been a laboratory for improvements in the care of the wounded from injury to treatment. Here, in the isolated mountains of West Virginia, hospital facilities were miles away, reached only by road, in double-duty hearses, used mostly for mortuary transport sans even a Band-Aid. Here he stood by, helplessly, waiting nervously for bits of news from the rescue team, along with the wives and children of the men still underground. He feared the prospect that he could suffer a flashback experience that would defeat his ability to be useful in the present situation.

Doctor's long wait finally ended as a chain of mine cars rolled slowly from the drift mouth entrance on the West Virginia side, bearing the dead and living bedraggled rescuers. Now he knew what the term "drift mouth" meant. He had heard it mentioned from time to time; it simply meant a flat direct entry into a mine where rails could bring the coal out to the tipple. Now it was disgorging human misery.

Rescue workers, some who had just escaped the explosion, their sad faces blackened with the interminable "black gold dust" they removed from the mountain for a miserable living, rode on the cars, accompanying the bodies of their friends and relatives. David could not hold back his horrific memory of a massacre that occurred above the village of Tunam, South Korea where thirty unarmed, critically wounded United States Army soldiers, and an unarmed chaplain, were killed by members of the North Korean army following the Battle of Taejon. Troops of the U.S. Army's 19th Infantry were cut off from resupply by a roadblock established by North Korean troops. To avoid the roadblock, they attempted to evacuate their wounded through nearby mountains only to become stranded. There they were discovered by a North Korean patrol. Only the medic managed to escape; all the rest were executed.

Dr. Cabot, the escaped medic, and other medical personnel, were ordered to return to the scene and document the incident including identifying the victims.[11]

---

[11]   One of the soldiers could have been Corporal Lonnie Bryant Hylton, Jr. of New Hope, Mercer County, West Virginia, who, for many years was listed as missing-in-action (MIA), but later showed up in army records as being kill-in-action (KIA).

L.B. Hylton was one of three Bluewell boys to serve in the Korean Conflict. The other two were Charles Hare and Me. L.B, along with his brother Kenny, were playmates. L.B.'s father grew up in Indian Valley with my daddy and they both immigrated to Bluefield, both working for the US Mail. One particular activity in which L.B. excelled was finding Chinquapins, a

Dr. Cabot desperately shook off the negative war images and tried to focus on the current situation where the bodies of the miners were being unloaded from the coal cars and taken to a mine company building where they were laid in rows so that Dr. Cabot and the other physicians and the county coroner could begin the grim task of establishing identification and, believe it or not, the cause of death. The examiners agreed that most of the first victims brought out of the mine died from suffocation rather than the force of the blast. The lack of physical trauma in many of the deaths probably saved David from being overcome by the scene's similarity to war. However, he nearly lost his composure when the last bodies brought out had been buried under

---

favorite autumn endeavor. "Chinkie pins" were a pleasant and profitable product in the Southern Appalachian Mountains. First off, they were real tasty and provided an extreme source of pleasure just having them, particularly as contraband in a school room with hulls covering the oiled wooden floors. More importantly, they were valuable, since they could be sold for twenty-five cents a pint which was big money back then. To put the market value of a pint of chinquapins into purchasing-power perspective, at that time, a loaf of bread was five cents, soda pops were five cents for a twelve-ounce bottle, potatoes were 25 cents/100 pounds, cigarettes were eleven cents a pack of 20, a loaded hot dog was five cents, a movie was ten cents and bus fare into Bluefield was ten cents. There wasn't a road anywhere in the fall of the year that did not find ragged kids alongside selling them. In many cases it was the only cash money to be found by a family. Blackberries were also a good cash crop selling for 25 cents/half gallon. We never had store-bought berries of any kind. Strawberries were favorites and only available picked from the surrounding hills. Nothing in the world was as good as wild strawberry preserves.

piles of slate brought down by the explosion, as well as the explosion itself. The task of identification was carried out mostly by a process of elimination since one miner was missing most of his head and others had been burned beyond recognition.

After scanning the horrible condition of the dead miners David was inexorably overtaken by déjà vu and rushed outside where he bumped into Jenn on her way into the building. He spontaneously burst into tears and extended his arms out to her. She responded by falling into his arms and returning the embrace. They remained so until Jenn slowly extricated herself and spoke to him as if he were a child.

"There, there; you'll be okay. Just remember what you are. You're a fine physician but first you are a fine human bein'. Now stand up straight and get on with the unpleasant job you know how to do. Later on, we can sit down to a quiet talk and work ourselves through this. It might appear to be amongst the worst you've seen but, believe me, you will see worse many times before you end your days as a doctor, especially here in the mountains where violence sometimes appears to be a way of life."

CHAPTER TWENTY-FOUR

TRUE TO HER WORD, two weeks later Jenn invited David to be her guest for supper at The La Saluda. Since it was a 'dinner out' it meant that Jenn would be dressed in her Sunday best and that was almost more than David could handle. Her in something more than the day-to-day nurse's uniform conjured up mental images of every fancy dress he had seen on the most beautiful movie stars. He unconsciously avoided her at work for fear she might change her mind. He discussed the date with Bill as if he was facing a Major Event. As if! This WAS a Major Event. Bill was not very sympathetic since, after all, Jenn was just a sister and certainly not special enough to cause the torment that David was experiencing. "Hey, Buddy, she's just another girl. If you like her, speak up. She'll appreciate it. Like any girl, she wants to be noticed and complimented."

David took offense at William's dismissal of Jenn as being 'an ordinary girl.'

"I beg your pardon," David practically shouted at William. "Under no circumstances is Jenn ordinary. Haven't you looked at her? She is the loveliest creature I have ever seen in my life. She is perfect."

Bill glared at David with a look of puzzlement that suddenly changed to astonishment. "Well I'll-be-doggoned. You're in love with her," Bill declared.

David's face turned to bright crimson. He sat, as if frozen. He tried to speak but nothing happened. He tried to casually laugh but he couldn't make it happen. He finally said in a whisper, "perhaps you are correct."

"Well, dang it man, do something about it," William demanded. "I think you would make a swell brother-in-law and truth be told, Jenn has no inkling of your hidden adoration. Jenn has never been around boys very much and the ones she has been are…well…just not her type, boy's already doing a man's job in the mines or…well, you know…I'll say it: poor white trash! She's as dumb as a post about…. courtin'. I taught her to dance and I am the only person she has ever danced with until I went away to school. Sure, she went to nursing school at the St. Luke's program in Bluefield but even there it was all women and old and older doctors. You are here providentially for a community needing a doctor. Don't you think that same providence might be a heavenly match up for Jenn? She is too precious to be wasted on 'old- maid-hood' if that is a word. Let me tell a story of a beautiful woman who lost out on the joys, heaven help me for saying this, of marriage."

"Up on the ridge there were two 'old maids' living in a very nice house with no one but the two of them and an orphan nephew. One was a very sweet, kind, gentle, accomplished, registered nurse…like Jenn. The other was as crooked as a barrel'a snakes and just as mean. I'll call her Miss Mean. The nice one, I'll call her Miss Nice, was our go-to person for minor injuries; Miss Mean was a flim-flam artist. She was the reason Miss Nice was never married. She was the oldest, dependent on her younger sister for her livelihood, and a gatekeeper to keep men out of their lives. Miss Nice had a boyfriend at the hospital but Miss Mean started rumors that he was…. well…. queer, causing him to leave to another state. This broke Miss Nice's heart and made Miss Mean, meaner."

"Miss Mean was my brother-in-law's nemesis as well as my nephew, Sonny. Miss Mean flimflammed both of them big time. She got Sonny and Joe first. She had a small field of hay, probably about three acres, that she hired Sonny and Joe to 'put up' in her barn. Sonny was only about fourteen at the time and Joe was two years younger. They used Leslie's Studebaker half-ton pickup to load and haul the hay from the field and unload it in the hayloft of the barn. It took two days and a tank of gas. Pay time came and she gave them a dime apiece for work that was worth at least $10.00 even in hard times, not counting the cost or the truck."

"She flimflammed both of them again the very same year. Leslie decided to put Sonny to work doing something useful until time for school to start. Sonny was hauling wood from a sawmill up on the ridge and stacking it at the barn to sell by the pickup load. He had hauled about 20 loads at the cost of fifty cents per load plus the cost of gas for the truck. Miss Mean came to Leslie and asked how much the wood was and he told her two dollars a load. She paid him the two dollars, and the next day while Sonny was in getting more wood and Leslie was at work, she showed up with a two-and-a-half-ton tandem wheel truck and hauled away the entire wood pile in ONE LOAD!"

David said, "I think I comprehend the first story as being a paradigm of unrequited love, warning me to not shy away from Jenn for fear she will sense rejection and therefore become an old maid. But the moral of the second story lacks not even a vague relationship to the first. Can you enlighten me?"

"They're not related. I was just on a roll so I thought I'd tell you a bonus story while I was so wound up in your affection for my sister. I'm on your side, man. Don't lose her by being as shy as she is," Bill chuckled.

"Laugh if you will, you infantile nitwit. I will become your brother-in-law just to torture you," David countered with laughter.

CHAPTER TWENTY-FIVE

THANKSGIVING DAY WAS APPROACHING and with it came numerous invitations to Dr. Cabot for a multitude of functions ranging from family dinners to institutional organizations including the Bluefield Country Club and the Elks Lodge also of Bluefield. David had no priorities except for one; he wanted to be wherever Jenn was. Of course, he did not make that wish known to her but he did drop a hint to Bill.

He and Bill had lunched together at Frankie's a couple of days earlier. David tried subtly and unsuccessfully to "weasel" information out of Bill on possible family gatherings to which he just might be included but in the words of Bill, there was nothin'-a- peckin'. Bill did invite him to go to a Turkey Shootin' match up at Hale's bottom run by the Hale clan. "Hey, how'd you like to go with me and Leslie, my sister, Lula's husband you remember, to a Turkey Shoot next week? We have lots of fun and Leslie and I nearly always win."[12]

---

[12] My dad and me used the same Remington 870, 12 Gauge (S8528) shotgun at shooting matches. It appeared to us, and

David, aghast, answered with abruptness. "No, of course not. You of all people should know that I am not amenable to the killing of animals for sport! Poor turkeys: subject to slaughter by a bunch of men bearing rifles."

Bill, laughing, said, "We don't shoot at turkeys and we don't use rifles. We shoot at targets with shotguns.

David adamantly proclaimed, "I saw the movie about Sgt. York of Tennessee and they showed a Turkey Shoot there. They positioned a turkey behind a log and the contestants waited for the turkey to protrude its head and the one that hit it won the contest."

"Well, maybe so, but that's not the way we do it. Bill countered. "The turkeys are the prizes and have been dressed for cookin'. Here's how it works: each shooter pays a fee to shoot at a target provided by the match sponsor that he has marked with an X and shoots at it from the same distance same as all the others who have marked their own targets. The shooter who gets the closest to the X wins the turkey. If the amount of money put up by the shooters goes over the cost of the turkey the winner gets the 'backdraw'. That's the real reason for the contest is to get the backdraw money. Nobody really wants the turkey but if the backdraw is part of winnin' the turkey then it isn't gamblin' and gamblin' is illegal. Got it?"

"Yes, I do indeed get it. Just another way you good mountain folks have devised procedures for avoiding the laws of your great state. First it was the private club to serve liquor and now a Turkey Shoot. What will it be next?"

---

nothing ever contradicted that view, that the shotgun delivered a pattern that gave us an advantage by placing our X in the lower right corner of the target paper and aiming for the center.

Bill laughed and said, "I don't know but try this one on for how to beat the law. As you have experienced, not too happily as I recall, only the government can sell hard liquor and wine in West Virginia made by controlled companies who are taxed at the point of shipping and receiving. But if the booze is made at an illegal still, it must be delivered some way because not everybody is handy to a source. So, moonshiners use bootleggers as their delivery system. Bootleggers may be locals on foot or mobile by way of specially built cars. Now, there's a difference between a bootlegger and a moonshiner. One makes and one distributes. There is a social difference between the two as well. A moonshiner is higher up on the social scale than a bootlegger who is often a low-life peddler pushing illegal liquor to hard-drinkin' people who are cheap drunks, or to alcoholics who want to hide their drinking problem, or church goers who don't want to be seen goin' into a state liquor store."

David, exasperated, said, "Good Lord, man, quit rambling and get to the point."

Bill whistled and said, "My, my, ain't we testy now. Okay, well, the motorized bootlegger in this part of the state can plan his route so that he crosses the West Virginia, Virginia State lines several times in a few miles. This puts up a barrier to the State Cops since they can't cross state lines thus giving the bootlegger a chance to stop and wait or to find another back road to where they are goin'. That didn't work after the state boys got radios because all they had to do was stop at the state line and call ahead for a BOL, that's 'be on the lookout' for you city slickers, thus causing the bootleggers to find other routes within their own states. The local constabulary just don't care, or might be customers themselves, or have family members in the business. Another thing…."

David interrupted emphatically, "enough, I have had enough for now. Besides I need to get back to the office or your sister will have my hide, as you frequently comment."

The day of the Turkey Shoot arrived. The snow was falling sporadically. Bill and Doctor approached the site of the activity leaving behind telltale footprints in the pristine snow. Bill said, "There's Leslie over next to the fire barrel."

There, beside the requisite fire barrel, a 55-gallon oil drum, stood a cluster of heavily jacketed men laughing and sharing a bottle. Two men stood, slightly apart from the drinking population, engaged in a conversation of their own.

"Over there," Bill said pointing, and then added, "Well I be dog bite,[13] that's Sonny with his Daddy!"

Doctor responded enthusiastically, "Splendid, finally I get to meet the famous Turman Boys."

Their approach was detected and all eyes turned to see Bill and his mystery guest. Leslie spoke first declaring, "Well, look what the cat drug in" extending a hand of greeting.

Bill grabbed Leslie's hand and pulled his top-rated-relative to him for a manly hug.

Pulling away he said, "Leslie, I want you to meet Dr. David Cabot, the new guru of medicine down at Boston Knob."

As they were shaking hands Bill continued, "And that long drink of water is his son, Leslie, Junior, better known around here as 'Sonny'."

---

[13]   My Grandpa Gullion was a very religious man who was adamantly opposed to 'cussing' so he created his own expletive, 'Dog Bite It', broadly used in appropriate situations such as hitting his thumb with a hammer—which he often did.

"How are you, soldier?" Doctor inquired still holding Leslie's hand. He extended his left hand to Sonny and apologized, "please excuse the left hand."

"Airman, and Ah'm well, thank you Doctor. And the left hand is, after all, the best since I am left-handed."

"Oh, no wonder you bear the title of family rogue. Do you, or have you ever had problems coping with authority figures or persons?" Doctor ventured.

Bill and Leslie simultaneously burst out in laughter and Bill inquired, "Does a bear poop in the woods?"

More laughter and the topic appeared closed but not before Dr. Cabot addressed Sonny with an observation. "As a physician in the military, I encountered an inordinate number of left-handed young men of apparent high intelligence who could not seem to fit the mold. I would like your viewpoint on that observation. Will you have time over your leave to visit with me?"

"Why, yes, ah would be glad too. How about you come by the house so you can meet Mama at the same time? Mama fixes the best fried chicken in the world." Doctor recalled a similar claim about Annie's chicken.

CHAPTER TWENTY-SIX

AFTER THE TURKEY SHOOT, the snow had fallen in earnest and had blanketed the area with about six inches of pure white. Here away from the mining it would remain so for several days. As he drove by the tipple the snow was already coated with black. The very efficient State Road Crews had cleared Route 52 and covered them with cinders. Jim was 'chauffeuring' the Doctor today so that he could take the opportunity to visit his mother up on Red Oak Ridge.

The Turman House sat on an artificially flattened area in the side of the hill above Old Route 52 just at the point where State Route 20 left 52. Snuggled within the juncture of the two routes was a small building with a large sign declaring this to be the 'L.W. Turman Store, Groceries, Feed, Hay'. A sign in bold letters on the door declared, 'Script Accepted'. He was aware of script as a company-specific form of currency usable only in the store owned by the issuing company, just another way to control the miners. The store was open. He entered.

The first sensation he experienced was the unique aroma of a small country store. Doctor looked to his right to see a ceiling-high stack of one hundred-pound sacks of cattle and hog feed contained mostly in colorful flowered fabric.

Hanging from the ceiling was a stalk of green bananas. To his left was a homemade counter with ceiling-high shelves full of canned, boxed, and bagged products of all kinds. Directly ahead was a meat case filled with rolls of baloney, boxed cheeses and soda pop. The counter top was covered with boxes of Moon Pies, both round and square, and like-choices. In the middle of that chaotic display stood a pot belly stove putting out a warm glow. He was the sole occupant of the building. Just for the novelty of it he went behind the meat case and retrieved for himself a twelve-ounce bottle of RC Cola. He then sat down on a stack of feeds and sipped his drink. Again, he surveyed the scene and further identified one of the dominant smells. A bright red painted square 'box' with a hand pump mounted on top contained 'lamp oil' according to a sign hanging from the pump. It briefly concerned him that the combustible liquid sat so close to the blazing stove. Next to the kerosene stood a wooden barrel of 'salt fish'.

The environment relaxed him. The ambiance was pungent but pleasant. He waited. No one came. Finally, he placed his empty bottle in a wooden departmentalized pop bottle case, left the store behind and walked up the hill, traversing the fairly steep incline by way of steps created with large flat stones. He topped the hill and advanced to a large, two step-up, roofed-over porch that would obviously take him to the front door. Directly in front of him, taking up one end of the porch, was a windowed room resplendent with live plants. True to this expectation the front door was there. He knocked.

His encounters with similarities reoccurred as a near-carbon copy of Annie, but obviously more concerned with appearance, answered the door.

"Hello, Doctor. Come in. Ah'm Lula. Welcome." she greeted with the same type enthusiasm as her brother William. "We've been waiting for you. Are you hungry? I've put the chicken on so we'll eat as soon as you say to. Everybody's in the kitchen. Come on in."

Doctor followed her through curtains into an unheated dining room, then through a bi-swinging restaurant style door into a wonderful old fashion kitchen. There at a large table sat Leslie and Sonny with coffee cups in front of them. The aromas were intoxicating. On a wood-burning cook stove, sitting forty-five degrees in the inside corner of the room, sat a cast-iron skillet, over an open flame, alive with the sounds of frying chicken. Pots with potatoes and home-canned beans were boiling away and homemade biscuits were going into the oven.

Doctor was told to "sit" and was given a fresh cup of coffee and directed toward sugar and thick, thick cream. He dipped the cream into his coffee and watched the butterfat drift to the top. This, he thought, must be what they mean as 'dessert' coffee.

An abundance of food was placed on the table with instructions "to eat."

To his surprise, there was no table grace offered. Conversation while eating centered around the snow, winter time drops in milk and egg production, and how he was enjoying West Virginia, coming from the North.

The meal was finished and out of the oven came a piping hot apple cobbler to be placed in bowls and smothered with sugar and the very thick cream. Sonny polished off two bowls but refused the offer of more.

There was a knock on the back door by a customer for the store. Leslie stood and said he would take care of it. Dr. Cabot and Sonny went to the 'front room' and sat in chairs close to the Heatrola, the trade name for a popular coal-burning stove, and visited.

Doctor broke the ice by asking, "Do they often leave the store unattended?"

"Seldom." Sonny responded with no further explanation then, leaning toward Dr. Cabot intently asked, "Do you think there is something wrong with people like me?"

"I assume you are referring to my observation of lefthanders?"

"Yes. Tell me what you have noticed."

"Of course, but let me state my hypothesis. It is my thinking that left-handedness is a neurological phenomenon affecting logic. Primarily I must say that, as a group, your mistakes are not the results of stupid behavior as is so often considered in reported infractions of the multiplicity of illogical rules we all encounter, but rather the reaction to stupid expected behaviors based on 'that's-the-way-we-have-always-done-it' demands. I should point out that in medical school we were exposed to very little on the works of psychologists. I do remember a lecture or two about brain dominance differences of left and right-handed people. The theory is that disorders, such as stuttering, may be caused by mixed brain dominance. Well, I am beginning to sound like your Uncle Bill. I will ask him a question and he tells me the history of the Roman Empire as part of the answer. Forgive me for rambling on."

Sonny alertly responded. "No sir, you really have my attention. You have noticed that Bill stutters sometimes, haven't you? This sounds like something I might like to look into some day. As for Bill, we have been very close. He and my Aunt Pauline have been so close to me that I don't refer to them as uncle and aunt, but by their first names. And

Bill has always been a talker. Pauline, by the way, was my fifth-grade teacher who finally got me to reading."

"And, as I have been told, you also are a bit legendary in your exploits," said Doctor.

"I don't see anything that I have done as 'exploits' but rather the act of taking advantage of opportunities. An example, right after the war was over, the WW2 that is, not Korea that caused me to go into the Air Force, an Italian family moved here in Bluewell, just beyond the schoolhouse down in the bottom. Nobody knew where they came from. They had no family here and all of the local Italian families that lived here for a long time tended to have nothing to do with them. A couple whispered that he might be running from the 'Mafia'. A few days after they moved in a brand-new Chrysler Convertible appeared under their carport attached to the garage. It just sat there; never moved. I had to know why so I went to their house, knocked on the door and this is how it went down.

The door opened and I said to the man who answered, "Fine looking car you got there, mind if I look at it?" I knew enough Italian to know that he said 'wait a minute' and 'speak English', so I waited."

"Shortly a pretty blond about my age or a little younger came to the door."

She said, "I know who you are. My name is Bonita Cordusio. I've seen you up at Frankie's and Mary said you are real nice. I'm listening to my record player. You like to jitterbug? I don't know how. I'm glad you stopped by. I haven't made any friends yet. The girl just across the road there and I have met but she has other friends."

Her English was northern and with not a bit of Italian accent. I asked her if it was alright for me to look at the convertible.

"Oh, sure." she told me. "You drive, don't you? I think I've seen you drive to the house across the road."

"Yes," I told her. "I have a driver's license."

All of a sudden, she said, "I've got an idea, wait here."

In a minute or two she came back with her Papa and introduced me to him in Italian. She then turned to me and said that she had asked her Papa if I could drive the car for her and he said, "Yes," after he took a look at me. I smiled my most winning smile and waited for an answer that came after they had a brief exchange.

After looking me over and asking Bonita several questions he finally smiled at me and said, 'Va bene' followed by what I didn't understand and then the word 'dollari' that I recognized as money. She was very happy and told me he said it was 'very good' and that he would pay me twenty dollars a week until school started. For almost three weeks I chauffeured Bonita to the swimming pool, to the show, to the drive-in; everywhere. Then, one day right before school started, Bonita told me that they were moving. She did not know when or where and for me not to come anymore. So, that ended that. I missed her, but I missed that convertible even more."14

---

14   This is a true incident that did not end here. Many years later in the 1970s I was in Las Vegas to present a paper at the American Speech and Hearing Association. A very attractive female friend and I were waiting in line at an Italian Restaurant when two well-dressed gentlemen joined the line. After waiting a bit one of them asked my friend where she was from and she informed him she was from New Mexico. In turn he asked me where I was from. I too responded New Mexico. The man said "No, I've been listening and you are not originally New Mexican. Where were you born?" I told him, West Virginia. He pressed me to be

"How are you faring in the Air Force?" Dr. Cabot asked.

"Okay. I'm in a very unmilitary setting. Most of my work responsibilities are to civilians of the Corp of Engineer personnel or retread officers who are engineers. I have had only one encounter with an officer that caused me to be disciplined but he turned out to be one of my best friends and an excellent teacher."

"That sounds intriguing. Tell me about it."

"I am, and was at the time, a well-respected architectural draftsman in demand for my ability to take a project and go with it uninterrupted, only to discuss changes not of my doing. We had a brand-new Second Lieutenant right out of college and ROTC who was unaware of the protocol, albeit unconventional militarily, that existed in our squadron. Lt. Little came to my work station the first week he was there and ordered me to empty his trash can. No big deal. I said 'Yes sir, I'll get to it shortly.'. In just a minute or two he returned and yelled, 'Airman, I gave you a direct order to empty my trash can. Now get to it'. That time I was not so polite when I told him to 'empty it himself or get Airman Bice, who's assignment that was. "I am working on a project that preempts all other assignments." Well, the Squadron NCO who works directly for the commander, came in the back door soon after, came to work station, and kindly told me to keep my mouth shut and go quietly to see the Colonel. I did as he suggested and reported, in good military fashion

more specific. I told him near Bluefield and he pressed again asking, "Where near Bluefield?" and I replied, "Bluewell." He laughed heartily and said, "I have a friend that lived in Bluewell. His name is Cordusio. I responded, "Cordusio, I drove for him!" Our dinner was free.

to the Colonel who was also a retread structural engineer who was pulled from a major national engineering firm to serve in the war. I approached his desk and snapped to attention and said, "Airman ………."

"Aw, hell, Turman, don't do that crap with me. Just tell me why you thought you could tell an officer where to get off."

"I tried to answer him but he cut me off and quoted the old military saw about the uniform, not the man in it, assigned me the task of washing all of the windows in the entire squadron over the weekend. I left his office and went directly to the fire house that was also located in our complex. I had done favors for most of the firemen, since I had access to the photo reproduction unit, and who are air force like me, and borrowed a firetruck, with crew, for Saturday. That Saturday I went and got my crew and we went to work. I sat top of the tank while the fireman directed the hoses to every window that I was ordered to wash. My heart sank when the Colonel's car entered the complex and he got out and walked towards his office. As he approached, he gave me thumbs up and entered the building. The next Monday morning there was an official letter from the NCO that said,' 'The Colonel said if there was a next time he would be more specific as to how the task was to be done.' I figure next time, every step of the command will be spelled out."

CHAPTER TWENTY-SEVEN

THE INVITATION TO THE family gathering came from Jenn and not Bill as David had expected. It was the Monday before Thanksgiving Day. Dr. Cabot had welcomed an invitation to join the Gullion Family for a feast of roast chicken and baked home-cured ham. This was his first visit to the 'home place'.

Grandpa Gullion sat at his usual kitchen-end of the big dining room table, Grandma sat at the opposite end with the requisite grandbaby in her lap. Except for the children, who waited second table, the balance of the clan was scattered on benches and stools down the sides of the table. David politely answered the less than polite questions thrown his way by a rowdy bunch of quarreling, bickering, and happy brothers and sisters and some in-laws who were treated as outsiders. The kitchen staff consisted of Lula, who provided most of the food and Virginia, Charlie's wife, a really out-of-place Yankee in-law from Detroit, who wanted so much to be embraced by a family as one of them. The seating arrangement was always the same. Grandma sat sideways at one end of the table in a position engrained by years of holding a child in her lap, brothers and sisters along one side of the table and in-laws, on a bench, on the other.

Grandpa sat at the end opposite Grandma and, as usual, provided the Blessing: "Our Father, we give thanks for these table comforts, forgive us our sins, in Jesus … AMEN," at which time he grabbed for the cream pitcher always placed in front of him, taking a healthy swig, followed by Grandma shouting, "Joe," and him responding with a happy, hearty, snicker.

This was the first table and as the food dwindled the adults routinely migrated in pairs to various corners, rooms, sheds, and even the outhouse for in-family gossip. The second table was for the food preparers and children. Lula always saved a chicken leg for Sonny because he was sickly. Bill rescued David leading him to the front porch even though it was a bit cool. They sat quietly for a while looking at the remainder of snow on the northeast side of a sixty percent grade hillside not too far from them. After a while, Bill broke the silence with, "Hey Doctor Dave; you remember the time when we were leaving the church and I told you to look at the bottom land behind the church and I would tell you a story about it later?"

"I do" replied David. "Please proceed."

"Well, it was really a mean trick my two nephews pulled but I still think it's the best prank I ever heard of. Anyhow, that flat lot between the church and the Sunny South Market was a favorite place for evangelical tent meetings. Throughout the summer there's no tellin' how many might set up there. One time a group set up for a revival right between the Bluewell Union Church and no more than 100 feet from the back of the dance hall. The revival started on Thursday night and was just getting warmed up on Saturday night at the same time the joint was really jumping over at the dance hall. It was a hot August night and all of the windows were open at the dance hall to let in some of the cool air for the revelers. At the same time the church goers were getting wound up and were speakin' in tongues so loud that the dancers complained that they could not hear the jukebox.

It just so happened that the Bluewell Union Church was havin' a Singing Convention on that very same weekend and, they too, had all of their windows open, and the tent meetin' was disturbing them as well. Well, let me tell you, Sonny and his cousin, Joe, were men of action! Right after the Union Church let out they decided to curtail the tent meeting annoyance by bringing in the power of the Holy Ghost. They went over to Leslie's store and borrowed a couple of banana knives. Their strategy was for Sonny to go up one side of the revival tent and Joe up the other, cutting the taut ropes holding the tent in place one at a time, while the congregation was engaged in tongue-speakin' and praisin' the Lord with shouts of joy! In their gleeful discussions of the plan the perpetrators imagined that the tent would collapse onto the activity within, reducing the sounds of joy into screams of fright; but alas, that's not what happened! The tent collapsed at the sides, okay? But the center poles didn't! The Rollers began to roll out from under the partially-collapsed tent looking for the source of the interruption while my two nephews made a rapid departure to the woods, where they hid in their tree house for hours after the event. The next day Aunt Sara, an honorary name for an old woman who had no relatives, and was one of the tent meeting attendees, came visitin' Sonny's mother, my sister, if you recall, and proclaimed that 'she knowed who done h'it but she warn't gonna tell.' Lula knew, too, but she just laughed because she knew Sonny-boy could do no wrong."

CHAPTER TWENTY-EIGHT

A NORMAL DAY WAS PROGRESSING at the clinic. Patients with cuts and bruises, patients with gout and children with ear aches sat patiently in the waiting room while similar complaints were being dealt with inside. Jenn efficiently performed triage, sorting the most needed judiciously in order to not appear to be favoring one over another.

Suddenly the door burst open and a frazzled old man shouted, "Hoot Colburn jist kil't his'self."

Jenn went into action and explained to the waiting patients, who had already heard what was going on, that they would have to wait or come back later. By then Dr. Cabot had heard the ruckus and stuck his head out the exam room door and asked. "Is there a problem?"

"Yes" said Jenn. "A man has shot himself and you are needed, probably to pronounce him dead."

Without being told Jenn brought the car around to the front and waited for Dr. Cabot to emerge from the building. Her reasoning was twofold: First, she knew the way and second, a severely damaged young man just might evoke bad war memories in the doctor and she didn't want him being alone in that event. She knew he would protest and she was right.

"I don't need a babysitter," he declared.

"Ah'm nobody's babysitter; Ah'm a nurse and you are a doctor. The nurse's role in medicine is to assist the doctor," she said.

"You think I can't handle a suicide, don't you," he blurted.

"How can you be so dadblamed stupid to not see when somebody just might care for you? I care what happens to you. You are special to me…I mean us…and I…we…want you to stay with us and be a part of us," she pleaded.

Dr. Cabot was stunned into silence. Jenn started the car towards Butt Holler. The roads to their destination were mostly paved. She took route 52 to the point where it intersected with the old route 52. They passed Hatcher's Mill where the locals had their grain ground and followed the paved road for another mile or so. Then she turned onto a well-cared-for dirt road that dipped down into a valley. The house they were looking for sat downward from the road decorated with multi blooming bushes and wild flowers. Jenn drove the car onto a natural lawn where the scene of the shooting became apparent. Dr. Cabot jumped from the car and rushed to the spot where people were gathered. Jenn followed close behind. Dr. Cabot pushed his way to a body slumped over a barbed wire fence with the hands touching the ground and the feet on the other. He rebounded as he saw the condition of the man's head.

"Lord help us," he cried. "What possesses people to do this to themselves; he is dead and there is nothing I can do. Call the undertaker," he demanded.

Jenn quickly moved to his side after having observed his unsteadiness. She took his arm as casually as she could and 'walked' him back to the car.

They sat there in the car for several minutes before David quietly said to Jenn, "Perhaps I do need a babysitter after all."

CHAPTER TWENTY-NINE

"HALLOWEEN IS A HOLY day in the hills. No prank – short of causing damage or hurt – was out of bounds. Turning over outhouses had been an age-old requirement but President Roosevelt's Work Progress Administration, fondly referred to as the WPA, dealt a blow to 'toilet tippin' by building the floor and stool out of concrete with metal strips embedded so as to provide an anchor for the main wood-constructed enclosure. Therefore, alternate pranks would have to suffice. For example, once a group of boys 'acquired' detour signs from the county road department and put one at the route 52 and 20 intersection in Bluewell directing all traffic to Red Oak Ridge. At the intersection of Route 20 and the Littlesburg road, traffic was sent to Brushfork where still another sign directed traffic to Route 52, right back where they started from, back to Bluewell. Very few people were caught in the trick but those that did were rewarded with cider and gingerbread cakes."

Again, David looked daggers at Bill and exclaimed, "Get to the point you windbag!"

Again, Bill pretended hurt feelings and continued: "Okay, sorehead! Sonny and Joe were, like many children in America, keeping track of my World War Two assignment on the B-29 Superfortress and set up a bombing raid of their own. By the way, there was no way of knowin' at that time that Sonny would serve in an adjunct role of the 509th Bomb Wing that dropped two atomic bombs on Japan. He was in the 812th Engineering Squadron that designed and built the facilities used by the 509th at Walker AFB. That's where he got all of his experience that allowed him to get jobs with the two architects in Bluefield after he got home."

"Bill," said David in exasperation!

"Okay, okay" said Bill as he continued with the story. "Route 20 from Bluewell east was carved out of a step bank. An older road, also carved out of the same hill, ran above the current roadbed, about twenty feet higher. They were so close together that the boys often cut grapevines from the trees growing between the two roadbeds and swing out over the new road."

"You understand me on this?" Bill inquired of David. "You have seen kids swinging on ropes over a river and then lettin' loose and fallin' into the river. Well instead of fallin' ……

"Yes, Yes. They were swinging out over the lower road from the upper road. I get it. Proceed."

"Alright; you don't have to bite my head off! Okay. On Halloween night Sonny and Joe got a batch of over-ripe cantaloupes from Sunny South and used them as bombs by holding them between their feet and swingin' out over the road and lettin' go just in time for them to splatter in the road. They sat quietly in their imaginary B-29 and waited for a car to come up the lower road. Their wait was short; Sonny opened up the bomb bay, put a cantaloupe between Joe's feet, and gave him and the grapevine a great push out over the road below. Joe was in great form and released the bomb just in time to splatter all over the windshield of

Constable Purdue's windshield! By the time Joe swung back to the upper road Sonny was gone! Joe found him hiding in the ever-present treehouse hideaway."

"Why… the little deviants" exclaimed Cabot. "Did the Constable apprehend them?"

"No, but next day he scared the living daylights out of Sonny. Joe had already gone back home to Bluefield. Sonny was leanin' against the pop case watchin' Mandy fix popcorn when the door burst open and who should appear but Constable Purdue! He stopped and stared for several seconds at Sonny; he said nothing…just kept looking and finally said, 'Hey, Boy, come here!' Sonny could barely manage to walk over to Purdue he was so scared. When he finally managed to get close enough to be reached, Constable Purdue handed him a dime and said…. with a grin… 'git us both a bottle uh pop.'"

The dignified doctor broke into laugher… a real hee-haw belly laugh when Jenn walked out the door and gave him a quick, light kiss on his forehead exclaiming, "My goodness it is so good to see you act human for a change." For the first time David had experienced two emotions that had generally escaped him his whole life, sheer joy and a reassurance of love.

CHAPTER THIRTY

Months later saw everybody resisting work on a magnificent spring day. The outdoors beckoned. Wild Rhododendrons bloomed everywhere. The Dogwood and Redbud trees added their profusion to the mountain ambiance as gentle breezes carried the perfumes of spring to every shade tree promising solace from winter's cloistered imprisonment. David had decided that it was a perfect day for a picnic and he had steeled himself to invite Jenn to Pinnacle Rock for a basket lunch that he had asked Annie to prepare, which of itself required robust fortitude of its own, and as expected, he was playfully teased by his lovable domestic gendarme.

He was particularly chipper having made a giant personal decision, he even felt like whistling, but his spirits were instantly dampened when he walked into the clinic and found Jenn wearing her professional attire and an all-business attitude. She had her back to him as she dealt with an elderly patient who was having difficulty following instructions. He stopped and admired the manner in which Jenn eased the tension; but as she turned, he noted something about her face that he had only seen once before – tears. He rushed to her but she placed a hand on his shoulder and held him back. Suddenly the hand moved and encircled his neck into a hug as Jenn whispered, "I am so sorry, there is bad news from Boston!"

"What is it? David asked.

Jenn quickly snapped back into her professional role, backed away from him and responded. "It's your father. He passed away last night."

CHAPTER THIRTY-ONE

H<small>E PURPOSELY PLANNED TO</small> take a train, rather than flying, so as to have time to think, (and perhaps mourn?) before facing his mother. She was a kind person but she hid herself in every way from the world giving an impression of coldness. When he faced her she would be in complete control and he needed to face her in kind. So, here he stood with his old army B4 bag packed with his best clothes. His best clothes; he was learning from his New World that best clothes meant only that you had one set other than work duds. Age didn't matter. It didn't matter if the lapel or tie was wide or narrow; it didn't matter if the fabric was wool, cotton, had a collar, was "high waters," had a cuff, or a shiny seat. Many of the dresses and shirts he saw were made of feed sacks[15]or cut down from bigger hand me down bigger dresses

---

[15]   My family could afford to purchase clothing but Mama still made my clothes out of feed sacks. One reason had to do with large quantities of feed we used resulting in an abundance of empty sacks; another was because of Mama's 'waste-not-want-not' philosophy. Our bedsheets were made of four 'white' feed sacks sewn together; all of Mama's everyday clothes were made of feed sacks. Only Daddy and my sister Dorcas drew the line

Feed sacks were greatly appreciated for home-made clothing.

on wearing feed sacks. I finally balked when I started to middle school where the city boys went to school. For six years of schooling I had been wearing feed-sack pants with permanent galluses to hold them up. I would hide them by wearing my shirt over top of everything. Since the pants were made solid, to pee, I had to take off my shirt, pull down my pants. That was in the warmer months; in the cold months I then had to deal with long underwear. Mama's conservation philosophy was active in the kitchen as well. We raised our own food for the most part and killed and dressed our own chickens. When a chicken reached the table not a portion was thrown away. Heavy quilts were made of feed sacks and used for warmth since we had no heat in the bedrooms. Fancy quilts were seldom made of feed sacks; rather they were made of scraps of mill fabrics and were hand stitched with designs.

to make smaller ones. Bib overalls were the required attire for both men and boys who often had no other trousers. During the depression feed mills, especially those producing animal feed products, realized that women in the Appalachians were using feed sacks to sew clothes for their families. Consequently, mills started using flowered fabric for their sacks. The manufactures' labels were removable by washing.

Once he was packed he drifted to the clinic to say goodbye. Business was moving on in spite of his absence. Nurse Jenn would handle many of the routine clinical maladies in his absence but he still felt he was abandoning his responsibilities. 'His People', as he now referred to his patients, were the most generous and understanding people he had ever encountered. Without a doubt, they thought well of him and had accepted him into the fold

Jenn saw him, stopped what she was doing, and asked, "Are you ready to go?"

"Yes," he replied. "Would you find Jim and tell him I need a ride to the train station?"

"Ah'm going to take you," Jenn informed him. "Let's go."

It was a short and silent trip to the station. Jenn aimed the Packard toward a curb marked 'passenger parking' and switched off the ignition.

"Ah'll walk you to the platform," she said as she exited the car.

David followed suit and fell in stride beside her as she moved toward the platform. They took up a position a distance from where several other prospective passengers waited.

"The weather looks good for travel," David opined.

"Yes, it does," replied Jenn.

"Jenn," David said and fell into silence.

"What," Jenn questioned.

As if reluctant to speak David began again. "Jenn, I…..I want to say……

Again, Jenn inquired "what?"

"Jenn, I …" David was interrupted by the noise of the train approaching. Suddenly, Jenn leaned into him, and kissed him on the mouth, quickly turned and ran off the platform toward the parking lot. He followed her with his eyes and was overtaken by a mixture of excitement and depression.

Dr. David Cabot stood forlornly still watching the parking lot long after Jenn had driven away. He became aware of another person standing close to him and turned to see a very dignified, well-dressed gentleman, with an impish smile looking at him. As Cabot turned in his direction the man queried, "Your wife?"

David looked back at the parking lot and replied dreamily, "No, my nurse."

The gentleman laughingly said, "That was no nurse's kiss; that young lady likes you. Do you share her feelings?"

David slowly turned his vision to the gentleman. "And who might you be to presume into my emotional state?"

"I'm sorry for my forwardness", the man laughed sticking his hand out in friendship and announced, "I'm Rob Dolan. Who might you be?"

CHAPTER THIRTY-TWO

AT THAT MOMENT THEY both turned at the sound of the mournful train whistle that David had learned to love. That sound had unique properties; it had the power of assurance that all is well plus it was an excellent weather forecaster. The black smoke spewing from the engine gave further notice that their train was just around the bend already beginning to slow for its short stop at the station. Both picked up their bags ready to board without a word. They gravitated to a group of vacant seats and sat down together as if by prearrangement.

Rob was the first to speak. "Well sir, as I said earlier, I am Rob Dolan from Bluefield, Virginia. I work at the Appalachian Power Company and I am on my way home for the weekend."

David was a bit taken aback at the forwardness of his seatmate. One thing he had learned about the people he had been experiencing for the past year was their willingness to engage in conversation, anytime, anywhere, so long as there were no uppity attitudes; that would put a halt to any kind of dealings. That's not totally true; Republicans, in the minds of the Majority, weren't smart enough to talk about anything since the State of West Virginia was as Democrat as it could possibly be.

David wondered if Rob Dolan was a Democrat and then he wondered why that thought even came to mind. His recent experience with politics indicated, to him, that most Democrats were uneducated, otherwise ignorant, and of fundamental religiosity and, but perhaps not all, looking for a handout many blamed on President Roosevelt's New Deal. He decided not to ask but it turned out that he didn't have to. The two riders talked companionably about politics, religion, and more intensely, the war in Korea. Rob had a son in the National Guard serving in Germany and a son-in-law in the USAF serving State-side. He spoke proudly of a brother-in-law, Elder, who served in the Second World War as the Executive Officer of the 14th Airforce, stationed in China. One of the Major's activities assigned to the "Fourteenth" was flying supplies, mostly gasoline, over-the-Hump to the shark-faced nosed Flying Tigers, piloted by volunteers from the US Army Air Corps, Navy, and Marine Corps, recruited under presidential authority and commanded by crusty ol' Claire Lee Chennault.

As the smoke-spitting train meandered slowly through the valley between tree-covered mountains, the switchbacks were so severe that the end car was visible from the rest of the train. Rob knew every twist, turn, bump, and village along the way and was as free with his travel expertise as he was with his political editorializing; David felt every twist, turn and bump as his stomach was doing some editorializing of its own. He knew he must be showing signs of motion sickness as they passed a small sign beside the road that said, "Falls Mills."

Rob took a glance at him and then spoke up. "Tell you what. If you stay on this train all the way to Lynchburg, you're in for a rough ride. Let's see. It's 11:30 now. Why don't you get off at Bluefield and spend the night at the West Virginian? We'll meet you there for supper at the hotel dining room. You can have a good night's sleep and you can leisurely catch the Powhatan Arrow in the morning at about ten-thirty that's non-stop most of the way to Lynchburg where you make your connection north. Besides, I want to show you off to my wife, Irene; she loves sophisticated professionals."

"Sounds like an ideal and restful time to contemplate my reason for this trip." interjected David. He was not looking forward to his home visit since he had no idea what to expect. Maybe this purported surrogate city of New York had so much to offer it just might prove to be very interesting. "I accept your generous invitation!" He said. "This is another example of the most wonderful Southern Hospitality that I have been experiencing in this magnificent hill country," he added.

CHAPTER THIRTY-THREE

Rob HAD GOTTEN OFF the train at Bluefield, Virginia with promises to meet David at six. The train barely had time to get started when it began to slow for Bluefield, West Virginia. David departed the train wondering if he should seek a taxi cab but after discussing the options with a porter he decided to walk instead. The porter told him more than he really wanted to know. He advised David to go west on Princeton avenue passing by the Colonial Theater and the Matz Hotel, continue until he came to Federal Street, then turn left and the hotel is three blocks south.

The weather was suitable for walking and his B4 bag was not heavy since he had packed sparingly. He crossed Princeton Avenue and soon came upon the theatre where 'From Here to Eternity' with Burt Lancaster and Deborah Kerr was playing and 'Roman Holiday' with Gregory Peck and Audrey Hepburn scheduled next, both first-run top movies. Back toward the train station the Rialto Theatre was showing 'The Outlaw" with Jane Russell. He wondered what talent she had to offer. He strode along noticing the variety of stores on the street including a large Woolworths, until he came to Federal Street, his turning point, when he abruptly stopped. There in front of him, on the corner of the next street, Bland was a classic example of the Romanesque architecture that had been a part of his early days in Boston. It occurred to him that the style was similar to that used by Boston Architect H.H. Richardson who had designed Sever and Austin Halls on the Harvard Campus and Trinity Church that he had attended with his parents as a child. However, he was also aware that it was a massive 'fad' design used in many cities around the world. (The building, the old People's Bank of Bluefield, corner of Bland Street and Princeton Avenue built in 1895, was one of the finest Victorian Romanesque structures in West Virginia. The architect was probably E. C. S. Holmboe of Chicago who had a branch office in Bluefield. Holmboe was heavy into Romanesque characterized by semi-circular arches. This style is seen in reduced form in many structures, including houses, in and around Bluefield and extensively in Bramwell.)

Former Peoples bank building.

Dr. Cabot vowed to find out more about the bank architect. His curiosity piqued, he decided to check into the hotel and find a source of information on local architects' past and present. He continued south on Federal street and was amazed at the degree of commercial, professional and financial activity condensed within the couple of blocks ahead of him. From where he was standing he saw three banks, The First National, the Flattop, and the Commercial, two department stores, Thornton's and A.W. Cox, two Kresges within a block of each other, and a Montgomery Ward. The West Virginian stood next to the Commercial Bank.

As he reached the entry of the hotel he noted the Woodlawn Florist and the Pinnacle Restaurant making a mental note to pick up some flowers for Rob's wife.

At the appointed time David drifted down to the lobby of the hotel to be with the Dolans. As he stepped off the elevator a well-dressed gentleman left the front desk and approached.

"You are Dr. Cabot? He asked in a southern dialect typical of the upper-class West Virginian.[16] "I'm T.P. Cole. Rob made reservations for the dining room and your table is ready if you would like to go ahead and be seated? By the way Irene is a cousin of mine on her mother's side who was ironically a Cabot. Her father is a long-standing businessman of Graham. Let me take you to your table." TP led David to a very nice table quite properly set as one would

---

[16] Except for William and Jenn and a couple of other people including Rob Dolan, he had not encountered this more 'proper' use of language of a very large segment of Virginia, West Virginia, Kentucky, Tennessee, and several other states including parts of Oklahoma, Texas and New Mexico.

expect from a first-class establishment. He saw that Doctor was seated and then, to Doctor's surprise, and pleasure, sat down for conversation.

"I gather you were with Rob long enough to get acquainted?" TP asked as a primer.

"We rode from Northfork to Bluefield on the train just yesterday" David answered. "He appears to be a very knowledgeable man."

"He and his brother have worked their way up in the Appalachian Power Company quite well and they did it as relative outsiders. Their Dad was a well-respected miller in these parts. He was associated with two or three flour mills in West Graham and Princeton, had several patents, I believe."

"Talking about me, I'll bet," loomed a voice from the door.

"Now Rob, be nice," Irene chided. "How are you, TP, Doctor Cabot," directing her attention to him, "so glad to meet you. Are you enjoying Bluefield? Isn't this a lovely dining room?"

TP pushed his chair back and announced, "I'll have Hayes take care of you. He is one of our best. You might remember him, Irene," and walked away without receiving an answer.[17]

---

[17] Hayes would be a black man. At that time there would be no women or white men waiting tables in higher-class restaurants. In the West Virginian all of the barbers were also black men. Bluefield was still segregated. The local bus station still had separate facilities including drinking fountains. On May 17, 1954, Brown v. Board brought integration to WV. Most counties complied without incident. Matoaka in Mercer County, in the heart of coal country and home for many migrant black workers,

Immediately a smiling gray-haired gentleman came to the table and dispensed menus. He inquired as to their comfort and informed them he would give them time to "pur'ruz" the menus.

Mrs. Dolan returned to her dialogue. "I have always found the roast beef with mashed potatoes here to be dependable. Is everyone ready to order?" and hailed the waiter without an answer.

Doctor noticed and thought 'She's ready therefore everybody is ready, just like my mother', then turned to Hayes and inquired. "My dear fellow, I am going to have the country ham for the second time in my life. What do you advise?"

"M'ah advice" said Hayes laughing, "is if'n you have had it'afore they ain' no time lah'k now to try it agin' since the cook here does the best job of almost anybody in fixin' it. On top'a that, ah know the man what cures air ham and he knows how to keep it from dryin' out. You'll need some fix'ns to go wid that an' ah su'gust some sweet tater kas'rol and red eye gravy that ain't on the menu to sop up air very good bread. The bosses here are real gud wif bread."

"Perfect." declared Doctor.

Rob took his turn and said, "I'll have what she's having."

---

experienced some disorder when black children showed up for school. To the credit of the coal companies, all were shorty integrated. However, several Eastern Panhandle counties were entirely segregated until the late 1960s.

CHAPTER THIRTY-FOUR

As promised Dr. Cabot was posited at the Bluefield, West Virginia train station just in time to board the sleek, streamlined Powhatan Arrow albeit still a coal-burning engine. The trip to Boston was mostly a daze. He slept some and snacked each time a vendor passed through hawking his wares at the infrequent stops. He would rouse only when the train passed through big cities. Ultimately, the trip was coming to an end as he entered the surrounds of Boston. He was saddened by the depressing vestiges of decaying neighborhoods that too often were doomed to fade as a result of their rail-side juxtaposition and a shifting demographic. Strangely, he felt a sense of home-sickness. That melancholy was replaced with a sense of dread as the train glided into South Station that seemed to have shared the deterioration of the rest of the rail-related scene. He assured himself that this feeling would subside once he was reunited with family and friends but this was not to occur. Instead, each encounter just exacerbated the depression.

His mother and her brother, Uncle Thomas, who was a retired physician, met him at the train station with stoic solemnity. His mother greeted him with a brief hug while Uncle provided a brief handshake. The conversation on the drive to the home-place was stilted if not formal. Uncle Thomas prattled on about the advantages of a Boston medical practice while his mother focused on the lives of his social peers, mostly female.

"David" she hesitantly began. "I have arranged for a special reception of those close to you and your father after the funeral tomorrow at the country club. I don't suppose you brought suitable attire with you? I assumed not, so I have arranged for a fitting for you tomorrow morning. Several of your old friends will be there and they are anxiously anticipating visiting with you. You remember Gloria Higginbotham and Suzan Cunningham don't you? Well, they have both acknowledged their intent to attend. You will want to look your best for the reunion."

His first thought was that his mother was meddling but he dismissed his disquiet as a result of his depression so he decided to remain silent. The event did, however, evoke thoughts of Bill and what his response to Mother's declaration would be. Bill would say that "He smells a rat."

His depression deepened as the house of his childhood came into view. While the 1906 vintage home was of excellent design and construction, it, like the balance of the surrounding homes, was showing signs of deterioration or just plain neglect, a result of creeping de-gentrification. It was obvious that the urban renewal activities taking place in communities all over the country were approaching the old home place. There was little verbal interchange as the small party entered the house. His mother opined that he was probably tired and suggested he retire to his old room to rest and "freshen up" before dinner.

CHAPTER THIRTY-FIVE

DINNER WAS AT A modest restaurant situated in a cluster of upscale chain stores featuring affordable clothing, shoes and hobby supplies indicating a change of residents' income for the area. David, his mother and Uncle Thomas entered the eating establishment and David noticed the absence of a requisite formally dressed Maître de but instead was greeted by a pleasant, simply dressed young woman who escorted them to a table for eight. David, turning to the hostess commented, "There are only three of us. Don't you have a smaller table?" To which his mother quickly responded, "This is suitable. Others will be joining us, thank you. "David reverted to a bill'ism thinking "Now my hackles are up. Mother is up to something of which I have not been informed." Before he could confront her, an assemblage of five well-dressed persons approached the table.

Uncle Thomas rose to introduce the individual members of the group by identifying each one with an open palm-up hand gesture. "David, you know Clara Cooper here on the left, And Dr. Tom Endicott and Nancy in the middle and Dr. Dwight Eliot and Ellen here on the right. They are here to bring you up to date on the status of medicine here in our little community. Now if all will be seated we can order drinks."

The group separated to move around the table. Clara moved directly to the chair beside David. Although she could have more easily seated herself from the left side where no one was seated, she, instead, chose to enter the chair by squeezing into the space next to David, brushing him casually. She immediately launched into a disconnected conversation ranging from her early association with David to her present situation as an available divorcee. Her physique, attire, coiffure, and most certainly the scent of a very expensive perfume drew his attention to her. He flushed to the warmth of her closeness as she had moved her chair to touch his. Clara was assuredly desirable but instead of being drawn to her he amusingly recalled the words of Jenn back at Frankie's La Saluda Club when he had suggested the ambiance to be romantic and she boldly replied, 'Don't get any ideas soldier. It's this or Lynn's Drive-in and I really don't like eating in a car parked beside a carload of teens'. David began to laugh out loud to the dismay of his mother and the bewilderment of the rest at the table.

The meal was winding down and coffee was being served. Doctor Eliot pushed his chair away from the table and inquired of David. "Well, David here you are back home for the first time since you were mucking about in that war in Korea supposedly practicing medicine. What are your plans now?"

David remained silent for several seconds while his thoughts went to "The cat is coming out of the bag." Eventually, he spoke. "What do you mean 'What am I going to do now? I will continue with my practice in West Virginia, I suppose."

Dr. Endicott, in a rather condescending tone interjected, "Come now, Son, surely you don't intend to honor that spur-of-the-moment fluke? Now that your father's successful

147

practice is yours for the taking, it would appear logical that you would return home and take up your legacy. Your mother desperately wants you to return to be with her and we are here on her behalf to implore you to comply with her wishes."

David again remained silent while he thought, 'Who in blazes are you to assume to call me, Son?'

Firmly, he spoke with a tone of voice that would have frozen a hot poker. "Am I to understand that you believe that I made a foolish decision in assuming a viable medical practice among people who are considered by many to be inferior to us?"

"No, no, nothing like that" responded Endicott. "As I said, your father has provided you with a far superior opportunity for a healthy financial future which would probably not be the case in such poverty as we hear about in West Virginia. Tell you what; why don't you take a look at your Father's set-up and give it some thought. Now, it's time for us old folks to settle down for the evening. Why don't you and Clara have a glass of brandy and visit for a while?"

"Slick" though David. "He just finessed my ace of trumps." Clara was thoroughly enjoying herself and making her presence known. David was loath to admit that he was enjoying her company. They had both enjoyed a brief flirtation many years ago before he entered medical college and her dashing off to marry money from a wealthy Boston Name. At the moment her history meant nothing to him. She was providing attention he had not experienced for many years and bearing on his thoughts of returning to Boston. The brandy and the lovely, willing girl were influencing his sense of judgment and he hesitatingly agreed to call it a night…..at her place.

CHAPTER THIRTY-SIX

HE AWOKE THE NEXT morning with a headache and a return of melancholia. His memory of the previous evening was somewhat vague. He stumbled downstairs to find his mother sitting primly on a kitchen chair apparently waiting for him to appear. She was wearing her uniform of the day that consisted of a gray pencil skirt and one-button blazer with a simple no-collar white blouse. Her shoes were the usual chunky heel black patent leather pumps with matching purse, her hat was a simple black satin pillbox and she wore the required white gloves. The presence of the hat, gloves, and purse was the only hint that she was prepared to go out otherwise she was dressed for a day at home prepared for drop-in visitors. "David, I want us to go look at your Dad's office. His receptionist is maintaining the office and will be there to show you around and to answer your questions. Now, you go get dressed and have a cup of tea and a quick breakfast before we go."

His first inclination was to rebel but he thought better since the visit was inevitable, so he might as well get it over with. "Mother, I don't drink tea for breakfast anymore. Is there coffee?" was his childish way of exerting a bit of willfulness.

"Do we call a taxi or do you have that planned out as well?" he inquired petulantly.

"We will take the family car if you can still drive" she responded in a motherly tone.

Sure enough the gleaming black 1951 Studebaker Commander Land Cruiser sedan stood elegantly in the garage set apart from the house. David held the door for his mother and moved around the front of the car rubbing his hand along the stylish protruding "bullet" nose that was unique to the post-war Studebaker. He found that the car easily accommodated his larger-than-average frame. He situated himself in the comfortable cloth seats and turned the key. To his surprise, the big 8-cylinder engine sprung to life with a single press of the starter. The trip to the office was silent and uneventful.

Both the receptionist and the nurse were there to greet the mother of their old boss and their potential new boss. The entire facility was spick and span but no amount of soap and water would be able to erase the effects of age. It was immediately evident that nothing had been updated in a number of years. The waiting room furnishings were worn and shabby. The walls were in need of paint of a less drab color and the tile floors were worn free of pattern. The clinical tools and apparatus were up-to-date as far as they went and were limited almost entirely, to pre-war vintage. It was clearly obvious that the clientele of this facility was no longer among the elite of the city.

He wondered why his father's old colleagues were pushing him to assume charge of such a pitiful scenario and out of the blue it hit him. They were finagling him to take charge of his mother! It was obvious. His father was gone and Mom had no one to care for her. She had always been dependent on father for almost everything and now she was helpless. Uncle Thomas, even if he was young enough, had enough problems of his own without taking on an aging niece.

For the first time since being home David looked at her from a different perspective. He had always seen her as too reserved, if not cold, domineering, and self-centered where, in fact, she was simply frightened.

CHAPTER THIRTY-SEVEN

I⟊ WAS A LOVELY day in Boston and David was decided against any future tête-à-tête with Clara. His thoughts were far too removed from his present location to consider other women. His mother was going through the motions of beginning the preparation of breakfast but it was obvious that her thoughts were elsewhere as well.

"What are your plans for the day?" she asked vaguely.

"Oh. Nothing," he responded equally as vague.

"Isn't Clara expecting you for dinner tonight?"

"Oh? Oh, right. I had forgotten. We were going to Michael's at Clara's choosing. I am not one iota interested but I suppose there is an obligation, at least family wise. But, mother, it's time for you and me to discuss more pressing problems. I know it's not a fancy restaurant but Shony's serves a good breakfast and there's one just up on the main street. Why don't we go over there and eat so that you are not distracted with preparations? I really must be thinking about returning home and to my practice as I have only begun to work through a very heavy schedule."

"Oh, home is it?"

"What? No, just a slip of the.....Yes, by heaven, HOME! West, by gosh, Virginia is now my home. I have friends and co-workers who care for me, and I am beginning to understand their ways. I have a wonderful home where I don't need to lock the doors even though hundreds of people live in poverty but are too proud to steal. I am providing a valuable, necessary service that is appreciated and too often paid for with chickens, a sack of potatoes or maybe no more than a genuine 'thank you' straight from an humble broken heart shattered by the shame of it all. I am offering up my skills, maybe it is shocking for me to say it, in the service to God. And last, but by all means not least, I have found a woman that I intensely admire. Yes, I need to go home."

The topic had finally been breached. He had no doubt that she was fully aware of his intentions. Yet, he knew that he must bring forth his must diplomatic forces to overcome the entrenchment of a mother from her familiar enclave. He steeled himself for the inevitable resistance.

His mother looked at him with the understanding that only a mother can muster and whispered, "Yes, you need to go home."

"Yes, I do. I apologize for my abruptness, Mother. My irritation is not with you. But we do need to discuss your future. Here you are in a decaying neighborhood in a home that was my home, and dad's home, as well as yours, for many years. When dad started his practice, this neighborhood was filled with professionals who could afford nice homes and country club memberships and all of the upper-class, heaven forgive me for making a distinction, niceties that only first-family status and money could afford. That is no longer the situation here now. The driveways are filled with pickup trucks instead of Buicks and Packards. The women are wearing short shorts and tee shirts instead of dresses and skirts. Break-ins are reported daily on the radio and in the newspapers. I cannot leave you here as a lonely, or maybe I should say, lone widow. Uncle Thomas is, sadly, well, let's admit it, getting old and lives clear across Boston from you, and additionally, has problems of his own. You know as well as I do that his situation with Aunt Helen's family would preclude any help from him."

He reluctantly looked his mother in the eye. He had expected to see a sad face but instead, he saw peace. His mother had an expression one would associate with beatitude. She sat silently for a long moment and then reached for his hand, gently squeezed it with both of her frail hands and whispered, "If you are working up to inviting me to go home with you let me ease your mind. "When do we leave for our new home together? Do you think I'll be able to learn to be a good hillbilly?"

CHAPTER THIRTY-EIGHT

THE DIE WAS CAST. His mandate was clear. His mind was cluttered with details but, at the same time, at ease. His thoughts drifted back to the times his MASH unit had to 'bug out' as enemy combatants threatened. The rapid deployment of a full surgical hospital appeared to be chaos. Yet, every member of the team knew exactly what needed to be done and the final outcome was an organized departure. The only emotion was fear. The here and now presented a totally different scenario. Here was an accumulation of forty years' worth of memories and collectibles. The memories are somewhat easy to transport; collectibles not so easy since they consist of a house and all of its appurtenances. The house itself has but one solution: sell it. The contents, then, become the real issue: what to take and what to dispose of.

They still sat in the kitchen without eating breakfast. Mother looked up at him and asked, "Well, are we going to sit here all day and worry over the future or are you going to take me to breakfast at Shony's?"

David jumped to his feet, bowed deeply and mockingly said, "Your ladyship, I am your servant. May I escort you to the local pub for grits and bacon?"

Leslie W. Dalton, Jr.

"Grits?" Mother giggled. "What in tarnation, see I'm already using the lingo, are grits?"

"Mother, I have learned that 'grits' is singular and you will learn that sometimes, in your home to be, they are the only food available for breakfast. Yet, the uppity folks eat them as a side dish, sometimes with cheese added, or even as a cereal with cream and sugar. As they say back home, 'grits is good'."

"Let me get my hat and we will be on our way. I think that we are ready to start moving. There I said it. You can now put your mind at ease and for your information, this has not been an impulsive decision brought on by your wise commentary. I have been considering what to do ever since your father died. I was only waiting for you to make a decision and, yes, an invitation."

David gave her a long loving stare and remarked. "Mom, you are a sly one. Here I thought I was in control. Speaking of being led down the primrose path!"

At the restaurant they sat in a booth, another first since her early school days, she eating pancakes and he bacon and scrambled eggs, she tea and he coffee, discussing tactics of the move. The final decision was determined to be a quick and clean break. He told her about the house and how it had been designed with two suites along with separate guest rooms to accommodate both long and short-term users. Her suite was on the ground floor with access to the library, sunroom, living room, and best of all, the kitchen that was active all day long from early morning to early evening, and all night if so desired.

Mother decided to cull treasures and leave the house and everything in it, including the car, to an estate liquidator. She decided a quick and clean departure would be less of a trauma. "Why linger over 'things'?" She asked her son. At first she thought that the car might be needed but David assured her that she had a car and driver at her disposal at any time.

The arrangements were completed in a few days. Travel plans were made. The bug out began.

CHAPTER THIRTY-NINE

As Dr. David Cabot mounted the steps into the waiting train with his mother in tow, he felt exhilaration greater than when the Korean War ended and he found out he was going home. Again, he was going home to West Virginia, West, by gosh, Virginia. The realization hit him that Boston was receding behind him and his mother and would cease to be their physical home. Was this really happening? The source of his early pride was fading in favor of a totally different society? With his sophisticated society mother beside him?

He had anticipated that Mom, as he had begun to call her as a part of the transition, would be somewhat of a reluctant traveler, but instead, she was as excited as a child on the way to a circus, and almost as difficult to control. She wanted a full travelogue of each station through which they passed. David opted for a Pullman Roomette for his mother while he settled for coach. That way he could make her comfortable and he could easily check on her. In the space of this short reunion he had developed a new protective fondness of his mother-child. She also seemed to be content with their new relationship.

The train left Boston, South Station at 6:00 PM during a front pushed by an Atlantic hurricane. His mother was frightened by the intensity of the storm so David stayed with her until she declared she was tired and ready to go to sleep. With the help of a porter Mom was left on her own until breakfast in the dining car while the trained roared on to Washington's Union Station, leaving the storm behind, after passing through New York while she slept.

Soon after leaving Washington they entered Virginia, passing through Alexandria and Charlottesville heading to Lynchburg where they would change to the Norfolk and Western lines that would take them through Bluefield, then home in Boston Knob where he expected Jim to meet them at the station. He had notified his 'colleagues' of his return and had specifically asked for Jim to be there.

The train route from Radford, Virginia to Glenn Lynn, Virginia/West Virginia meandered along the New River providing picture book viewing. The road was quite curvy requiring the train to move at a rubbernecking speed. Harriet Cabot was thrilled with the abundance of flowering shrubs and trees. Talk was offered by a young lady going home from Radford College for spring break. She was further fascinated that the train stopped at a house alongside the tracks for her host to disembark and run quickly into a thicket of a million blossoms to a fairyland house. As the train began to move again Mrs. Cabot looked back to see the front door of the house open and a lovely grey-haired matron emerge before the view was lost by the accelerating train moving towards Bluefield, its next scheduled stop. There, from the train window, David exhibited his new-found knowledge of the city by pointing out the West Virginian Hotel where he had stayed the night on his trip to Boston and the First National Bank. He focused on the Bank building because of its architecture that mimicked many of the buildings his mother was familiar within Boston including her church, Trinity, and a couple at Harvard, his school, Sever and Austin Halls. He promised his Mom that he would bring her to the "New York City" of West Virginia for a shopping trip and dinner at the West Virginian. Next stop, HOME!

CHAPTER FORTY

THE TRAIN BEGAN TO slow. The blossom-covered mountains were lovely but beginning to become tedious, David thought. He watched for the station platform to come into view where he expected to see Jim waiting. Instead the platform was overflowing with people. The parking lot was filled to capacity and cars were parked along the road. This was no spontaneous party. This was a planned activity. He dug into the possibilities and came to the conclusion that some dignitary was on the train and the gathering was for him. Assured that he had an explanation he helped his mother into the aisle and proceeded to the exit. He carefully helped his mother down the steps watching to assure she took each step without stumbling. Then he followed still looking downward.

Suddenly a great din erupted startling him. He abruptly stopped and was amazed at what he saw. Across the top of the station door was a sign that declared 'WELCOME, DOC'S MOM'.

The town's mayor stepped forward and presented her with a document declaring her an 'official' resident of the State of West Virginia surrounded by a beautiful hand-made wild-flower wreath. The Doctor was not ignored. His heart did flip-flops when Jenn approached him and welcomed him with a generous hug and kiss on the cheek. He stood there stunned and speechless. William, standing close by shouted above the noise, "Well, don't just stand there with that silly grin on your face. Hug her back. She's glad to see you."

Jenn grabbed his hand and led him towards the inside of the station to hoots and hollers and teasing shouts as the crowd parted to let them pass. David felt like a little boy who was being accused of having a girlfriend. He was thrilled but too embarrassed to enjoy it. Someone shouted, "Is thar gonna be a weddin'?"

David wanted to melt into the floor as he entered the building where a bluegrass band was pounding out their version of 'Happy Times are Here Again'. He looked around for his mother and found her wearing a gold crown and carrying a magic wand thoroughly enjoying the party and, yes, the attention. This was a crazy and new world for her.

Ultimately the party melted away. Jim approaches Doctor with the question, "Ya'll bout ready ta'go?"

"Thank you, yes, Jim. Come and meet my Mother."

"Tha's her rat thar?"

"Yes, I'll introduce you to her. She will be depending on you a great deal. Is that satisfactory with you?"

"Sho'nuf. If'n she's enythang lahk yew she's a fahn person."

They walk across the room where his mother was exchanging niceties with a group of people, and to his amazement, showed every indication that she was enjoying herself. The group included Jenn and Annie. When he saw Annie, he became a bit concerned because she was, for certain, the matriarch of the existing clan, including him. It occurred to him momentarily that she might consider Mom as an intrusion. However, his fears were quickly abated as he approached close enough proximity to hear the conversation.

"…..ah'n you kin hep aw yew wan'ta be uh'doin er yew kin pick wha'cha lah'k ta'do, mak's no mat'er ta'me," Annie was saying.

"Well, bless your sweet heart," Mrs. Cabot said boldly. "Perhaps I can relieve you of some of your chores and make myself useful."

He had never, in his whole life, never, heard her use the expression, "bless your heart." Was she assimilating that rapidly? He hoped so. He had been anticipating a reluctance to even tolerate his new clan, let alone acceptance. Was the compliance for his sake or will she truly blend in and be a part of the family? His doubts were dissuaded as he saw Jenn point to his Mom and give him a great big wink and nod.

Jim helped by voluntarily approaching Mrs. Cabot with a cheerful "Hah'de ma'am. Mah nam's Jim and I ah'm at chur al'aroun' service. Wh'ever yew need yew jus call me an' hits dun. Ah'm a gud safe drah'ver an I kin fix anythang. If'n you wan'uh far in yor farplace, ah kin keep hit up fir yew. Jis ask, okay?"

Mrs. Cabot's response was again, "Why bless your heart," as she gave him a motherly hug. Jim took her by the arm and escorted her to the Packard where he opened the door politely for her and averted his eyes as she slid into the plush seats. He carefully closed the door and went around helping Jenn enter from the other side. Jenn laughed to herself because he had never held the door for her before. Jim was working hard to impress Mom. Jenn's approval rating for Jim jumped several notches.

The drive to the house was extraneous dialogue until they reached the entrance to the property. Mrs. Cabot suddenly sat erect, and her comments were excitedly favorable, as she viewed the serenity of her new home. When she first saw the house her only comment was a whispered, "Oh, my."

CHAPTER FORTY-ONE

THE DAILY ROUTINE RETURNED to normal with Mom readily fitting into the mix. Annie was thrilled to have her in the kitchen and the two became fast friends. Additionally, Annie now had a 12 hour-a-day audience for her tall tales and family recollections.

The medical clinic was running smoothly with a steady flow of appointments and the usual walk-ins. The number of hospitalized patients increased rapidly requiring daily visits. This he did not mind for it gave him the opportunity to return to surgery, that being his primary training and military contribution. He never went into surgery without Jenn even though the hospital supplied a full complement of surgical nurses and technicians.

One day following the completion of their hospital activates with time to spare, Jenn inquired of Doctor, "How brave are you?"

Such a question was so out-of-the-blue that David was not sure how to answer.

"Well, I spent about two years of my life performing surgery near or under hostile enemy fire or threat of fire. Does that qualify me as brave?"

"Not entirely," Jenn retorted. "Since we have some time I would like for you to meet my Aunt Nan Dickens who lives down the river from Maybeury. It's just a mile or two out of our way, on the Bram'ul road, if you have the guts for it."

The gauntlet had been thrown down. Who was he to refuse a challenge from a mere woman? Well, maybe 'mere' did not fit in Jenn's case. Anyhow, he bravely, if not arrogantly, declared his acceptance of the implied dare.

"You're on. Lead the way to this daring venture," he replied with gusto.

Jenn, who was driving, guided the Packard through the winding road until she came to a turnoff from Route 52 where the Bramwell road, The N&W railroad, and Elkhorn Creek ran side by side for several miles. A clearing to the right came into view with two poles about three feet apart standing sentinel over their side of a suspended bridge across a deep gorge containing the Elkhorn Creek and two identical pole pairings standing on the other side. Each set of poles was secured by guy cables that were also the suspension cables for a wooden plank bridge swinging precariously across the gorge. The opposite end of the bridge terminated at the railroad. A path ran across the track, to what looked like a million steps, then ascended to a neat little house on the side of the mountain.

"That's where Aunt Nan lives. Up There."

"You don't expect me to risk my life crossing that…. that….thing," David moaned.

"You took the dare, you wimp. Come on. There're hand cables to hold on to. I'll go first. Just do as I do," Jenn teased as she blithely stepped on the swinging bridge with a tantalizing 'swing' of her lovely derrière as she sashayed in sync with the bridge.

"You will be the death of me. You cannot assume that I will risk life and limb just to please you. I may be beguiled by your charms but that does not make me a fool."

From the other side of the bridge now came a taunting cry. "Sissy, sissy, cut and run. Sissy, sissy never has no fun."

"How dare you. I am your boss." Doctor shouted. "You are fired, you hear me. Fired for…. disrespect of a superior officer…. or something akin to that." David shouted back suppressing a laugh.

"Okay, you asked for it. I am crossing now solely for the purpose of doing harm to your bod." David threatened as he proceeded cautiously. As he approached the end of the bridge Jenn backed away from him and began to run as if to escape from him. He had no difficulty catching her by the hand. She responded by turning and placing a generous kiss on his lips. He spontaneously returned the kiss but suddenly broke away and said, "I thought we were here to see your Aunt Nan. Is this visit a personal call or a professional call?"

He was still holding her as she replied, "personal."

"Right," he said and returned the kiss. The bridge proved to be dangerous after all.

CHAPTER FORTY-TWO

THEIR VISIT WITH AUNT Nan had gone well. They returned to the clinic with hardly a word spoken. He invited her to stay for supper but she shyly declined using laundry as an excuse.

"Please, stay. You have not been at our table since my mother arrived and I think she would enjoy meeting you again, especially.... now."

She relented since she was hungry and also because she was curious to see if Annie's cooking had changed since she had a new mouth to feed. And, so she could sit next to him while they ate.

As soon as they entered the house Jenn excused herself to 'go freshen up'. When she returned she gave a new meaning to the expression 'freshen up'. Her beautiful hair was no longer up in some sort of knot that she usually wore at work, her face was red from scrubbing and embellished by a nominal application of makeup. But what caught David's attention was the dress she wore. It fit her perfect figure like the proverbial glove yet it was not provocative. She wore a shirtwaist dress with a fitted skirt made of pink cotton checked gingham. He could not resist asking her where she got it. She answered, "Thornton's in Bluefield. You like it?"

"Of course, I like it. But I didn't mean from what store originally. I meant where you got it here and now?"

"Oh," she smiled sheepishly. "I have had a closet in Annie's house for a long time since I served as Dr. Fields's hostess after his wife died. I can continue if you like."

He did not have a chance to respond since Annie, in her best hog-calling voice, announced that supper was ready. He took her hand in his momentarily and then tucked it under his elbow to escort her to the dining room.

They gathered around the table with Annie seated in the 'jump seat' at the end nearest the kitchen. David usually sat at the other end but the evening he announced that he wanted to be on the side facing the windows so that he could enjoy the changing weather outside. Mom Cabot sat across the table from David. Jenn sat next to him by pure accident. Jim would sit to the side at the other end of the table as soon as he brought the meat in from the outdoor oven-smoker. The only point of contention emanating from Mother was her disapproval of the 'help' (her label choice) eating with the family. David squelched her conservative thinking by pointing out that without the help the table would be practically empty, and very dull, as Mom was about to learn.

Jenn spoke. "David, Dr. Fields always had wine with the evening meal. He….

Annie interrupted loudly. "Humph. Hit ain't bad'nuf that jes' bout ever man up this holler air a drunk. Jenn, yew ort'a know that since ever dang one of your brothers, excep'un Bill, air addicted to drink."

"Annie, not a single one of my brothers would touch wine, you know that. You also know that the drink of all of our alcoholics is hard liquor, legal or otherwise. You know your bible; Jesus turned water into wine, didn't he?

I know you take Paul's letters as preaching the Gospel of Jesus Christ and he told Timothy to 'Drink no longer water, but use a little wine for thy stomach's sake and thine own infirmities' and that was straight out of your official King James Version, right?"

"Well" retorted Annie. "Drinkin' enythang with alke'hol in'it will lead to heavy drankin'. Hits lahk gittin' in'na tub of hot water. First yew pu'ch toe in and next thang yew know yew air in'it whole hawg. Yes sir'ee bobtail. Drink'un leads gud pep'l to no gud. You take yer brother in law, Lula's husban'. He's the smartest man I ever seen. When he ain't drinkin' that is. One time he was all dressed up for a picnic in'a fancy new white suit, got drunk and sat down in a cow pile thankin'hit was a rock. 'nother time he drove his car in'a crick next to a bridge he was goin' to cross. Somebody as't him why he did hit and he said 'they was two bridges and he tuck the wrong one'. So, you see, li'ker kin make a smart man int'a fool."

Everybody laughed, even Annie herself.

CHAPTER FORTY-THREE

D<small>R. DAVID CABOT WAS</small> now a transitioned and genuine Mountaineer. He could not believe that almost three years had passed since that auspicious meeting with Jenn at the Bluefield airport. He still marveled at his position in the community and even more so about his relationship with Jenn. On several occasions his memory flashed back to the first-sit down meal with Jenn at The La Saluda: 'Don't get any ideas soldier. It's this or Lynn's Drive-in and I really don't like eating in a car parked beside a carload of teen-agers'. For years he feared asking her to share even a sandwich together for fear of being rejected. That had changed.

This evening they were going to a formal Fourth of July dinner-dance at the Bluefield County Club where he was invited as a guest. Jenn was tingly with joy and made no effort to hide her excitement. She had selected a Tanpell Sleeveless, floor-length mermaid gown of matte black satin with lace straps as her choice for the occasion. No one would ever believe the lovely garment had come mail-order from Sears-Roebuck after Annie altered it to fit snugly to Jenn's perfect figure. The neckline was a bit revealing to suit David's mother but for David it was so perfect that he went to Alfred Land's Jewelry in Bluefield and purchased a double string of pearls as enhancement.

The dinner had been marginal and the fireworks display over the golf course was meager. But to David and Jenn everything was perfect. Nothing could dampen their excursion into a near- fairyland experience. The dance following the fireworks had been pleasurable given the opportunity for David to hold Jenn close in public. The small band was excellent and specialized in simple versions of current popular songs. Jenn's favorite was 'Smoke gets in your eyes' mainly because David had taken her to see the remake of Roberta, (Lovely to Look At), with Kathryn Grayson singing the song herself instead of the usual practice of a beautiful actress with a lousy voice lip-syncing an unseen singer. The band was notable for its unusual makeup of WKOY radio personnel as well as the instrumentation of vibraphone, bass violin and piano. David was particularly delighted by the absence of drums.

Midnight approached and the band segued into 'Goodnight Ladies' signaling the end of the party. The crowd drifted to the exit and their automobiles for the drive home. Jenn and David followed suit with many a male glance at her glamorous dress. David was totally unaware of those admirers since he had only fleetingly looked at anything but her for the totality of the evening. For once he was driving the Packard and guided the fine car over Cherry Street Cutoff to Route 52 and the road home. Jenn had snuggled close to David as they passed The Ritz Curbway just across[18] Easley Bridge doing a booming business with

---

[18]   The Ritz Curbway, later renamed the Bluefield Drive-in, was one of my favorite places to eat because of their footlong

the loud speaker flooding music over the randomly park cars nosed into the drive-in restaurant.

"Want something to eat? Perhaps a foot-long hotdog with all the trimming?" David teased.

"Hush your mouth. That would really be too much sugar for a cent, after all of the hors d'oeuvres I had at the dance." Jenn protested. "Now, I could go for a big thick juicy steak at the La Saluda," Jenn joked.

"No, you wouldn't if you heard Annie describe where his meat comes from."

"Doesn't matter if it's cooked like most people around here like it, unlike present company who eats steak almost uncooked." They laugh happily.

The radio had been playing quietly in the background and Jenn suddenly reached for the volume knob and turned it up to hear Doris Day singing 'Sentimental Journey'. Except for the music, all was quiet.

As they approached Pinnacle Rock, Jenn suggested that they stop for a walk through the park. David complied by turning the big Packard into the deserted parking lot.

The park lights provided sufficient illumination but still David fussed over Jenn's progress up the stone steps ensuring that she did not trip on her gown. She could have managed quite well without his focused attention but she leaned into him as if she needed the support. They sauntered through the moonscape of the park until they found a large tree guarding a rocky prominence protruding outward toward the valley below where individual efforts of single skyrockets unsuccessfully challenged the lightening-filled sky. He leaned against the tree and she leaned into him, both focused on the valley below, watching flashing lightening embroidering lace doilies onto the green mountains below. Autumn would integrate the colors on the Maker's palate, like a child's finger painting, into a panorama of color unparalleled anywhere in the world, followed by winter displays of dazzling white that could paint the devil himself into a picture of purity.

After a long silence she looked up into his face and queried, "A penny for your thoughts."

He pondered the intrusion of such a personal question and for the first time he revealed his inner self to her. "It has oft been said that home is where the heart is. You have my heart, so I must be home."

"Me too." She said.

CHAPTER FORTY-FOUR

ANOTHER GLORIOUS DAY AHEAD of him, Doctor jived down the back hall of the clinic. Everything around him glimmered with a new brightness. An irregularity in the wood wainscoting was seen as a piece of Mondrian art; the old, obscure pictures on the wall shone with a new significance. Four men stood side-by-side posing for the camera: An army colonel, and three men, one fairly well dressed, but bedraggled, wearing a felt dress hat, one in coal-mining attire including a hard-hat, and a fourth, much younger than the other three, dressed in what looked like a lab coat. His curiosity piqued, he called out to Jenn to come and explain the origin of the photo and why it was on the wall of his practice. "Oh, that?" She sighed with a hint of respect. "That happened long before my time with Dr. Fields. He had just started his practice here and was sort of drafted by the Army to go up on Blair Mountain to treat the wounded in a fight between what some sources claimed was around 10,000-armed coal miners and maybe 3,000 deputies and strikebreakers. It was all started by coal mine owners when miners tried to unionize." Jenn paused and asked Doctor, "Do we have time for this? It's a long story and we have patients coming before long." "No, any time alone with you is not wasted time," he murmured. "Just give the edited version." "Okay," she purred giving him a surreptitious kiss on the cheek. "Jenn!" He chided. "What are you thinking!"

"Heck, everybody but you already knows. Even your Mom. She asked me the other day if our relationship is likely to cause disruption in the clinic."

"Don't tell me your response! Really, now. Get back to the story."

"I'd rather drag you into your office and engage in a bit of hanky panky."

"Jenn! Shame on you!"

"Okay, if you're going to be a prude, I'll finish the dang story. Many people think it really started when the mine owners sent agents to evict miners from their company houses. It was raining at the time on a normal work day and only the women and children were home but that didn't stop the agents from throwing them and their belongings outside. When the miners came home and saw what had happened they retaliated and a gunfight started with several men on each side killed. The whole incident became known as the Matewan Massacre. You know where Matewan is, just over the hill that way?"

"Yes, I recall."

"Well, the whole affair kept brewing until it finally broke out into a wholesale war with machine guns, and even a Gatlin gun. The Army was finally sent in to break it up and most of the miners sneaked away and went home after hiding their guns so that they could go back and get them later. I'm told that times were scary for the miners; they even had bombs dropped on them from airplanes, mostly filled with some chemical, maybe lye."

"And Dr. Fields was up there through the whole affair?"

"No, only a short time. When the Army came in their medical people took care of both sides. Their medics were part of a peace-keeping effort and treated all wounded the same. They figured what's 'sauce for the goose is sauce for the gander' and didn't discriminate. Now, let's get to work. You have a couple of black lung patients, a woman with a boy she says his teacher thinks has something wrong with his eyes because he can't read, and another woman that is about to bust with a baby and hasn't seen a doctor up until now. That's no big deal around here but she says it hasn't been kicking like it used to."

"Let's see her first in the event we need to send her to Bluefield. Put her in room three, it's a bit more cheerful than the others."

"Yes, Doctor," replied Jenn, quickly returning to full professional mode. Doctor Cabot had gone to his reference book for some guidance when Nurse Jenn knocked, entered, and said, "She's ready."

Doctor steeled himself for he knew what was coming. He tried to appear cheerful but failed miserably as he saw an emaciated little woman before him that looked much older than the age he knew her to be. In order to avert his eyes even momentarily, he went straight to his writing table and feigned reading her chart. Finally, with great effort, he turned to her and asked;

"Are you in any pain, Mrs. Gates?"

"Ah don't thank from the Baby, no."

Puzzled, Doctor asked, "Are you having other problems?"

"Hit all start'd when mah hus'bun come home Sa'tee nahght drunk an' beat me'un two of air kids. Ah never seen him so mean drunk. He blamed me 'cause he had been fard frum his job. Ah tol' him what wif' all the ma'chens comin' in, hit was bound ta' hap'n. Ah thank he kilt mah baby. The

176

good Lord knows ah don'need 'nother one. We can't feed the ones we got."

Doctor quickly stood from his chair, excused himself, and left the room.

Jenn followed close behind and found him in the back hall in tears.

He turned to her and lamented, "I cannot believe that I am of the same species as the man who tortured that poor, pitiful woman. If there is a god why would he create such a monster? What did that poor woman do to deserve such treatment?"

Jenn tried to hug him but he withdrew. "How can you love any man if that's what we become? How can you be sure that such behavior does not lie dormant in me? Such behavior can be possibly understood if it's man against man in war, but to a poor, pitiful little woman that appears to be the soul of innocence?" He stood there against the wall for several minutes before he was able to say:

"I need to call the sheriff and have him take Mrs. Gates to the hospital in Bluefield. She needs more than we can provide here and that also serves notice to law enforcement regarding a crime of assault."

Jenn, realizing that the next step was hers, informed him that she had a patient waiting. He acknowledged her directions and walked slowly back to the exam rooms where he found a very prim, well-dressed mother sitting in the extra-room chair and an equally well-attired boy that looked to be about ten, leisurely ensconced on the exam table. Doctor glanced down to the chart to find a name and introduced himself.

"Good afternoon, Mrs. Peters and Calvin. I'm Dr. Cabot. How may I help you?" addressing his question to the apparent mother.

Mother was a real beauty. She wore quality clothing and wore it well. Her sitting posture was proper and she spoke with a general American dialect, probably Ohio.

Instead, the boy responded. "They're all stupid."

"Calvin," his mother said calmly. "Talking like that don't help."

Dr. Cabot caught the grammatical error and almost jumped to an erroneous conclusion. Before he could respond Mom continued.

"The school says he can't hear. There's a woman that comes through here selling hearing aids who gave him a hearing test and told me he hears the tones on her hearing device and I should see a medical doctor to look at his ears in case he has wax in them. My husband stays busy and told me to get you to look at his ears and if he needs more we can go someplace where they have an ear specialist." She relaxed as if a burden had been lifted.

Doctor opened a drawer and retrieved an otoscope. He turned to the boy and said, "Let's have a look at those shiny clean ears of yours."

The boy in rebellion reached up and pushed the instrument away. "Don't touch my ears!" he shouted.

"He don't like men," offered the mother.

"How so?" asked Doctor. "He allowed his hearing to be tested, didn't he?

"That was a woman," said mom.

"Ahaa," said Doctor. "Let's see what we can do about that." He left the room and called Jenn. The boy sat perfectly still while she looked into his ears. He recoiled slightly when she pumped the air bulb to see if the drums were compliant and reported the ears to be free of wax and the drums to be normal. She handed the otoscope back to David and, with a large smile, left the room.

Dr. Cabot went through the physical examination to the extent that the child would allow him. He checked the growth/weight vs age charts. He read the school report that depended on academic performance and teacher-subjective behavioral assessment. Also, in the report was a report of an evaluation administered by the psychologist employed by the West Virginia Division of Maternal and Child Health Clinic headquartered in Charleston with a satellite clinic held monthly at the Mercer County Health Department facilities on the Bluefield/Princeton Road. The psychologist had administered The Wechsler Intelligence Scale for Children (WISC), developed by David Wechsler in 1949 as an individually administered intelligence test (IQ) for children between the ages of 6 and 16. Doctor noted that the test reported results on two subtests organized into Verbal and Performance scales and provided scores for Verbal IQ, Performance IQ, and a Full-Scale IQ. Obvious to even a novice was the big gap between Calvin's two scores even though the Full-Scale IQ was rated as being above normal. The psychologist had written a narrative questioning the validity of the fairly new procedure that was just beginning to work its way into various programs that encounter underachievers formerly considered mentally deficient and routinely held back in school.

"Mrs. Peters, your son is healthy in all regards physically. The report from the psychologist covers a test with which I am unfamiliar. Psychology of that type is a developing field and medical people like me are really not versed in its attributes. So, here is what I suggest. I have a close friend who is about to complete his degree in a related field at the University of Virginia. I would like to take Calvin to their clinic so that we can all learn what is in the works for children like your son who has been falling through the

179

cracks, so to speak, of the educational system of the past and today. What do you think?"

"I'm all for it but I'll need to run it by my husband who will go along with whatever I want to do anyway. When would we go?"

"As soon as I can set it up both here and there. When you give me the go-ahead I'll call UVA and set it up. Call me when you are ready, okay?"

"Thank you, Doctor, I feel better already. What do you think, Calvin?"

"Do they have hotdogs?" inquired Calvin focusing on something on the ceiling.

CHAPTER FORTY-FIVE

DR. CABOT WAS MENTALLY exhausted and decided to sneak up to the kitchen to see if Annie had the coffee on. She had some sort of uncanny ability to always have a fresh pot ready when he showed up in her domain. Bo trailed along behind.

"Annie, I need a cup of coffee ree'ul ba'yod," he said mocking the local dialect while entering the kitchen.

"Fresh pot is ready, Your Grace," answered Annie returning the mockery.

"Annie, I just spent a most exhausting hour with a young lad who is very intelligent but can't progress in the educational system."

"Th'ut mus'be an untol'ur'bu thang for him an' his ma an' pa,' Annie commiserated. "Mah l'il'un hain't smart an' ah tuk her out'n skul caus'ah was afreed that she wuz lef'out'n ever'thang. She don't see hit but ah did. Hit's ruff on folks when chil'len hain't rahght. Yew knows wahy Jim quit school don'cha?"

"I have suspected it was mostly sociological," suggested Doctor Cabot.

"If'n that means cause of who he is, pro'bli that, too, but mostly cuz he wus book dumb but handi as a handl' on a bucket. You see that don'cha? His Pa saw hit and tuk him aut'n school an' put him ta'work a'fixin up old bicycles and sell'um fur a gud profit. Jim can fix enythang what can be fixed. But he can't read a lick. Nosiree bobtail, not a lick."

"Annie, you ol' fox; you just opened my eyes to an unforgivable misapprehension on my part. I have been remiss in not seeing Jim as a failure of our educational system instead of a lack of familial guidance. Jim's dad took the correct action that allowed Jim to learn a useful trade. Jim has been a bastion of support of which I have been totally unaware. You knew it all along. You knew of Jim's value to this place. Why didn't you make me aware of his value?"

"Well, I recon'ed yew wuz smart nuf to see hit fer'u'self. He' hep'ed yew e'nuf times fer yew ta'see hit yer self."

Bo attentively followed the conversation.

"You are indeed correct, Miss Annie. Twice today I have been made aware of young boys who are being ostracized for problems that might be neurological instead of intellectual doldrums. I must contact Sonny at UVA and discuss my concerns with him. My last conversation with him indicated that he had some ideas about language learning disabilities. An old professor of mine, as I recall, a PhD instead of an MD, once told us that in any diagnosis, 'it's not so much what you see but what they say', may have been prophetic."

Dr. Cabot had just given the operator the instructions to call the Speech and Hearing Center at the University of Virginia in an effort to locate Sonny Turman. He was sitting at his desk, deep in thought, waiting when Jenn entered the room.

"A penny for your thoughts," she asked.

He looked up startled out of his reverie and blurted, "The last time you asked that question it almost evoked a proposal of marriage out of me," David replied.

They both laughed. The phone rang and Jenn started to get up but David put up his hand and in a 'wait' gesture and said, "Hold on. If this is the call I'm waiting for I want you to hear it."

It was. The operator said "I have your party on the line sir. Go ahead."

"Hello, is the speech and hearing program?"

"Yes, it is. This is Mary. May I help you?"

"This is Dr. David Cabot calling from Boston Knob, West Virginia and I am looking for a student from West Virginia that is enrolled there."

"We have two students from there in our program, Leslie and Thelma."

"That would be Sonny."

"Hold on please, Doctor. He's here. I'll see if he is available."

David held the phone away from his ear and said to Jenn. "Sonny has developed an interest in the use of EEG in the study of how the brain processes sound. The last time I talked with him he was using radio technology in the development of a special hearing test. I don't know the status of his research but it occurred to me that we might try his ideas on Calvin. I'm convinced that he is not hearing…." He heard the phone being picked up.

"Hello there, Doctor, where are you?"

"At home. I am calling to inquire as to your research progress?"

"Perfect timing, Doctor. I have been discussing a new auditory stimulus for assessing the central auditory processing system with a psychiatrist over in the medical school. We have put together a pilot project and have been testing with some limited success. Why, what do you have in mind?"

"I have two patients that have piqued my curiosity because of the similarities in their clinical histories. Both appear to have normal hearing but neither can read. One shows big differences in that new test called the WISC? Have you heard of it? The other is a whiz with his hands and, likewise, cannot read."

"We use the WISC here along with several other tests that measure language usage in an effort to correlate the two. Tell you what; if you can get the boys to us we will be glad to include them in our research. It's a perfect time to visit Charlottesville. As mama always said about the fall and spring in Bluewell, 'I've never seen it so beautiful' and that's what I would say about the show spring is putting on now. You'll want to take time to visit Monticello because 'Little Mountain' is outstanding this year. Let me know when you are coming and we will be ready. We would love to have you stay with us but we live in the old slave quarters on Fox Haven Farm and we are crammed into our space as it is."

"Thank you, no. Your aunt, Jenn, will be along and we will stay close to the patient. The more we observe beforehand the better informed we will be. I will write you the details. Thank you and we will see you in Charlottesville." Doctor said and broke the connection.

As soon as the phone hit the cradle Jenn asked, "Am I a part of 'we'?"

David smiled at her as he looked on his desk pad for a phone number. He dialed a number and waited for an answer.

"Mrs. Peters, this is Doctor Cabot. I just got off the phone with Charlottesville and we are invited to be a part of their research any time that you are agreeable."

Mrs. Peters responded excitedly, "We are ready and my husband has even offered us the use of the company airplane. It's a DC-3 and holds a bunch of people so we can all go and come as we please even if we have to make several trips."

David's curiosity about Mr. Peters had led him to delve into the man's source of income. He thought he had become familiar with most, if not all, of the wealth in the area since it was posted on any number of mines, buildings, roads, and even churches and schools. The name Peters was significant by its absence. This caused a bit of pause in Doctor's willingness to accept gratuity of any kind from him. The mother's expensive apparel and her uncharacteristic dialect, yet not 'upper class' grammatically, was puzzling. He decided to have someone associated with the law look into it for him and decided to call William.

He called out to Jenn who was busy with a patient in the room next to him. "Jenn, when you are free will you please call my attorney for me?"

Sticking her head in David's office door she said, "Your attorney? I didn't know you have an attorney?"

"Your brother, William, and you know that! That's why I asked you to call him!"

"Oh, him?" laughed Jenn.

"Smart aleck," responded David.

Moments later Jenn called out, "Bill on line two, Sir."

"Smart aleck," David repeated not realizing he has already picked up the phone.

Bill said, "You interrupted my deeply involved legal activity just to call me a smart aleck?"

"That remark was directed at your smart-mouth sister, and I have a serious matter to discuss with you."

"Ah have my lawyerly ears on so go ahead."

"Do you know a business man named Peters?"

"Ah've heard the name but nothing specific comes to mind. Care to tell me why you are interested?"

"His son is a patient of mine for whom I have asked Sonny to arrange an evaluation. Sonny is engaged in some exciting new research at UVA. Mr. Peters has offered his plane for transporting us, along with the boy and his mother, to Charlottesville. I plan to take Jenn along since the boy relates to her."

"Oh, sureee she does," teased Bill. "Ah am so verrrry sure that's the onnnly reason for Jenn going along."

"My heavens, William, why can't you two ever be serious?"

"Okay, seriously, I'll look into it and get back to you; satisfied?"

"Most certainly, yes. I will await your call. I must go now as your clone is calling me to get to work."

CHAPTER FORTY-SIX

Annie and Harriet had become close friends although neither was fully free of distrust of the other's cultural background. They worked together in the kitchen where they spent many hours working and talking harmoniously. On one occasion they were duly engaged when a voice called through the screen of an open door, "Annie, air yew in thar?"

"Come on in, Ellie; door's open."

A youngish, rail thin woman came in with a basket laden with eggs and butter. She gingerly set the wares on the counter and said, "Annie, this here is to settle air bill with Doctor. We ain't lik'ly ta have no cash money eny time soon so maybe this'll hep until sech time as Tom git's uh'job. Hi'de'doo, Ms. Cabot. How'yew doin? They's a quilt n thar that maybe yew can find a use fer. Ah been workin' on hit since Chris'mus and I done a pur'ty gud job if'n ah do say so mah self."

Mrs. Cabot, taking advantage of the use of the woman's name in Annie's initial greeting, was prepared to use a name when she offered, "We are so pleased to receive the fine produce, Ellie. Let me see that quilt. I have just the place for it in my quarters. Thank you for inquiring as to my wellbeing and you can be assured that your bill is paid in full."

Mrs. Cabot delved into the basket of goodies and found eggs that had not been washed, butter molded into a round shape with a flower bas-relief embossed on the top. At the bottom of the basket, folded carefully, was a lovely handmade quilt with exquisite, tiny stitches the likes of which she had never seen before. She abruptly took in a breath and exclaimed brightly, "Why this is the most beautiful bit of handwork I do believe I have ever seen! Is this your work, Ellie?"

"Yes, um," Ellie responded meekly.

Mrs. Cabot removed the quilt from the basket, shook it out to its full glory, and spread it over the dining room table. She placed her hand against her cheeks, cooing her joyful satisfaction. She turned to the thin little woman and spontaneously pulled her into an embrace filled with explanatory jargon.

"Ah think she lahks hit," Annie ventured dully.

"Like it! It's the finest gift I have ever received in my entire life. I will treasure it forever!"

"Ah'm real glad," whispered Ellie. "Well, ah best be a'goin'. I left the kids by they self."

Ellie left hurriedly and Harriet followed along with praise. When the screen door slammed she turned to Annie and said, "I know money would help on a one-time basis but I so wish that there is something that I could do that is more lasting."

"They is, and you jes threw hit over the table ovah thar." Annie offered.

"Really?" puzzled Harriet.

"Yep. Clear as day. Ellie cud sell all of them quilts she cud make but at a price so low hit wud do her no gud. City folks frum a'roun here com awantn' locals to make stuff fer'em but they 'spect them to mak'em fur less than yew cud git'em at Kresges or Woolworths if'n they had 'em. Why don'cha open a store whar all the handi'crafts here'abouts cud be sold at a fair price?"

"Annie, you are a genius!" sang Harriet!

The entrepreneurship seeds had been planted. Annie and Harriet decided the first thing was to put a plan on paper so that they would enter the enterprise organized. First, they decided, a survey of the potential source of goods to be sold must be done. Annie cautioned Harriet that there would be suspicions about the process and that some method of assurances should be developed to get the flow of stock started.

Harriet had a ready solution. "I will pay for the first item from each new contributor placed in the store and then put that money into an individual account earmarked for that contributor only."

"Good idee," praised Annie. "That account book can be on display, so's that ever'body kin see just what they kin git if'n they do the same thing. Now, none of these folks have ever had a bank account so we best allow them to draw from their accounts if'n they need hit fer food and sich."

"Okay," said Annie. "That takes care of pro'kur'munt. Let's look at fah'nances."

The next item on the business plan was financing. Harriet solved that problem post haste.

"That's my responsibility, move on. I'll start a list:"

"Next," said Harriet "is an outlet. As a perceived snob myself, I believe the best place for a market would be where the snobs go."

Annie quickly disagreed. "I think somewhar bu'tween the snobs and the artists would be best."

Mrs. Cabot, taking satisfaction in Annie's use of the word 'artist', readily agreed. "Next item on our business plan is 'location, location, location' as the realtors are want to say. I would venture to say that the combination of our experiences make for a fine team."

"Yeah," said Annie. "Mah mama always did say that 'two heads'er better'n one even if one is uh sheep's head."

CHAPTER FORTY-SEVEN

Dოctor Cabot was just finishing up with a patient when Shirley, the receptionist, handed him a letter with the comment, "Th' mail jes' got here an' I thought yew would want this rah't away."

He thanked her and asked her to tell Jenn he was going for a cup of coffee and to join him. He entered the kitchen, followed closely by Bo, to find Annie and Mom deep in conversation over supper preparation.

"I suppose there is no fresh coffee to be had amongst the founders of the mountain crafts executive business meeting?" He asked pleasantly.

"They'air, Dr. Smarty," Annie yelled back. "Hit jest finished perkin' and yew kin hep'ya'self, cause, as yew kin red'ly see we air busy."

"Never let it be said that I was an impediment to progress," said David.

Jenn bounded into the room with her usual zeal and yelled, "Coffee hot?"

"Indeed, it is and I have a cup ready for you inasmuch as the kitchen help refuses to provide any consequential service. I have a letter here from Sonny about our trip, I suppose. Sit. We'll read it together."

Annie yelled, "Any excuse to sit clos'ta each other," and she and his Mom laughed with glee.

"Mind your own business," demanded David who then turned and whispered to Jenn, "She's right, you know?"

Jenn responded with a sneaked kiss and said, "Open the letter."

David pulled the letter from the envelope, placed it on the counter in front of them and began to read.

Annie and Mrs. Cabot stopped what they were doing and turned to listen.

> *Dear Dr. Cabot:*
>
> *I am very excited about your visit. I am really glad to hear that Aunt Jenn is coming. I don't recollect her ever going anywhere, vacation or otherwise. I think she will enjoy Charlottesville. She, of all of my relatives, I think, will appreciate my research since she will remember my difficulties in school. Ask her about the time I came home crying, during school hours, because the teacher had paddled my left hand with a ruler to force me to write with my right hand.*

Jenn interrupted and asked, "You remember that don't you Annie?"

"Ah shore do," replied Annie. "He wuz devs'tated an' his ma was mad as'uh wet hen."

"Don't interrupt," demanded David.

"Will if Ah want to," declared Jenn.

David resumed reading.

Coincidently, and serendipitously, handedness and brain dominance are part and parcel of my research springing from my clinical training in existing procedures of hearing science.

A common question people ask me is how did I make the jump from architecture to audiology? At first blush there appears to be a giant gap between architecture and audiology/speech/ language disorders. But really the basic precept in all things new is discovery. In architecture the task is to take a piece of raw land and design a unique edifice suited to the site. The comparison breaks down when considering the prolific information available to the budding architect via centuries of standing structures to emulate. An architect can simply copy something. Therefore, in architecture the choices were, copy or create.

In my new profession there is little to copy and what is there has been unscientifically determined. A few communication disorder models are available for deafness, language development, aphasia, and stuttering and speech production with neurological justification based on the invasive brain mapping of Wilder Penfield who demonstrated that stimulation of the right side of the motor brain would cause a response on the left side of the body or—contra laterality. His book is required reading here. A second book on the required reading list is by psychologist Helmer Myklebusts who hypothesized that auditory processing disorders are different from language learning difficulties. He coined the condition 'psychoneurological learning disabilities' defined as Deficit learning ability coupled with adequate motor functioning, normal intellect, auditory/visual and emotion. He developed a 'modality-based processing model' for identifying and remediating children with different sorts of psychoneurological learning disabilities.

Around the same time a group of Italian researchers, led by Bocca and Calearo set up an experiment testing auditory perception to different speech signals going to each ear and found a way to test cortical hearing in temporal lobe tumors.

Now my reason for going into so much detail is that I have been developing a hearing test stimulus that shows different electroencephalographic (EEG) patterns for left and right-handed subjects in (EEG). The test results are positive but what is surprising in our preliminary data is that there are a disproportionate number of left handers in our psychoneurological learning disabilities group that we have here in the UVA Speech and Hearing Clinic. Finally, our results correlate to the WISC.

We only need a week or so advance notice in order to reserve the EEG.

One other late item to report. I have been offered a position with the W. Va. Department of health. More on that when I see you.

Best regards to you and my love to Aunt Jenn.

Les

David handed the letter to Jenn who proceeded to reread it.

"Wuz that letter in Ah tal un? Ah didn't unner'stand a word of hit." Annie asked.

"No." interceded Mrs. Cabot. "It was a perfect letter that reminded me of the letters David's father used to write. Jenn, it sounds like your nephew is a very bright young man."

"That's what we all say and he is making the transition in his education with apparent ease," interjected Dr. Cabot.

Annie spoke up again. "Air yew plan'n on havi'n him see Jim?"

"Most certainly," answered Doctor. "He is one of my reasons for the initial inquiry. He fit the subject requirements perfectly even to his left-handedness. We have plenty of room in the plane for him and I'll pay for everything else. He will need some new clothes. We can do that here before we leave in case there is any need for tailoring."

Annie roared with laughter. "Now if'n that ain't too much sugar fer a cent? A tailor fer Jim? Hit's nuff yew agon'na git him some hep. He ain't got to be dress't up fer that. A'new par of over'hauls is all he needs."

"Annie, that boy has a fine sense of dignity. With minimal assistance I believe he could go over to the county vocational school and successfully supplement his natural skills to the degree that he could open and manage a shop of his own. Of course, I am happy to have him here but I do believe he would love his independence."

"He cud'nt git no more indee'pend'unt," mumbled Annie.

"Oh, and Annie, I failed to mention. We will need someone who has known Jim for most of his life to accompany us on the trip and I suppose you will suffice."

Before Annie had time to react, David continued. "And of course, Jenn cannot possibly travel unchaperoned with an unattached male, so Mom will be employed in that role. Now, I think I have covered every contingency; sound satisfactory to you, Jenn?"

The chatter in the room drowned out her response for everyone but David.

"I have never been anywhere further away than Bluefield. Did you know that? Bluefield! No more than thirty miles away! You asked me if going to Charlottesville with you and the whole damn town of Boston knob, including your mother, is satisfactory. Well. The answer is, No! No, it-is-not! At first when you told me that we were taking Mrs. Peters and Calvin I was so excited. I thought we would be with them only during the hospital visit and we would have the rest of our time only with each other. I imagined seeing the sights with you, eating out with you, maybe even going dancing with you. Just you. Can't you get it through your thick skull that….."

David was speechless. He felt frozen to the floor. Finally, he took her in his arms, hugging her close and pleaded, "Jenn, forgive me. I am so…so…such a clod! I am so afraid of showing…offending…driving you away that I assume too much about how you might…may…Oh, dog bite it," not knowing anything else to say, he quit talking, lifted her chin, and kissed her firmly, ignoring their audience, Annie and Mom, who in unison called out, "Well it's about time!"

Mrs. Cabot excitedly exclaimed. "Okay, Annie this is what we are going to do. Do you think we can get everything together by next Sunday?"

"We shore kin," turning to Jenn and David she asked, "Do ya'll want a church weddin'?"

David practically shouted. "What a doggone minute. I did not ask Jenn to marry me."

"Ah hear'ed hit, didn' yew Harriet?"

"I most certainly did and even if you did not, Annie and I say that was your intention. Jenn, do you want to vote?"

"Ah do. Don't those words sound good to you, David?"

"Yes, Jenn, they really do. Let's make it legal: will you marry me?"

CHAPTER FORTY-EIGHT

DAVID SAT ON THE balcony of his suite looking out over the woods. The sky above was an artist's brushing of puffy white clouds and the bottom of wooded areas were edged with the many colors of multiple flowering trees and bushes. Life was good. Can't see the forest for the trees? Who cares?

A voice called from below. "Penny for your thoughts," called William from below.

"Keep your penny. I am betrothed to your sister because of that question," David answered with a happy laugh.

"So, I heard you proposed."

"I didn't. I was shanghaied, pure and simple, by a tribe of wild women. They are in there now plotting my doom. Come on up. I've got a pot of hot coffee on."

Bill didn't bother to go into the house and use the steps. Instead he climbed a trellis covered with vivid red roses, hopped onto the balcony, and inquired, "Where's the coffee?" David pointing said "in there."

"What's the good news?" Bill inquired.

"Really and truly, the exceptionally good news is that you are going to be my brother-in-law."

"That's good news?"

"As I have often heard hereabouts, does a bear poop in the woods?"

"Ain't the way I heard it," Bill said.

"I'm not vulgar like you," David said.

"Yeah, I forgot. You are of gentility," Bill said.

"You win, as always," David conceded. "What's new?"

"I have a dossier on your plane-man."

David responded with a querulous glance. "Dossier is it? Sounds sinister."

"I would say so. It appears that organized crime has been doing some probing in the area concerned with drugs, specifically marijuana.

"What does that have to do with Peters?" David inquired.

"The plane he has access to is registered with the FAA under a corporation operating out of Cincinnati that deals in a host of unexplained businesses. I dug as far as I could and found a connection between a couple of the board members of a mining company and real estate. That's about as far as I got that I can hang my hat on."

"So, you put two and two together and came up with a conspiracy, am I correct? David asked.

"Most likely," Bill replied.

There was a long period of silence while the two sat fraternally. Ultimately Bill spoke. "When's the wedding?" He inquired.

"Don't know. The syndicate hasn't informed me yet. All I know, I was told that I proposed and they accepted. Other than that, I'm on standby."

"Better that way. Just go along; it'll work out."

"Indeed."

William took his leave abandoning David to his musing. Almost immediately after he left another voice called from below the balcony.

"Hey, Doctor, it's Sheriff Hare. Gotta minute ta talk? Bill said you're not doing anything."

"Why of course, Sheriff. Go on in through the sunroom and I'll meet you in the kitchen for coffee and a viable substitute for a donut."

Doctor descended the steps just as the Sheriff entered the sunroom. They performed the ritual handshake and greetings and Doctor gestured toward the kitchen.

"Annie" he said. "We have a visitor from the law enforcement community whom I would venture to say is already among your acquaintances?"

Annie looked up from the oven in which she was looking and gleefully declared. "Little Sonny Hare. Course ah know him, ah remember th' day his wuz born. His ma is salt'a th'earth people and a gud quilter' too. Coffees' hot and ah got goodies comin' out'a the oven. Sit'cha self-down and ah'll git'em fur ya," she ordered as she retrieved the coffee pot and cups.

Dr. Cabot inquired tentatively. "Is every boy around here named Sonny?"

"Pert near" said Annie. "Any Mom aron' cud go ta'th door an' yell 'Sonny, supper's ready' and ever' kid in the neighborhood wud com runnin'. Not only that, they'd be welcome at th'table too."

"That's' right," added the sheriff. "There was five of us named Sonny within yellin' distance of all of our houses. One of those Sonny's got a new name one time when he went in one of the poorest families' house while they were eatin'. The usual invitation was offered and Sonny said, 'Ah see ya'll air finally down'ta nothin' but jelly'un bread'. After that his name, for that family anyhow, was 'jelly bread' later shortened to 'Jelly' that stuck with him forever."

Everybody joined in a healthy laugh and Sheriff turned to Doctor and asked, "Got a minute?"

Both sat down at the table and no one spoke until Annie had poured coffee and placed a platter of oatmeal cookies in front of them leaving them with the comment, "Now ah've got work'ta do. Ya'll go'ahead and enjoy."

Sheriff broke the ice by speaking first. "Doctor, it ain't no coincidence my showing up about the same time as Bill. He is your lawyer, ain't he? Never mind, none'a my business actu'ly. What is mah business is why he was lookin' into the business of a man named Peters for you?"

Doctor Cabot bristled momentarily but decided to answer a question with a question. "You suggest that Mr. Peters is a concern of yours?"

Sheriff looked short of a response. He ducked his head and scratched his temple, finally he said, "We ain't sure what he does and we're lookin' into 'it."

"Are you suggesting that he might be engaged in shady endeavors?" asked Doctor Cabot.

"Well…yeah, you could say that. Okay. Here goes. Tit for tat. Let's draw a profile of this man. He shows up and all of a sudden, my officers see an increase in unusual activity such as an increase of out-of-state license plates. We are beginnin' to see an increase in prescription drugs for pain and we're seein' more amphetamine and barbiturate usage. At the same time Peters shows up with no visible means of support. Am I crying wolf? We are wondering, why are you?"

"My dear sheriff…" Doctor bristled as his first inclination was to tell the officer that it was not of his affair but decided cooperation would serve his own interests… "Mr. Peters' son is a patient of mine. Possible answers to the nature of his disorder are lacking here in our medical community and I have referred him to the University of Virginia. His visit there avails me of a continuing education opportunity and I am making plans to be at Charlottesville to observe the evaluation. Mr. Peters has access to a sizeable aircraft in which he intends to transport his son and the son's mother to the UVA Hospital for evaluation. Since there will be excess seating in the plane Mr. Peters has generously offered me, and anyone I wish to accompany me, to ride along. Now, since the receipt of gifts and accommodations in most cases is considered unethical, and particularly so if those favors may be benefits of ill-gotten gains, I simply had my attorney check into the source of that offered gift so as to cover my ethical butt, as William so colorfully put it." Doctor concluded with a look of determination suggesting that the topic was closed.

"Ah sure understand and I won't bother you on that topic again. Ah do advise you to get to Charlottesville some other way since we have doubts about what might be on that plane besides passengers."

For the first-time realization hit. Dr. Cabot's boorishness diminished as he realized that the sheriff was actually concerned about him. "Thank you, Sheriff. Why didn't you come out and warn me rather than beat about the bush?"

"We sheriffs have ethics too, you know. Ah had to let you give me a reason to warn you without unethically revealin' something about Mr. Peters. What if he's innocent; maybe he is and maybe he ain't. Maybe we'll never know."

Sheriff Hare sat quietly for a very long time with his elbows resting on his knees, just looking at nothing on the floor. Slowly he sat up straight and looked over Doctor's shoulder focusing on nothing behind him.

"Doctor Cabot, I gotta' another problem that you might be able to help me with.

"We found a young man drowned in Bluestone Lake on the West Virginia side where the lake follows the West Virginia line for about two miles in Mercer County and that puts it in my jurisdiction. We ain't got no reason to believe it's anything but accidental."

Doctor Cabot interrupted Hare's questioning, "I don't see where this concerns me?"

"Oh, Ah think it does," the sheriff responded emphatically.

"He had no identification on him. All we got is this wad of dirty paper found in his shirt pocket. Can you tell us anything about it?" handing the 'evidence' to Doctor Cabot.

Doctor took the paper and unfolded it carefully. The paper had been torn leaving only part of a hand-written message: *"contactez le Capt Cabotin Bluefield."*

Doctor examined the filthy piece of paper and read it again. Puzzled he said, "It's in French translated loosely as 'by contacting Captain Cabot in Bluefield'. Means nothing to me," he said.

"But that last name is either yours or the same as yours. Could it be you?"

"As I just said. Means nothing to me. Sorry. Besides, I was a Major. Yet in the back of my mind…….? No nothing. If I make any sense of it I'll give you a call," finalizing the conversation.

Doctor saw the sheriff to the door and bade his goodbyes. He returned to the kitchen, found his cup and went for a coffee refill. "Annie," he said, "I think I have painted myself into the proverbial corner. I am now engaged to be married, a potential participant in criminal activity, getting ready to embark on a research mission in autism, and probably a recruit in a new mountain artist gift outlet. Can I handle all of that, and practice medicine too?"

"Aw boy, don't blow up ever'day thangs in'ta problems. Why, they're too small to be seen on a gallopin' horse."

"You are probably correct Annie. Why should I burden you with my perceived problems?"

"Time'll tell; time'll tell," Annie prophesized.

CHAPTER FORTY-NINE

Dr. Cabot was settled into the protective cocoon of the kitchen with a fresh cup of morning coffee' just placed in front of him by Annie, and the 'on your porch before breakfast'[19] newspaper—The Bluefield Daily Telegraph— when Jenn barged into the room with a dour look on her face.

With little fanfare and no hesitation, she rudely declared, "The weddin' is off!"

Annie reacted first: "What in tarnation you rantin' on uh'bout girl? Even if'n hit's th truth that ain't no way of goin' bout uh'tellin' hit!"

"Ahm sorry Miss Annie," she apologized. "The mother of that boy we scheduled at The University of Virginia just called and canceled everything."

---

[19]   The Bluefield Dailey Telegraph ran a contest of slogans of businesses in Bluefield, the object being to see who could name the most. For example, Warlick Furniture Company's slogan was "Cross the bridge and save a dollar", Alfred Land Jeweler's was, "I'll stand on my head to please you." I asked my Grandma Gullion the pick whose slogan was "On your porch before breakfast," and she quickly responded "Chicken doo."

Dr. Cabot, having been dumbly monitoring the exchange up that point, finally reacted. "Did she give a reason?"

"Something about her husband 'putting a stop to it."

"Well, that concerns me about the boy, but it is father's decision to make…in Annie's words, it's a fly in the ointment but is only a brief hindrance as far as the wedding is concerned. We will just have it right here." Doctor said unenthusiastically. "It will be even better since we can invite more people and have a gargantuan party."

"Glory be," exclaimed Annie. "That's what ah hoped fur in the first place. Jenny, me and yore Ma will put on the best weddin' this here part'a th'woods has ever done see'd. We'll git yore brother's band to play th'music. Won't that be good, Jenn?"

Jenn was not listening. Her mind was on Jim. He had been reluctant at first to be a part of the Charlottesville 'study' but as the time for the trip became shorter he was, in his words, rarin' t'go'. Finally, she turned to leave and distractedly said, "I'll see you when you're ready to see patients."

Doctor took longer than usual at the breakfast table dreading facing Nurse Jenn and her bitter-tongue of anger which she would take out on him, as usual. Finally, with a big sigh, he rose from the table, thanked Annie for another fine supply of buckwheat pancakes and dragged himself to the clinic with faithful Bo, in an apparent similar state of mind, following closely on his heels.

Jenn's strong feeling that she had let Jim down with the Charlottesville cancellation continued to plague her even though that evaluation would have offered nothing toward career training. She had considered several possibilities but the one she was actively pursuing was Bluefield State College where two-year certificate programs were being introduced as well as specially scheduled single semester job training courses. However, Jim's academic preparation, as well as his questionable intellectual level, probably precluded any academic choice.

Jenn's search led her to the State Unemployment Office where she found recently introduced Federal employment and training programs where the Area Redevelopment Act provided subsidized training to workers in depressed areas. Further, The Economic Opportunity Act created an array of new employment evaluation and job training programs, including Job Corps. She found Welch to be a hub of those opportunities and a decision was made, pending Jim's acceptance, of course. She was pleased to find that for the trade schooling there were no educational prerequisites. However, the applicant needed to pass an *age-level verbal-skills test of understanding* she took to mean that the student needed to have the ability to follow normal verbal instructions. That, Jim could do easily.

CHAPTER FIFTY

O<small>NE COLD AND BLUSTERY</small> day, somewhere north of Morgantown, West Virginia near the Township of Connellsville, Pennsylvania, a history-changing meeting in the annals of organized crime took place—particularly in the southern Appalachian Mountains—since the purpose of the enclave was to discuss territorial rights of the rapidly changing crime market. Moonshine was losing its luster as the illegal mood-altering drugs extended their cruel tentacles into chronic poverty where hope had long-since been abandoned. Marijuana was becoming an ideal cash crop since it was a native plant of the mountains, often growing wild amongst the rhododendron, dogwood, chinquapins, ginseng, and trillium. Change was on the march and organized crime was right in step.

The delegates of the meeting were a heterogeneous representation of locales and peoples quite different from any other organization with similar goals. A newcomer to the alliance sat reverently aside of the assemblage studiously acquiring an image for himself. What he saw were demigods of crime attired in the 'robes' of power purchased from the best shops but lacking 'taste' in their sleaziness. He took note of this and decided he would stay with off-the-rack garments that did not call attention to what he had been forced into. His work environment was among simple folks who scoffed at people who 'put on airs' and generally were distrustful of 'outsiders.' He had observed the vehicles in which the other participants had arrived, and he decided that he would stick to his plain ol' Studebaker. Really, he thought, this meeting was doing a good job of teaching him what he should not be. He had arrived at this meeting in a 'company' plane and he decided that its use placed him too much in the public eye and that, too, was detrimental to his ability to gain the trust of the independent people with whom he must develop an involuntary working relationship.

He was first and foremost, an accountant. He had studied his market and found a changing Southern culture; Appalachian moonshiners were following the market and switching to marijuana. The 'Feds' were finding more marijuana patches than moonshine stills. In one location agents found only 90 stills, down from 1,200, while running into 20 patches of marijuana ironically planted in rows with corn. His research showed that moonshine was a local product generally transported by 'runners' in modified automobiles. Marijuana, on the other hand, was a national market even finding acceptance as a medicinal product. As the demand for weed grew, so did the demand for a more potent product leading to the 'Mexican connection' providing stronger stuff to mix with the poorer quality mountain-grown marijuana. Investigating this more marketable product was his 'mob' assignment. But, he had a problem; most of his potential growers were from fundamental Christian backgrounds where moonshining was considered a government restriction having nothing to do with religion. Drugs? A whole different ballgame.

CHAPTER FIFTY-ONE

THE FIELD MANSION WAS abuzz with excited activity as the board of directors and craft providers of the Community Arts Cooperative celebrated the acquisition of a rent-free building visible from Route 52 in Simmons that was once a company store. They decided to call their new store The Mountain Crafts Company Store. The location was near perfect since the boundaries of Bramwell, Freeman and Simmons were fuzzy at best. Route 52 heading north, dropped down the mountain side from Pinnacle rock and confronted the Bluestone at the mountain's foot. The road to Bramwell cut sharply and uphill with its modern high school appearing to the left just a short drive west. Freeman and Simmons sat a stone's throw further up on the banks of the Bluestone river. The community of Bluewell was four miles south, half way between Bramwell and Bluefield. Speculation by some suggested that Bluewell got its name by taking the first part of Bluefield and the second part of Bramwell as a credit for being a 'half-way' point between the two.

Doctor, Jenn and Bill sat on the balcony of the living room hidden by quilts. Down below there were Antimacassars, doilies, afghans, hot pads, lace-edged towels,

210

trivets, coal-carved statuettes, wooden toys, stools, chairs, bird houses, yard-art of all kinds, and much, much more. All lovingly created for the new store. They were being totally ignored by Annie, David's Mom, and the gaggle of ecstatic folk artist thoroughly enjoying their role as creators of the art scattered about the large living room.

Bill spoke: "Jenn, did you know that our grandparents on Papa's side of the family are buried just east of Simmons?"

"What? No, I didn't. Wonder how come I didn't? How is it that you knew, and I didn't?"

"The reason, I guess, is that before I went into the army I used to take Papa over there to clear the graves. After I was drafted Sonny took over that job until he went into the air force and by then Papa wasn't able to do it anymore. Sonny told me he tried to find the place once by himself but the location eluded him. \ I guess they're still there. I drove up the road myself a time or two, but it's just too grown over with weeds and trees along there to get even an idea where it might be. Earth to earth, I suppose. I never have known why they were buried there. The only tie that I know of about the area is that Aunt Nan lived out that way."

David perked up and said. "Hey Jenn, that's where you took me see your aunt across the swinging bridge isn't it? I'll always remember chasing you down the railroad tracks…." he exclaimed before he realized what he was saying and turned a vivid red in embarrassment.

Bill, never one to let an opportunity to tease David, latched on to the comment by declaring, "Oh, so Simmons Road is now lover's lane?"

Jenn joined in gleefully, "He finally got up enough gumption to realize that I was more than an office nurse to him."

David jumped up from his chair and headed for the kitchen gruffly pronouncing, "I was chasing you because of your abominable behavior on that dangling footpath. You scared the wits out of me by willfully swaying that…thing so dangerously. I…. Oh, I cannot win with the two of you against me. I need a cup of coffee." He left with laughter striking him in the back. As he entered the kitchen he caught a glimpse of a police car pulling into the back entrance of the house. He walked back through the sunroom to meet Sheriff Hare at the door. Greetings were exchanged, and coffee was offered and accepted.

"Doctor" the sheriff began, "I need your help. It's no small request and ah'd not blame you if you told me that I've become plum' addled. Ah want to deputize you."

The room fell silent. Doctor was speechless. He finally leaned forward and opened his hands in a questioning gesture. "You…want to deputize…Me?" he inquired incredulously. "What in…in tarnation for?"

Sheriff inhaled deeply, leaned back in his chair, and huffed out his breath before saying: "It's a long story."

"I am intently listening," exclaimed Doctor.

"I'll start by askin' you if you recall the piece of paper I showed you that had 'En contactant le capitaine Cabot à Bluefield' written on it? Pardon my French."

"Don't be ridiculous, Of course I do. Go on." Doctor testily responded.

"Well, first of all, we found that item on the young man found drowned in Bluestone dam. Or at least we thought he had drowned in the dam. An autopsy was performed on him and routine lab studies showed he had drowned in chlorinated water, not water from the lake."

Doctor tried to interrupt. "I do not see wh…."

"Just listen to me…please. You and your family are in danger if you don't follow along with me and maybe if you do. Organized crime, Ah don't mean a few moonshiners from a bunch of relatives, Ah'm talking about Chicago, Pittsburg, and places like that where the nasty stuff goes on; you know what Ah mean since you're a big city boy. Are you with me so far?" the Sheriff inquired.

"Yes, but…"

"Ah ain't finished," the sheriff continued. "The potential is such that the Governor issued an executive order creatin' a secret unit of the State Police sent out of State to study with mob crime specialists who have been dealin' with it for many years. Part of that was because West Virginia has only had to deal with locals, mostly in the liquor business, and partly because honesty in the local police departments ain't the best when it comes to moonshinin'. Any effort to try to change the way we do business as cops will meet with the hillbilly stubbornness that is a part of us; change is a tough row to hoe in these parts. So, while we're runnin' around makin' and peddlin' moonshine, the savvy outsiders see a growing market for far more evil things such as drugs. We are hearing a lot about the popularity of marijuana but here in the mountains it ain't anything new. Why, people here have been using it for asthma for years. You don't need to go to no crime boss to buy it; it grows everywhere around here but it likes the side of roads makin' it easy to pick. It ain't considered no worse than Cubeb[20] and people wonder why all the hullabaloo over a dang 'ditch weed'."

---

[20]   I have been an asthma sufferer all my life. When I was a teenager, an unsuccessful political candidate, Mr. Nub P., left unemployed as a result, opened a variety and used book

Sheriff stopped to catch his breath and Doctor interjected a comment. "We briefly studied the benefits of Cubeb in medical school. It never really caught on."

Hare ignored him and continued. The problem now is that they're startin' to bring in the strong stuff and breedin' it with the prolific natural stuff here creatin' a whole new very valuable product. The people doin' this ain't locals but major crime syndicates lacking the morals of the true mountaineer. Nobody wants that, least of all my people."

"I still don't see my role in any of this," said Doctor Cabot.

"Ah'm getting' to that," sheriff continued. "Ah contacted the sheriffs of Giles and Bland Counties, both very long-time, dependable and ethical friends of mine from way back. I met with them in Bluefield 'cause it's kinda a central location for one thing and another is Ah don't feel secure using the phone anymore. I told them about the water in our mystery man's lungs and about it maybe not bein' an accident. Neither was surprised because of strange behavior in their jurisdictions. Now I told them about a note that was found and that I planned to start an investigation about its source. Ah didn't give them details about the content of the note or hints as to how Ah was goin' to go about it but they agreed that we should not involve any local authorities

---

store in Bluewell. While browsing his wares I discovered a box of Cubeb Cigarettes. Curious, I read the label and was surprised to find that smoking Cubeb was 'good' for asthma. I spent a dime for a pack and was astounded to find that Cubeb would, indeed, relieve an asthma attack as good, or better, than inhaling nebulized epinephrine. My source dried up when the store abruptly closed and the owner became a post master, a frequent reward for those who ran and lost.

in any investigation. We are going' to work together in documentin' unusual doin's in our three counties. We discussed the geographical importance of our counties—and the jurisdictional restrictions caused by state lines—because of the many roads going in all directions without passing' through any big cities and the number of airports we have available. We have set up our own Tri-county Crime Task Force and…that brings me to you. First you already have skin in the game and second what better person to freely mingle with all sorts of people but a doctor."

"I sup'ose ya'll hav'uh plan for me?" Doctor whined mockingly, well aware that he was beaten, and he might as well 'go with the flow'.

"Most certainly, my dear fellow. We have considered your options and have drafted the following scenario, whuther you lah'k hit er not," Sheriff Hare shot back in kind.

CHAPTER FIFTY-TWO

THE DC-3 FOLLOWED A straight approach over the curvaceous New River into the New River Valley Air Port (NRVA) at Dublin, Virginia. The plane had departed Joseph A Hardy Airport at Connellsville, Pennsylvania earlier in the day with no flight plan and three passengers aboard. The DC-3 landed smoothly, taxied to the gate area, and did a one-eighty before coming to a stop. The steps momentarily dropped disgorging one passenger who quickly passed through the small empty terminal to a waiting car that moved out before the door was closed.

The drive spoke first. "How did it go."

"Ridiculous," replied the passenger. "They're still a bunch of Capone wannabees. Thank goodness we're pretty much on our own down here and that's the way I like it. Take the back-way home."

The 'back-way' avoided major roads. The NRVA was on RT 100 north of Dublin. going north to Poplar Hill and west on the Wilderness road that led to RT 52 and on to Bluefield to the north and the coal fields beyond or south to his farm-home. By staying on RT 100 to Pearisburg one could also avoid major roads in getting to the coals fields. Another reason for using the NRVA had to do with an

Executive Order issued by the governor of West Virginia that established a secret—short lived secret as it turned out—tactical strike force (TSF) made up of selected state troopers to combat the illegal manufacture, sale, transportation, and use of narcotics and collect and disseminate intelligence on organized crime activity throughout the State. All airports in West Virginia were under surveillance including Bluefield and Beckley. To combat this minor inconvenience, the major mobs were reducing the size of their aircraft to smaller planes that could land on any flat field surreptitiously. This reduced the payload but that was just a price of doing business. This was quite satisfactory for Peters since this reduced the number of mob-provided soldiers. He was living on a rented farm in Bland County, Virginia just south of Rocky Gap where he maintained a grass runway kept in tip top shape as a part of his lawn thus provided a resource if there was a need for a plane. Living with Peters was a former beauty queen, whom he had befriended, and her retarded son whose father was unknown.

CHAPTER FIFTY-THREE

IT WAS MID-OCTOBER. THE foliage had been spectacular. The doctor business was booming so much so that Doctor Cabot was becoming bored with general practice as his only activity. Every day the same people with the same problems highlighted by men dying, hopelessly, with black lung. He longed for some variety; maybe some surgery? After all, he was a trained surgeon with extraordinary experience in Korea at the MASH unit. He had been encouraged repeatedly by fellow members of the Mercer County Medical Association to accept the proffered privileges at both Bluefield hospitals. Finally, he capitulated and was now spending one day a week in surgery that, as it happened, was good for him, and his practice. He was wool-gathering at his desk after a very busy day of black lung, sore throats, a broken arm and other routine cuts and bruises when Jenn briskly entered his office without knocking as she was want to do and to which he was not, in the least, annoyed. She plopped herself in the chair beside his desk, and addressed him in a very business-like manner.

"I have a serious question for you." She said.

"I know" he pleaded. "I am so sorry about the wedding …."

"Nah, not that," she interrupted. "I got you hooked so Ah'm not worried about that. It'll happen soon enough. What Ah'm wondering about is the large amount of money someone is spending to get the Company Store up and runnin'. Your Mom had agreed to provide the funds for a modest start but this gung-ho investment from an unknown source is too good to believe. Here Annie, your Mom, and a host of excited mountain folks are hustling to stock a large building that has been restored into a first-class retail outlet. It has 'place to go' written all over it after the article in the Telegraph was picked up by the Associated Press. Oh, Ah'm happy as a lark about it. People from all around are comin' in and payin' outlandish prices for whatever is available no matter the quality. Oh, Ah'm not saying that any of the work is shoddy but, let's face it, some is better that others, and some of it is, well, really, just junk…no, not junk…frivolous? Haven't you wondered?"

David could not resist laughing as he responded. "I have indeed puzzled over the situation. I have even entertained the possibility of money laundering but quickly dismissed that as a big city activity."

"Money laundering?" Jenn questioned. "What's that?"

"Hum. Let me see how I can explain it. Okay, try this. Organized crime in big cities generate a large amount of ill-gotten cash, say in drugs or illegal liquor. That money is not spendable because it has no legal source of record. So, the crooks 'buy' legal businesses and put the ill-gotten gains in the cash register, counting it as part of the day's profits and, then legally, putting it in the bank. Dirty money into clean money—hence laundered money. Got it?"

"Yeah, Ah got it." Said Jenn. "But how could money be laundered through a non-profit like the Company Store since the crook doesn't get any of the passed through cash?"

"Maybe it buys good will," opined David.

CHAPTER FIFTY-FOUR

DOCTOR CABOT SAT AT his desk with his head resting in the cradle of his hands and his elbows tripoded on the desk, when that most beautiful voice in his world requested a "penny for your thoughts." He raised his head to look at her and felt that familiar never-ending heart-leap that was reserved for her only. He soaked in her loveliness for more than a brief moment before responding to her question. Then he spoke.

"I cannot get that note out of my mind."

"What note?"

"You know; the one found on the young man who drowned that the sheriff has been hounding me about. Out of the blue, awake or asleep, there appears a brief glimpse of a scene-past, but the instant I try to focus, it's gone. The more I think about it the note is personal; it is addressed only to me and I should recognize it. Several times in the past three or four weeks an image of a time or place briefly appeared but, like a butterfly, flitted away. The vague fuzzy edges of the apparition are…I don't know, maybe from a suppressed memory?"

"It'll come," suggested Jenny as she edged around the desk to give him a quick kiss on top of his balding head, "But, I came in here with something else on my mind."

"That tone of voice and faraway look generally portends a disruption of my stolid existence, am I correct? May I assume that the delay in our nuptials is bearing on your mind?"

"Nuptials? What? Heck no. Why do you always think Ah'm in a such a big rush to marry you? Heck, I ain't even sure I like you enough to call you a friend, much less a husband, Yuck," she jokingly declared.

"Well, as your rejected fiancé I am properly scorned, and I fall before you humbly seeking a restoration of your good graces," he pleaded.

"Aw hush up. I came in with a serious concern and you have turned the conversation into a Burns and Allen[21] comedy bit. Now listen to me, will you?"

Doctor realized her seriousness, got up, encased her in his arms and pleaded. "Forgive me my love. Let's go get a cup of coffee, and I promise you my total and undivided attention."

In the kitchen they found the usual unexplained, perpetually fresh, pot of coffee and equally predictable 'hot-out-of-the-oven' treats. This time they were miniature popovers. Instead of sitting at the kitchen counter, as usual, David led the way to the living room.

After they were situated David softly said, "Go."

"As you already know, I was raised by church-goin' parents and I have missed that in my life. It's mostly my fault since I have been afraid to say anything about church knowin' that your religious experience was in a fancy big city 'proper' church where the preacher was called 'priest' at

---

[21]   Burns and Allen was an American comedy team very popular on radio up until about 1958.

church and 'father' everywhere else. I remember the time you went to church here with Bill and how you were put-out by the way it was done. Now, I can't give an appraisal of… high church…? because I haven't ever been to one. Here in the mountains the Catholic Church is so misunderstood that I probably have a gross misunderstanding of any church that is called liturgical and since the Episcopal Church, the one you go to, does many of the same…. activities…? Well, you understand?"

David started to speak. "Jenn…."

"No, wait a minute. Let me finish. Ah'm not done yet."

"Okay, let me warm my coffee and you will still have my full attention, and, if the truth be known, my understanding. Be right back my most precious one," he said as he kissed her gently on the mouth on his way out.

Doctor went in search of his mother. He found her and Annie working on the Company Store inventory. Why he sought his mother he did not know; probably in the back of his mind she could provide something that he could say to Jenn? His intentions were to simply ask her how to approach the apparent…gap?... between two differing religious backgrounds but he found that he did not know what question to ask. Both women looked at him expectantly. He stared back and finally said, "Never mind," and turned to leave.

His mother was the first to speak. "David, wait. You are concerned. Tell us what it is. You will be addressing the top brains of the court of mediocre advice in this household."

Annie piped up with her input by offering, "You bet'chem Red Ryder. Gud ad 'vice and hit's cheap. Have we ever led you astray?"

"Mom, Miss Annie, this is no laughing matter. Jenn has confronted me with the desire to get involved in…well…

going to church. What do I tell her? We grew up in such differing philosophical settings that I do not see a middle ground."

Annie took the challenge first. "Tel'me, my lad. What's the purpose of religion anyways?"

David mulled the question for a brief period and hesitantly responded, "salvation?" vaguely recalling something from his Episcopal catechism as a boy.

"Rah't cha'air," exclaimed Annie as his mom nodded enthusiastically.

"And salvation is'uh heap lahk butter" Annie reasoned. "Yew git butter frum milk frum all kind'sa cows, black, white, brown, Holstein, Jersey, but hit don't matter none, cuz hit's still butter after hit's churned. Most rele'juns air 'bout the same in that respect. Oh, some air fancy with the preacher wearin' robes and big hats, readin' out of big ol bibles, held up by'uh little boy wearin ' a night gown, with the congega'shun bouncin' up and down, sayin' things lahk 'and also with you,' while simpl'r ones jest git down to redin' the bible, preachin' 'uh'bout hit and sayin' a prayer in thar' own words about somethin' goin' on local, lahk the need fur rain, or askin' God to take ker of a sol'chur boys, cause we air always in'a war sum place or 'nother. Anyhow, what's important is they're all gittin' to the same point, mostly about Jesus, ain't they?"

Mom, nodding her head vigorously, put the exclamation point on Annie's soliloquy by adding, "Amen, like they say in your church, Annie."

David marveled at the bond that had matured between the two since his Mom had moved into the Fields Mansion.

"But Annie," pleaded David, "what am I to do? I am an intellectual snob, you know that all too well; part of that attitude is that my concept of worship was ecclesiastically formulated into me as a child. Intellectually, the choice of religion and consequentially the church one attends, is not a matter of self-determination but rather a part of historical heritage. Jenn and I were raised to our 'faiths' and we took them for granted. In my case however, I have considerable doubt about the relevance of the church altogether, liturgical or otherwise, and their declaration of faith stated in 'creeds' that are contrary to my intellect that stand in the face of new knowledge that most churches seem to ignore in favor of 'tradition' based on archaic protocols. I must admit that I lean towards the simplicity of Jenn's teachings since they do leave room for critical thinking outside the parameters of the rigidity of the liturgy."

"Unfort'unate," Annie offered, "they all seem ta'have some petty ah'dees 'bout which'ns rah't and which'ns wrong, lah'k sprank'lin or 'e'murshun, but all that stuff kin be ignored if'n hit's jus' not turn't into an issue. The important thang is if'n Jesus Christ is the central focus all th'time. If'n He ain,t then do what Jesus told His disciples, and Ah'm not just talkin' about the twelve original one's , but us too, He told them, in Mathew 10-14 to 'shake the dust off'n your feet and move on.'"

"Mom…Miss Annie…the two of you comprise an unbeatable team. Thank you. I know what to do now," said David as he rushed out of the room to continue his conversation with Jenn.

He found her, more composed, sitting primly on the sofa patting her eyes with dainty lace handkerchief. He sat beside her, gently taking her hand in his and spoke.

"Jenn, I have been a dunce; no not just a dunce, but an arrogant dunce. What I know about religion will not fill a thimble. I went to church on Sunday Morning with my parents because it was the proper thing to do in Boston.

I was required to remain silent, and motionless through a dreary, mind-numbing, monotonous ritual that never deviated except for the addition of equally boring liturgical-season changes that lengthened the torture I endured. I suffered through the catechism…"

Jenn interrupted him in mid-sentence stating, "I know that catechism is a class that Catholic Children had to go to because I went to Junior High School with Italian kids when we were bussed into Bluefield. I have always wondered what it was."

"During the Protestant Reformation," David began, "you know what that was?" He inquired of Jenn.

"Well yes, Ah'm not that ignorant." protested Jenn. "If Ah didn't learn it in Sunday school or bible class in junior high, I read about it in romance novels that we passed around during nurse's training. People were becoming unhappy with how the catholic church was being run and several theologians took them to issue. Most of them were excommunicated, just in case you don't know, that means thrown out…"

"I know what it means, Miss Smarty Pants," David laughed. "Wait a minute." He backtracked. "Did you say bible class in school?"

"Ah did, and it was fun. It was a required course unless you were exempt for religious reasons such as being a Jew. It was taught by an itinerant teacher that did nothin' else. She used a flannel board as a visual aid to illustrate the stories. In particular Ah remember the lessons on the reformation not associated with the major people like Luther but by what she called 'The Radical Reformation' that were called Anabaptist and Mennonites and…maybe Quakers?… She said that their attitudes were the foundation of most of

American fundamental churches. That's about all I know about it."

"That, my dearest, is an amazingly detailed summary of something I know absolutely nothing about. Admitting that, I have an idea for an exploratory plan. Both of us have science-based professions. We never make a diagnosis without a case history and basic physical, do we?"

"Yeess…?" replied Jenn hesitantly. "Go on."

"Well then, it appears to me that you are longing for a church affiliation and you think I am too snobbish to approve of what's available locally."

"Now hol' on jus' a dog'gone minute mister better'en-anybody-else. Don't you go puttin' words in mah mouth!" Jenn, reverting to her hill-country dialect in her anger.

"Whoa, whoa," rejoined David. "No offense intended; just stating a fact. Didn't I admit that I am a snob."

"Well, yes but you did infer that local churches are… well…unacceptable…?"

"I implied no such thing but that could possibly be true if we took an objective look at all of the possibilities? A diagnosis, as it were?"

"Ah accept your apology."

"I did not apologize."

"Yes, you did. And I accepted it. Move on."

David laughed heartily and said, "I love you, you stubborn beautiful Hillbilly."

"Ah ain't no hillbilly."

"Yes, you are."

"No, ah ain't, but ah accept your compliment about bein' beautiful. I really am ain't Ah?" as she leaned into him seductively.

"This ain't workin'" David laughingly surrendered. We *will* solve the church problem. Jes' yew wait'un see."

CHAPTER FIFTY-FIVE

DOCTOR CABOT WAS SURPRISED, after a very tiring day in the clinic, to find sheriff Hare sitting at the kitchen table having coffee with Jim. He said nothing as he moved to Annie's perpetually-fresh coffee pot and poured himself a steaming mug of the world's best. He was steeling himself for what he knew was coming.

"Jim, have you been properly catering to our Chief County Law Enforcement Officer?"

"If'un yew mean am Ah bein' nice to the sheriff, then, yes sir."

"And Sheriff, have you been heeding to the sage advice of one of my most treasured advisors?"

"Ah have, and he tells me things are relatively stable here'bouts. But he also confides in me that there are new people workin' the area in shady-like activities. You know anything about that?"

"Not at all. I am much too engaged in the practice of primeval medicine here in Utopia. What goes on amongst the proletariat is of minimal consequence when compared to the carnage created in the name of industrial progress by the absentee coal barons," Doctor Cabot lamented.

"Doctor David, ah do d'clare that you air the mos' confoundin' talker Ah ever did see. What the heck did yew jus' say?" Jim inquired.

Sheriff Hare laughed and said, "Jim, he's just bein' sarcastic."

"That don't hep none," pouted Jim.

"Okay, Sheriff, you are most certainly not here for congenial banter, what's on your agenda? Asked Doctor.

"What I have to say is a bit sensitive…"

"Hey, I ken tak'uh hint," mumbled Jim jumping to his feet. "Buh'sides Ah got chores ta'do. Ya'll 'scuse me?" Jim said over his shoulder as he stomped out of the room.

From the kitchen came the voice of compassion. Annie called out, "Jim, fresh cookies jus' out'a'th'oven. Come fill up before you go out."

"There's one of the finist women you'll find anywhere. Her sense of passion is a model to us all. Known her all my life and she just gits…well, better if that's possible," observed the Sheriff.

"She is my moral guide, solace, jester…I don't know how I would have managed, or continue to do so, in my life's transition here without her guidance. Now, continue with your purpose for being here," Doctor requested.

"There are some rumblin's' detected around the tri-county alliance that I told you about. Nothing new, really. One note-worthy observation was a couple of practically touch'n go landings of a DC-3 at the New River Valley Airport. Only one time was anybody seen gettin' on or off but they only have one guy there most of the time. You could probably load or unload an elephant and he wouldn't see it. Neither time did the DC-3 request landing information or permission. Also, over in Giles County a kid keepin' track of license plates told a deputy that he had seen several cars, or one car several times, from Ohio on back roads. It could be nothin' but it sorta fits the scheme of things."

Sheriff Hare paused for a long spell causing Doctor to intensify the focus of his attention for the first time. Doctor asked, "Am I to anticipate the dropping-of-second- shoe?"

"Well…maybe…something like that." stuttered Sheriff Hare. "The dispatcher of the Bluefield Police Department got an anonymous call a while back asking if they had a Captain Cabot on their force. When the dispatcher said 'no' the caller hung up."

A cold chill ran up the Doctor's spine. Now they— whoever 'they' were— had his full attention.

"Sheriff Hare," declared Doctor, "I do believe that it is in my best interest to become one of your deputies. Please proceed with the swearing-in ceremony. All I ask is that I remain anonymous and that I am not required to carry a weapon."

"Ah believe I can assure that your best interest will be guaranteed," said the Sheriff. "We should have a couple of witnesses but considering the need for confidentiality we'll go without.

The necessary participants were assembled. The Sheriff instructed Doctor to hold up his right hand and repeat the usual affirmation after which the Sheriff welcomed him to his department.

"Here is your credentials jacket. Inside is a badge and a picture ID. Carry these with you always and display them only when absolutely necessary, and not then, if you can bluff your way out of it. You are a special investigator that does not require you to be in hazardous situations resulting in an arrest. Never enter a situation where you might be in jeopardy. Your firearm is strictly for protection of yourself and your loved ones who might be threatened. Are these instructions clear?" asked the Sheriff.

"Wait a moment, my dear man. Clarify, if you will, the morsel about a 'firearm?' I believe you gave me your assurance that I would not be required to bear arms?"

"Ah made no such assurance. Ah believe what Ah said was that 'Ah can assure you that your best interest will be guaranteed' and that is what Ah will do. And besides, the law requires that all my deputies be armed. End of argument. Now to what you can do to help out. First, the people around you are the drivers of our community. Miss Annie and your Mom, for example, are the heart and soul of the new Company Store and therefore in a position to notice unusual cash flow. A business like that is a fine pass-through for illegal money."

"Perhaps it is more than coincidence that you mention money laundering. Just a few days ago I used the Company Store as an example of a business conducive to exploitation by organizations seeking sources for legalizing ill-gotten gains. Jenn was puzzling over why an anonymous donor would dispense such extravagance upon such an unlikely endeavor," said Doctor.

"You're right on target and for that reason I think that we should maybe hold a small conference with your enclave?" Sheriff suggested.

"Indubitably," said Doctor. "We can meet at the clinic, but you will need to be the organizer and moderator. If it comes from me they will most certainly dismiss any concerns as the mental aberrations of a big city fear monger."

CHAPTER FIFTY-SIX

DR. CABOT WAS READING the morning newspaper when an announcement caught his eye:

Church to present Handel's Messiah

The combined choirs of Christ Episcopal, First Presbyterian and Immanuel Lutheran Churches, accompanied by The Bluefield Symphony Orchestra along with the entire music department of Bluefield College and the Beaver High School Acapella Choir, will present Handel's Messiah in special concert at Westminster Church on December 4th. The concert will feature John Ingram of Philadelphia at the pipe organ. There is no charge for the concert, but reservations will be required due to limited seating. Tickets may be obtained at the offices of any of the participant organizations. Live remote broadcasts with be provided by WKOY radio to the Granada Theatre, where high

> quality sound is available, as well as the
> regular radio audience.

Doctor grabbed the phone and asked the long-distance operator for the Westminster Presbyterian Church in Bluefield. He waited for the call to go through only the hear the operator inform him that that number did not answer. He asked her to try Christ Episcopal and got the same answer. Becoming disheartened, he requested her to try the Immanuel Lutheran Church. He waited several moments when the operator informed him, "I have your party on the line. Go ahead."

"Hello, to whom am I speaking: Doctor inquired.

"This is Pastor Linebarger," came the replay.

"Oh, thank Heaven," Doctor said. "Pastor this is Doctor Cabot, in Boston Knob, down toward Welch. I just read an article in The Telegraph about the upcoming presentation of the Messiah…"

"Well, Hello, Doctor. I know who you are. The Cole family belongs to this church and one of them shared your experience with the moonshiners. I hope you got over it." Pastor inquired.

"How profoundly embarrassing," exclaimed Doctor, "I should have hoped that my reputation was based on something more inspiring."

"Your reputation is intact, I assure you. To add to that assurance, you are welcome to join our homebrew group where we make the best beer agoin' from a 'blest' recipe developed at the Southern Lutheran Seminary. Oh, excuse me. You called. What can I help you with?"

"About the Messiah; I am seeking reservations for the live presentation. Are you in a position to assist me in obtaining four seats?"

"I am. Give me a second or two while I find the reservation sheet. Hold on…here it is. Four seats, down front?"

"No thank you. I would prefer the balcony for a more panoramic view as well as the blending provided by the distance from the performers."

"There you are then. Four seats, front row balcony are… now…yours. Give me your address and I will mail you the confirmation, or would you rather pick them up? I've got an even better idea. Why don't you visit us at church some Sunday? We would be delighted to have you. Please do."

"That is a splendid idea," David opined. "We will see you there."

CHAPTER FIFTY-SEVEN

Mrs. Cabot and Annie were busy in the kitchen chattering away about their many joint activities when the house phone rang. Mrs. Cabot answered it, paused a bit and exclaimed excitedly, "Everything?" as she looked incredulously at Annie.

"What is hit? Somethun' wrong? Queried Annie.

"Mrs. Poe down at the store says that a man is there and wants to buy everything in the store. He has cash to pay a flat price for the entire inventory. What do we do?" pleaded Mrs. Cabot.

Tell'um ta'hold on. Ah'll get Doctor. He'll know wha'ta do. Jes' hold on. Be right back."

Annie dashed down the back steps to the clinic and bumped into Jenn in the hallway. "Jenn, we have th' makin's of a disaster, down at the store. Some man is a'wantin' to buy ever'thang. What do we do?"

"Whoa," said Jenn. "Everything?"

"Ever' thang; they're holden' the phone 'til we tell'm what ta'do," Annie said.

"Ah'll get David; he can tell you the best thing to do."

Doctor Cabot was just finishing up with another black lung patient when Jenn knocked on the examination room door and said, "We have a nonmedical problem and need you, stat."

"Alright, I'll be in my office shortly," Doctor acknowledges her intrusion and calmly finished up with his patient.

When he entered his office, Jenn and Annie were anxiously waiting for him and Jenn spoke first. "The Store is on the telephone and some man wants to buy everything. What do they do."

With his usual calm manner, as if he were examining a patient, Doctor inquired, "Does he have cash?"

"We don' know," answered Annie. "Come on up star's and tel'us wa'ta'do and don' give us none'uh yor smart mouth."

"Right. On my way," He said.

As Annie hurried ahead to the kitchen Jenn said, "David, wait a minute. Do you think this is what you were talkin' about some time ago? You remember…? Money laundering? It sure sounds fishy to me. Somebody coming in to a no-profit store and offering to buy everything?"

"I believe you have correctly assessed the situation, my love. The timing of the execution, however, is surprising occurring much sooner than I would have anticipated. I think it best that you become the spokeswoman for the telephone portion of this transaction. If this is truly what it looks to be we need to keep the relationship active for legal purposes. We are not so much interested in the income as we are of documenting the exchange of funds. So, here is what you do. Tell them that to simplify the purchase, the Store will accept a single payment, in cash, of five thousand dollars. If that is agreeable with them, then have the Store attendant tell them that she is not authorized to accept a payment that large and that an officer of the Non-profit will be there shorty to complete the transition. You will need to remain here to tend the clinic until I return."

They arrived in the kitchen to find Mrs. Cabot apprehensively clutching the phone to her breast. Jenn took the phone from her and asked Mrs. Poe to give it to the potential buyer and to stay within earshot so she could hear that end of the conversation. Rustling sounds emerged from the phones' receiver as it was given to the buyer.

Jenn inquired, "Who am I speaking to?" she asked.

"Name's Wilson. Are you the one that can take care of my offer?" inquired a surprisingly cultured voice.

"Not directly, no. Ah'm the temporary secretary of the non-profit, citizen-run, Company Store. You have offered to purchase the entire inventory of the store?"

"Yes ma'am. We have ready-buyers from up-scale retailers ready to market your crafts. We are offering wholesale value for your inventory."

"Fine," Jenn replied. "I have our Association President on his way and he will be there directly to handle the deal. By the way, how do you anticipate payment?"

"Sounds good to me, and we will be paying in cash." replied Wilson.

"Gotcha," whispered Deputy Investigator Doctor Cabot.

CHAPTER FIFTY-EIGHT

THE TRADITIONAL GULLION CLAN Thanksgiving Day gathering was presented with a panorama of Heavenly proportions providing undeniable evidence of a Supreme presence. It had snowed. Oh, how it had snowed, the depth of which could almost cover the sins of man. The ugliness of strip mining, of clear-cut timbering, the filling of deep valleys with lovely mountain tops to make roads; no artist could capture it and no poet could describe it.

Bill had called and insisted that he provide David and Jenn with transportation since he had put chains on his pick-up truck tires that, in this type of snow, barely slowed it down.

"I'll swing by and get Jenn and pick you up on the way back," offered Bill.

"Come straight here. Jenn's here."

"Oh, the snowstorm get to her?"

"Yes and no, she is residing here now…" Before David could finish the sentence.

"Without the benefit of wedlock?" Bill chimed in.

"You, my dear brother-in-law-to-be, are a scandalous reprobate. For your information the Simmons-shanty that your Uncle Henry left you, in which she has been 'living,' partially collapsed under last night's heavy snow. I have been trying to get her to move into the suite next to Mom for a while now. I suppose decorum does imply a more imminent wedding date to mollify people who reason as you do."

"Aw, come on down from your high-horse. Common-law marriage has been a way of life around here; it keeps you from marchin' down the aisle." Bill retorted.

"The consummate lawyer who must have the last word. Come and get us before that herd of vultures you call relatives devour the victuals."

"Vultures don't herd; they flock."

David hung up the phone as a definitive statement. His angst was somewhat abated by informing Jenn of her younger brother's vulgarity. That would teach him a lesson he would not soon forget.

Bill, soaked with melancholy, took a slight detour to the gathering and guided his truck to the-top-of-the-hill where in previous years they would have descended to the old homeplace. It was gone, buried under over one hundred feet of fill dirt, yielding to a wider, straighter, quicker road to the coal fields. He recalled sitting in the 'front' room of the cozy old house and listening to his father reflect on the convenience of the new road based on a survey stake just twenty feet or so outside the window. Bill was glad 'Papa" had not lived to see that that stake represented a point far above the roof of the home he had, single-handedly, built many years before and where he and 'Mama' had borne thirteen children and raised them on thirteen acres of hillside land. Thank goodness, the snow covered this as well. He turned his attention to Jenn and saw the glimmer of a tear on her cheek. She too was probably thanking God for the beautiful blanket of snow obliterating the scene of the present, but not the memories of the past.

The partakers of the festivities had, of necessity, parked their cars at a good distance away and walked to the house, the footsteps of the previous arrivals leaving a meager path to be followed and the smoke from the chimney, providing a friendly beacon of welcome.

The gathering reflected the progressive dwindling of numbers, a result of migration and death. Three sisters and four of their offspring were there when the Boston Knob contingent made a noisy entrance. They were warmly welcomed by their hostess and were given prime seats at the huge solid oak round table that was stacked with a turkey—complements of Bluewell Pharmacy where Sister Lula worked since Leslie's retirement—a home-cured ham from the smokehouse, green beans, peaches, homemade chow-chow from the garden, candied yams, homemade rolls and topped off with—*fresh strawberry cobbler*! When queried about the source of the fresh strawberries, Lula simply replied, "Seek and ye shall find."

CHAPTER FIFTY-NINE

THE CLINIC HAD BEEN typically busy this cloudy and dreary day. People prefer not to get sick on nice days. While trying not to be impersonal, Doctor often found himself preoccupied with matters not associated with the task at hand. It was one of those days precipitated by a letter that had arrived in the morning mail from Sheriff Hare.

The letter was short and to the point: "Thank you for the very valuable report. Follow-up belongs to people with more resources. Are you planning to attend the Medical Meeting at White Sulphur Springs next week? Important that you do. Please advise." It was not signed.

The referenced report was the sale of the Company Store inventory that had been hand-carried to the sheriff by Jim along with the untouched cash involved in the transaction. The shouts of protest from the Store's management—Mom and Annie—still rang in his ears but he had convinced them to allow him to hold on to the money and not to disperse it to the membership of the co-op for a while. He had appeased them by dipping into his own savings that they quickly dispersed to the co-op contributors to the great pleasure of all. He had been assured that the funds would be returned once they were fingerprinted and traced, if possible. He would be hounded unmercifully and with regularity, until the full amount was handed over to the board of directors.

He was not unhappy with the idea of spending a couple of days at The Greenbriar. He immediately contacted the hotel and reserved two rooms in anticipation of inviting Jenn to go along as a special treat. He held a slight uneasiness about her fears of 'what people might think' but his fears were quickly assuaged when she squealed with excitement and declared, "Ah don't have a thing to wear!" A trip to Bluefield solved that problem.

To get to the Greenbriar they had to go through Bluefield. They took US 460 to Rich Creek where they picked up US 219 most of the way. The road was surprisingly straight and level except for a few miles along the Seneca Trails. Farming appeared to be a dominant activity even in the hillier areas. At Union the land took on the characteristics of the Shenandoah Valley of Virginia with lush farms as far as the eye could see in every direction.

They drove into White Sulphur Springs on US 60 and found their destination easily. David guided the big Packard onto the tree-lined Village Run Road and followed its winding route to where the opulent elegance of the Georgian structure jumped abruptly into view with its commanding gabled façade lovingly supported by four very smart Doric columns.[22]

---

[22]   The Greenbrier was built in 1913 by the Chesapeake and Ohio Railway. 26 presidents have stayed at the hotel. Dwight D. Eisenhower was the last. In 1942 the hotel was commandeered by the U.S. Army for a hospital. They converted the resort into a 2000-bed facility that opened on October 16, 1943. The

Jenn's eyes became the legendary saucers as they approached the resort. "Oh, my," she repeated numerous times as they left the car with the parking attendant. She oo'd and ah'ed as they entered one of the several lobbies. The one they had entered was resplendent with a large green leaf design and gold wallpaper and draperies of art nuevo patterns. A grand piano stood to one side of the room. The room was so enormous that the large gathering of people was dwarfed. They registered and were escorted to their rooms by a uniformed bellboy who opened the door to Jenn's room first to find that her bags were there already.

"It's beautiful and lovely and gorgeous and...and... swell...oh thank you David for this trip. I love it...and you," she bubbled.

The room broke all the rules for color coordination. The carpet was a checkered royal blue and the walls were papered with a green floral on a beige background. A pseudo canopy of lagoon blue, and olive green with red trim served as a headboard between massive four posters. The bed skirt was also lagoon blue and the folded-down bedspread was a bright red and green floral pattern. An arm chair and luggage racks were a mix of olive and turquoise, the chair a floral pattern and the racks stripped. A large fireplace was ablaze with wood enough to last awhile. The bellhop informed them that the wood would be replenished as

---

hospital treated nearly 25,000 patients before closing on June 30, 1946.

The Greenbrier was the site of a secret underground bunker meant to serve as an emergency shelter for the United States Congress during the cold war. The Bunker is now open to the public.

needed if the do-not-disturb card was not on the door. He then turned to David and said, "I'll show you to your room sir. It's right across the hall."

By the time they reached the dining room the novelty of the opulence had partially been satiated. It too, was lovely with a large chandelier dangling from the center of a large bas relief circle. The walls were painted tangerine orange. The windows were big and arched. The floor was highly polished hardwood.

Jenn and David had dressed for dinner, not so much to meet the dress code, but for each other. Jenn wore a simple black short sleeve, knee length, stretch cocktail dress with a scooped neckline that fit perfectly. Accessories consisted of a single strand of pearls and red medium high-heel shoes. David chose an off-the-rack tailor-fitted Hart Schaffner & Marx grey worsted wool suit. They made a striking couple and stood out amongst the large crowd of well-dressed couples.

They were seated, after a short wait for a table in the crowded dining room by an attractive young woman, and were immediately swarmed by waiters bearing miscellaneous items and menus. Jenn viewed the menu and pitifully moaned: "Oh, David ah don't know what any of this is. Chicken liver what...? Pattie? And Tiger Shrimp? Salmon Gravlax? Sounds like a laxative! Don't they have any just plain food like fried chicken or roast beef? And look at those prices. What is Free Range Chicken anyhow?"

"Free Range means they were not raised in cages, they supposedly run free. To what degree, I don't know. Perhaps still in very crowded conditions." answered David.

"Well heck, that's the only chickens we ever had at home. They were shut up in the shed at night but run loose all-day long. Why don't they write the menu in English? What's all of this…French? Oh, well, new experience. Here goes. Ah'll have the Chicken Liver Pattie for the First Course, Cream of Five Chicken Soup for the Second Course and the Mint English Pea Ravioli for the Main Course. Ah'll have ice tea with m'ah meal and coffee with desert."

David chose the Salmon Gravlax, Romaine Salad, and the Prime Filet Mignon. In so doing it gave Jenn an opportunity to sample other menu choices. The room was abuzz with conversation. A grand piano fought pitifully to be heard over the cacophony. Jenn and David ate silently except for the on-running critique about the food by Jenn.

"This smashed-up liver tastes just as bad as the liver puddin' Mama used to make every year at hog-kill'n time. She made it like so many things, chit'lens and crack'lins so as not to waste any part of the hog. You know they could make a mint out of pig knuckles with the people here since they seem to like the leavins' of a hog killing. Pigs' feet would go over big, and that onion soup with ramps and shallots was nothing but a thin onion broth with little green onions and slices of just another onion in it. Ramps and Shallots, my big toe; just fancy words for little green onions and full-grown onions." David smiled affectionately and shared tidbits from his plate to kindle further amusing analysis of the cuisine. He did not reveal his own opinions that, curiously, agreed.

David signed the check and they left the restaurant to the tune of Jenn's continuous indictment of the food with such opinions as, "if the desert had been a teaspoon smaller there wouldn't have been any," and "the coffee cups were so tiny they wouldn't hold a robin's egg." They sashayed along the plush corridors to the Ball Room where the conventioneers were gathering for an official ball.

Jenn excused herself to 'go powder her nose. Doctor meandered through the wandering crowd unconsciously looking for familiar faces. He was mildly startled when a well-dressed man touched his arm and inquired, "Dr. Cabot?"

Doctor answered in the affirmative as he searched the inquirer for recognition—that did not occur. The man responded by presenting official credentials for Doctor's perusal.

"I'm Captain Blake, Commander of the Governor's Taskforce on Organized Crime. May I see your ID please?"

Flummoxed at the request Doctor hesitated several seconds before remembering that, he too, had a badge. He reached into his inside coat pocket and, with an authoritative gesture, flipped open his badge and photo ID. He was pleased with himself for remembering to heed to the Sheriff's instruction to carry his badge and a gun always. However, he still refused to carry a weapon.

"Thank you, sir. I'll be brief. The money used to buy the inventory of the Company Store was not traceable, but it did yield several fingerprints, most not on record. One identifiable print did pop up for a Tom Duggan, U.S. Army. He was discharged in 1953 sometime around the end of the Korean war.

"Tom Duggan, humm…" pondered Doctor. "Duggan… Duggan…somewhere in the back of my mind…no, not there. Not familiar with the name."

"Also, we looked closer at the water in the unknown drowning victim's lungs and concluded that it was probably from a swimming pool based on the amount of chlorine present. The note that allegedly had your name on it? It had no chlorine on it, so it was put there after the drowning and before the body was placed in the reservoir. An interesting error on that note is that the name Cabot was preceded by the rank of captain. You were a major, weren't you?"

"Yes," replied Doctor, "During my entire tenure as active military."

"Well, may mean nothing. One more thing and I'll let you go. Our agents were surveilling a gathering of suspected crime bosses up in Connellsville, Pennsylvania. Three of those attendees were observed there departing Joseph A Hardy Airport on a DC-3. One of those persons of interest is from Maybeury, last name of Peters. Our new request for you is to learn all you can about him, very cautiously understand. We will be in touch. Thank you for your help, Doctor…Detective? Few people would step up as you have." He then melted into the assemblage of people leaving David just as Jenn emerged from the ladies' room.

They checked out late the next morning after a really fine breakfast that offset Jenn's disappointment over the evening offerings. At the front desk when Doctor asked for the bill he was told that it had been taken care of and all he had to do was sign a voucher that was placed in front of him. The issuer of the voucher was the Governor's office. He hastily placed his arm between Jenn and the voucher to block her view. He glanced her way to see her giving him a puzzled look. An inquisition was inevitable.

CHAPTER SIXTY

THE TRIP HOME WAS uneventful. Jenn chattered endlessly about their experience at one of the world's premier resorts showing how unimpressed she was. She concluded that if that is what high society was, then she would prefer being a lowly hillbilly. "Lots more fun," she opined. She was particularly put-off by the food as being "too uppity." Yet, she prattled on and on to Annie and Mrs. Cabot and Shirley at the clinic about how beautiful everything was and how fine the restaurant was, and how pretty the food looked. David decided that she really did have a good time and her criticism of the adventure was to hide naivete from him. His suspicions were confirmed the following morning as he entered the kitchen to the chatter of three women preparing breakfast. He stopped at the door and eavesdropped as Jenn regaled the other ladies about the opulence of the Greenbrier.

"There was a big bowl of fruit of all kinds, and fresh flowers in the room when we checked in. The colors were so different. They mixed greens and blues and olive and stripes and florals. Things we would never do. The bathroom had all kinds of soap, lotions, shampoo; everything anybody would want or need. And towels! Must'a been six or seven different sizes and enough of them that you could dry every part of your body on one and still had clean ones left over."

"Sound's a bit too fancy fer me," opined Annie. "How much did all'a that cost?"

"Ah think each room was about uh'hundred and fifty dollars."

"What? Uh'hunner'und'fifty fer one room? Y'all shoud'a stayed in the same room. What'a waste."

"We aren't married, Annie. That wouldn't have been proper."

"Proper m'ah foot. You air purty clos'ta bein' married. Close enough."

Mom, feeling a need to support Jenn interjected, "Now Annie, she's right. It would have been improper for them to share a be… room. Was the food good Jenny?"

"It was pretty and strange. Everything had a fancy name and there wasn't much of it. And it was expensive! A couple uh teaspoons of liver puddin' cost nine dollars. A bowl of onion soup was twelve dollars. David's steak was thirty dollars."

"Thirty dollars fer a piece'uh meat? Yew cud buy the whole dang cow fer that," protested Annie.

David decided it was time to make his entrance. He rounded the corner and the room fell silent, but not for long. He became the focus of the interrogation that delved into every aspect of the trip.

The Clinic was buzzing with activity as they caught up from the absence. As usual Black Lung prevailed, allergies running a close second. He was listening to the familiar sounds of a defective lung when Shirley called down the hall that there was an emergency coming in. Doctor apologetically excused himself and rushed to the waiting room were a man on a stretcher was just being brought in by the rescue squad. His face and hands were loosely covered with dressings that had been moistened. One of the EMTs expertly summarized what treatment they had employed before and during transportation. Doctor lifted the gauze from the patient. The damage was extensive on the face, but the eyes seemed to be unaffected. "What happened?" Doctor inquired.

"A Battery explosion," replied the EMT.

"A battery explosion?"

"Yes. Damage appears to be mostly caused by battery acid, the EMT said.

Battery Acid…battery acid? "BATTERY ACID…! I know who the note writer is, C'est le cuisinier! It's the cook!" Doctor practically shouted to the puzzlement of all of those around him.

"Forgive me," pleaded Doctor Cabot. "another time, another place. Let's get this man on his way so that treatment can commence."

Jenn, who had witnessed the whole episode, did not remove her eyes from David until he replaced the bandage onto the damaged face. She then whispered, "What note?"

"Tell you in a moment." He then turned to the EMTs and said, "Excellent work. There's nothing more than I can do that you have not already done. Now he needs a hospital. Please transport him."

"Which hospital? Welch or Bluefield?" asked the EMT.

"The closest. Your choice," Doctor replied. He then turned to Jenn and said, "Come with me."

They went to David's office where Jenn took the chair behind the Doctor's desk and he sat in the side chair.

"Explain," she demanded.

"On the day I finally was transported out of Korea, I was gathering wool in the sunshine in what was left of the

MASH compound. I had been left by the unwritten rule of 'first one in first one out' to attend to a couple of wounded boys until proper transport became available. The helicopter that had finally extricated them made a return trip, it turned out, to get me. While I waited a young sergeant came out of the mess tent…"

"Mess tent. What's that?" Jenn interrupted.

"Dining hall of sorts. To continue. He exited the tent and approached me with a big smile on his face. He was carrying a pot of coffee and a mug. He asked me if I wanted a cup of 'this battery acid'. I don't remember his name. We chatted on for a while, partly in French. His name escapes me, try as I will, but I well remember the French because he had cooking experience with an old Mess Sergeant who had been a French Chef before he was drafted and made an army cook. In our conversation I revealed to him that I was heading to West Virginia and he said he was from Rocky Gap, Virginia. While we were chatting my transportation away from that miserable MASH experience arrived."

Jenn, her frustration growing, said. "So, his calling coffee 'battery acid' and the mention of 'battery acid' today triggered a significant memory to…of…what?"

"That is not the end of the story," David continued. "The sheriff recently sought my advice regarding a drowning in Bluestone Dam Lake. A note had been found in the victim's pocket. It was in French and said, *'En contactant le capitaine Cabot à Bluefield* that translates loosely as 'contact Capt. Cabot of Bluefield'. Sheriff thinks that that is me."

"Holy Moley, David! Does he think you know something about the dead guy?"

"No, not specifically but he is concerned with the possible incursion of organized crime, here in this local, associated with the popularity of marijuana nationwide and

250

the suitability of West Virginia as a product source. He is asking people who might encounter strangers to be vigilant. That is the reason he called me," he fibbed.

"Humm," pondered Jenn. "Do you suppose that the cash deal at the Company Store might have something to do with it? That deal was in cash; did you suspect anything illegal in that deal? Sounds crooked to me. That man comin' in with all that cash and buyin' a whole lot of stuff. Of course, he got his money's worth and he can readily sell it for a whole lot more than he paid for it to rich folks in a city. Right?"

CHAPTER SIXTY-ONE

ANNIE WAS IN A cheery mood when Doctor entered the kitchen. It was a bright sunny day with a blanket of light snow providing a canvas for the sun to draw intricate shadow patterns with bare-tree branches.

"Good morning, Miss Annie. How are you and your family today?" inquired Doctor.

"Ever'bodi's fine. My Hubby's black lung aint'gittin' no better as you well know. Ah don't thank he kin last much longer. One day at'a time as the ol' sayin' goes. My girl is beginnin' ta'read a little bit. She's got a new teacher that seems to understan' retards a little more."

"Annie, what did I tell you about calling your sweet daughter a 'retard'? They are now referred to as 'special' or 'exceptional' children."

"She's special alright but she is still a retard in school, hit don't matter what the proper name might be. The big problem with children like her is they ain't no jobs they kin do. She's uh willin' worker but nobody'll hire her. She's still school age and not allowed to work no job but hast'a go to school by law. We been talkin' about seein' if'n the health department could set up a program where non-profits like the Company Store kin har' them under some sorta special exception, but so fur we ain't hear'd nothin."

"That is a commendable suggestion and bears looking into. I will take it on as a project. Meantime are you ready for the big day at the Messiah Concert? I am rather excited about it."

"Me too. I jes' don't know what to expect. Air they any preachin."

Doctor answered seriously. "No preaching."

"Whada'bout an invitation? Will thar be any?"

"Invitation? I'm not sure what you mean. We have our seats reserved. The invitation for the recital was a note in the Telegraph."

"Naw, Ah mean, will somebody git up and try to git us to jin their church after everthang else is done?

Doctor Cabot had to smile at such a thought. "No ma'am. That activity is generally reserved for regular services in some non-liturgical churches such as the Baptists."

"That's gud, cause I git's tired of that after ever sermon cause most of the people air already saved. Corse, they's always a backslider er two sittin' out thar that could stand a bit of renewal of the spirit given' the 'mount of drunkenness in air part uh th' woods. Will they take up a collection? Should I take some money with me?"

"My dear Annie, you just go, you and Mom, and enjoy yourselves. No one is going to expect you to do anything but experience the joy of the music. It is a most special musical accomplishment. It has been a Christmas tradition for many years bringing the true miracle of the Season into focus."

"Ah jes' hope hit ain't too hi falutin' fer me. Ah ain't had no music trainin' ceptin' fer a couple of sangin' conventions at the church when ah was a girl."

"You do not need training to appreciate the classics or any music for that matter. What is a singing convention?"

"Hit's whar a music teacher come's around to schools and churches and teaches how to read music. We larned square notes. Unfortunate, none of the new song books uses them eny more."

"Square notes? I don't think I am familiar with that method."

"Yes, you do; Do-re-mi-fa-so-la-ti-do; ever' note has hit's own shape. 'do' is a triangle layin' on hit's long side, 're' is shaped like a water dipper, 'mi' is a lopsided squar', 'fa' is a oval, 'la' is a rectangle; all of them have tails on-um. Unner'stan?"

"Yes, strangely, I do. I believe they are more frequently referred to as 'shaped' notes."

"well, hit don't matter none since ah don't sang enythang excepti' by mem'ry now enyhow. Ah still lahk the ol' songs. This new stuff ah don' lahk a'tal."

The rest of the family began to assemble in search of breakfast. Jenn and Mom stepped in to help Annie in preparing a hearty meal since they would not eat again until supper because of the recital that was to begin at 2:30 in the afternoon.

They arrived at the host church a few minutes before the event was to begin and found their perfect seats on the center balcony. This location placed them slightly above eye level with the last row of the choir loft. The choir loft was not adequate to contain the combined choirs, but the church had been creative in spilling the participants into the areas on both sides of the communion rails. The small orchestra was grouped strategically around the organ to complement the antiphonic capabilities of the fine old treasured instrument, the main reason for the selection of the recital's venue. The organists had been with the church for about thirty years and was quite accomplished adding appreciably to the eminence of the performance.

Annie was as fidgety as a wind chime. The presentation was limited to about one hour, focusing on what has been named the 'Christmas Portion' of the Messiah with the first thirty minutes including several solos. During that time, Annie acted if she was about to bolt. The solos, particularly the soprano, seemed to increase her agitation. But when the Hallelujah Course was begun, with organ and orchestra at about fifty minutes into the concert, she perked up and sat in a near state of rapture to the fading echo led to silence. The congregants sat in respectful solitude until the lights were gradually turned up. Then, a totally unexplainable event occurred; the normal burst of applause did not occur. In near total verbal silence, the church emptied; only whispered conversation was evident.

They reached the car, parked on the street close to the church before anyone spoke. It was Annie who finally chirped, "Well, ah ain't never seen nothin' like 'at before in my whole life. Is that what them lur'cal churches do when the service is over?" she asked.

Mrs. Cabot answered her. "No, Annie. That was very unusual. It was if we were all mesmerized. I can say that I have never heard the Hallelujah Chorus rendered with such a combination of tenderness and vitality. Having them sing acapella made all the difference in the world. I think the sweetness of their performance created a holy solitude that followed. In my experience the Hallelujah Chorus is met with enthusiastic applause."

"I fully agree with you mother," David interjected. "That was the Beaver High School Acapella Choir made up of volunteer students directed by Miss Liz Sheldon, according to the program."

"Well, whoever they were they were special. If only we had a church choir as half as good as them somewhere nearby, I would be there every Sunday."

"I think I would be inclined to join you," declared David.

CHAPTER SIXTY-TWO

THE NEW YEAR WAS celebrated via an open house at the Field Mansion hosted by Mrs. Cabot. She was at her graceful Boston Matron's best and the party was a monumental success. Particularly noteworthy were the members of the Company Store Association made up of the volunteers and arts and crafts contributors. It was a strange mixture of peoples brought on by a successful community collaboration. People who previously seldom mixed socially, or otherwise, joined together in celebration of a new year and a new fellowship.

Annie was in full command of the refreshments and circulated continuously to be certain no one was feeling neglected. Platters of ham biscuits, fried chicken livers, corn muffins slathered with a black-eyed pea chutney, and pickled peaches predominated the non-dessert table. The dessert table was a masterpiece of sweets including a layered cake, cookies, brownies, and cobblers. Non-alcoholic eggnog, apple cider, bottled soft drinks, coffee and hot chocolate sat available on another table.

Jenn and David wandered politely through the happy party-goers until the party begin to fizzle directly associated with the reduction of food and accompanying appetites somewhere around ten o'clock. Jenn went to her suite to settle in for the night and David went to his office for a nightcap of brandy. His mind had been occupied with the 'Mystery of the Drowned Man' and his role as a reluctant investigator. He had before him a list of occurrences, facts, assumptions. The one single 'piece of evidence', that seemed to be his alone to pursue, was the note that appeared to be from a Tom Duggan of Rocky Gap, Virginia who's fingerprints on the Company Store money further muddled the mystery. He sat broodingly for several minutes pondering a strategy that would appear to be a casual visit to Rocky Gap. An obvious ploy would be to have Jenn with him and they could be looking for antiques, but in January? Probably not a good idea.

Bo became impatient that his adopted master was not coming to bed. Try as he would to convert, 'that dog', as Annie referred to him, Bo was fully in charge of Doctor's clinic off-time. So, like a good master, Doctor changed into his night clothes and pulled back the covers on his side of the bed. Bo was already lying crosswise underneath the pillows on *his* side of the bed. "Goodnight Bo. I don't suppose you have any ideas as to how I might proceed into Bland County without suspicion, do you?" Bo just groaned and passed a whopper of a stinker, silently of course.

After airing out the room with January night-air, Doctor appreciatively crawled under the cover waiting for Bo to change to his final night time sleeping position; sprawled lengthwise as close to his master as he could get. His warmth was as steady as an electric blanket and had become a source of solace in a strange sort of way. Doctor had just reached the twilight stage of sleep when he remembered—or dreamed—a story Bill told him about Sonny's Dog, with the paradoxical name, Petunia. He was a big solid Gordon Setter who got his name from sleeping in Lula's flower bed.

[23]Petunia loved to travel. He would hitch rides in or on any conveyance that would stop long enough to mount. On one occasion, he rode all the way to town on the sloping trunk of Leslie's 1946 Studebaker Coupe. Most of his chauffeurs would bring him back home on a return trip or call for him to be picked up. His coup-de-grace was a trip to Bland, Virginia on top of a load of hay. He had to stay there for two weeks until the truck came back through Bluewell. Doctor spoke out of his reverie and said to himself, "That is what I will do. I'll go in search of Petunia. Everybody would appreciate that, particularly in such cold weather."

The next morning Doctor Cabot woke with a realization that he really did not have a plan. Looking for a dog, indeed! Any child would see through such a transparent ploy. Circumventing the truth leads to doubt and suspicion

Sunday rolled around with light snow falling—again, being part of the approximate 62 inches annual average. Bill had invaded the premises for one of his frequent forays seeking gossip and other extraneous news. The family was congregating for Sunday Dinner of roast beef, mashed potatoes, home canned green beans, hot rolls with fresh butter, miscellaneous jams, jellies and pickles and desert of apple pie. Bill was his usual irreverent self. He endeared

---

[23]   Petunia was a real dog and his travels were notorious.

himself with his sister with the query, "Are ya'll still cohabitating?"

Jenn took the bait and physically attacked him with a spoonful of mashed potatoes that she was preparing for the table. He ducked but not before she struck the bridge of his nose with a robust whack splattering his face with hot potatoes, following the blow with the question, "Why can't you be civil just once? You always try your very best to humiliate me in front of people."

Bill stood looking at her with surprise on his face— underneath a layer of potatoes— and David commenced laughing joyously. Jenn then saw the expression on Bill's face and followed suit with the whole family finally joining in. Bill had his come-uppance and sheepishly said, "Guess I kinda' touched a sore spot, huh?"

Jenn removed her apron and gently wipe Bill's face. "Just be grateful Ah was dippin' up the tater's and not the gravy 'cause the gravy is boilin' hot," she said laughing. "Now go to the bathroom and clear off the rest before I whoop you." Bill meekly complied mumbling something about how big sisters were always picking on their little brothers.

There were extra places set at the table this night. Annie's daughter and Jim were sort of guests of honor since they both had birthdays this month. Jim's birthday was unknown, so Annie had designated his birthday to coincide with that of her daughter since they appeared to her to be about the same age when Jim appeared at their doorstep— apparently having no home and too young to relate his story— to be taken in by Dr. Fields. Annie had originally resisted Doctor Cabot's efforts to meet her daughter, Margie, but he persisted, and she finally complied. When he had first come to West Virginia Annie had told him she had a Mongol'd and he did not challenge the name since that was the common referent for the genetic defect at the time. He had since learned that Down Syndrome—after English physician, John Langdon Down. John Langdon Down first classified the syndrome as a separate form of mental disability in 1862—and he had counseled Annie accordingly.[24]

Jim came in through the back door with a hearty greeting for everybody. Annie called out, "A'fore yew take off yer boots, go git Margie, will you Jim?" Jim complied on two counts; he went next door to escort Margie to the birthday party and took off his snow-covered boots and left them in the mud-room.

"Margie was a surprise to Doctor Cabot. She was Definity a Trisomy 21—an extra copy of chromosome 21 in every cell— the most common form of Down syndrome, with a prevailing symptom of obesity. Margie was stocky, but not over weight, indicating extraordinary parenting. She entered the room with a princess-like bearing and

---

[24] Until around the 1980s people with Down syndrome were generally ignored by educational institutions according to The Global Down Syndrome Foundation. While working for the West Virginia Health Department, Division of Maternal and Child Health in the early 1960's, the only Down Syndrome cases I saw were in mental institutions. That does not mean, however, that all DS children were in institutions. Many were well cared for by their loving parents often under very stressful conditions, such as schooling. Few grew to adulthood due to medical problems. Some were even 'terminated' at birth. It is important to remember people with Down syndrome were among those targeted in the eugenics movement in the United States that has been claimed to have influenced Hitler's first mass murders in 1939.

introduced herself to everyone in the room, including those whom she already knew, with, "Hello, Ah am Margie and Ah kin write mah name. Jim is mah best frin' an' yew kin be too."

Annie sat Margie and Jim next to her in her usual 'jump seat'. Everyone in the new extended family had yielded to the placement of Annie as the reining Matriarch, at the dinner table, at least. Without preamble, she said, "Ever'body bow yer heads fer a blessing." she continued. "Dear Lord Jesus, bless these here birthday children and thank you fer makin' them so special to us. Bless this here house and all in't. Amen."

A hearty "Amen" was added by everyone.

Bill, the gregarious one, started the table conversation with a question aimed at no one in particular. "Tell me how the concert went. The Messiah. Did it go well?"

Mrs. Cabot responded first with an exuberant, "I have heard it many times and I would say it was among the best renditions I have ever experienced. Wouldn't you agree David?"

"Yes, Mom. It was well done I thought…"

Annie interrupted. "Well, Ah wish't ya'll would es'plain the whole thang ta'me. Hit didn't make a bit'a sence excepten' that part ya'll called the Hallaluh course. The firs' part seem'duh be a man bellerin' lahk a bull an' uh woman skreemin' her head off an' lookin' lahk she wuz agoin' to jump offen the platform that she'wuz'a'rockin'back'n forth on. Why don't they jus' stand an sang normal instead of screamin' so loud. An' some uh'those people playin' instru'munts keep jumpin' roun' and jerkin' lak they had the heebie jeebies. Fer uh'while thar Ah thought Ah was at'uh holy roller meetin' with all that shout'un and jerk'un goin' on."

Jenn broke in to defuse Annie by suggesting, "Ah thought we were here for a birthday party. Let's eat so we can cut the cake and I believe that there's a present or two to be opened?"

The rest of the party time was ruled by Margie who took over as hostess and did a rather commendable job of it. She and Jim blew out the candles and shared the task of cutting and distributing the cake. There was ice cream too.

CHAPTER SIXTY-THREE

W INTER WAS THE QUINTESSENCE of frustration. Snow provided a unique beauty for a short spell only to be painted black by the mines and trains. Folks were longing for Spring and the Jonquils were sending up probes. The forsythia were sneaking peeps with yellow buds of promise. Crime too, was emerging from Winter hibernation as witnessed by a reminder from Sheriff Hare. Doctor decided that he would wait for the Dogwood, Redbud, Rhododendron and other colorful Spring glorifiers to make an appearance before he set out in search of his former MASH contact. For now, he would bide his time. One of his favorite pastimes during lulls in the Clinic was to browse the bookshelf bearing the book selections and personal notes of Dr. Fields. He was currently engrossed in a thick loose-leaf notebook of hand written personal historical interviews collected from the first days of Dr. Fields' practice in Boston Knob. Most were passed down by word-of-mouth through families and, often, in the family bibles.

A particularly noteworthy interview of one immigrant planted the idea that people of Irish descent were shipped to the new country as captive 'white slaves' outnumbering black slaves and enduring worse treatment at the hands of their masters. Dr. Fields, being a scientist, sought the truth of that claim and found that, like impoverished people of Ireland, Scotland, and many other nationalities, came to America in the 17th and 18th centuries as indentured servants. He found that a small number were forcibly exiled into indentured servitude during the period of the English Civil Wars, but that was a unique case. He also found that indentured servants often lived and worked under less than suitable conditions and were sometimes treated cruelly. Furthermore, unlike Black Slaves, white indentured servants had legal rights and were not considered property. indentured servitude played a strong role in the survival and growth of the original 13 colonies. Those who could not afford the travel were brought from Europe under contract to work off their passage, room, and board over a period of two to seven years. About half of the immigrants who came to the New World during the colonial period came as indentured servants.

At this point Dr. Fields departed from the third person to the first person expressing his view on the concept of indentured servitude.

"In the Science of General Semantics an axiom declares that 'the word is not the thing'. Alfred Korzybski published a book called *Science and Sanity: An Introduction to Non-Aristotelian Systems.* In that book he presented the hypothesis that language, while a powerful communication advancement for mankind, is still flawed in that it is a major abstract tool. First, words are arbitrary symbols assigned to indicate an object, but it might also be used for another purpose, even another object. When the object is 'real' like a chair, confusion can be averted. But when there is no object and the word is applied to a 'feeling' or 'situation' then the resultant intended concept is fuzzy."

"Thousands of Irish people delivered, against their will, into indentured service is a fact. When a person is forced, against his/her will, to work for another without the option to leave, the question is whether they are fulfilling the role of a slave. The labor they are doing is slave-like and refusing to call it slavery is pedantry. Any form of forced labor can be called slavery. But what do we gain by doing so, besides blurring historical distinctions? As I become acquainted with the people of the area, I see people who were born into slavery by their dependency on coal. Yes, they can quit, but what can they do? They probably went into the mines with their fathers rather than going to school. They never have any cash money, only script issued by the mine owners redeemable only at the company store. They are inextricability, Slaves: Slaves to their heritage, Slaves to the Coal mines, Slaves to the Company store, and Slaves to a certain, slow, painful death by Black Lung. Slaves they were born and Slaves they will die leaving their progeny to the same fate."

Here his essay ended leaving Doctor Cabot deeply depressed.

A light tap on the door failed to rouse him from his reverie. Jenn pushed the door open and informed him, "You have patients…my goodness! What's wrong with you? You look like you just saw a ghost!"

"I believe I just did, Jenn. Have you read any of Dr. Field's essays in his diaries? I just finished reading one that presented a scenario so disheartening that I fleetingly realized the fruitlessness on my endeavors here for the future. I am not practicing medicine; I am a subordinate of the Grim Reaper, preparing men, women, and children for their death brought on by a centuries-old system of indentured servitude…NO…call it what it is…slavery."

Jenn gently closed the door and went to David. She took his head in her hands and gently pressed him to her breast saying, "My dear sweet man, you need a break from this. I have a great idea. Let's get married and take a long honeymoon? It's about time you know. We can go anyplace you want to. How does that sound? We can have a really nice wedding right here in the house and invite lots of people. You kind'a liked Pastor Linebarger from the Lutheran Church in Bluefield so you could ask him to perform the ceremony. I would rather not go away from here because of the travel problems for locals. It would be fun to take a train all around the country where we could stop anywhere we want to and stay over…"

"Whoa, slow down. I am not contemplating an escape. I might entertain a change of venue someday. Right now, I just need to reacquaint myself with a former unseen reality that was obvious to Dr. Fields but has escaped my awareness. What he implies in his thesis is intriguing but by no means a rationale for alarm. Depressing? Yes. Cause for immediate action? No. Now, as pleasing as my resting place is at the moment, kindly release me so that we can return to work."

Jenn had released her hold on him and sat down looking at him with concern. "Are you mad at me about something?" she asked.

"Of course not. I could never be angry with you. That essay by Dr. Fields just initiated some concern about my professional future. Is this what I want do to the rest of my life? With your life? Look at our social life. We have none! In the length of time we have been here together we have been to the Greenbriar for one night and the Country Club once. That's' no life for…well…for a beautiful, talented woman like you. You merit better. While my skills are still sharp I should be in surgery every day, not checking off the days of dying Black Lung victims. And you, you have excellent nursing skills and manners. Look at how you spend your days. What a waste of talent!"

"Then Ah tell you what you should do. Go find the openings for surgeons anywhere in the United States… anywhere…and contact them stating your interest in their position. We…or just you…can go look at any offers you get and if you find something that really looks good, and you are sure you like the area, and the people better than you do here, we will move there. Okay?"

CHAPTER SIXTY-FOUR

As had become an adventitious custom, Bill showed up for Sunday dinner at the Field Mansion. However, there was a noticeable difference in his countenance. He was polite, but the usual banter was clearly subdued. He gave Jenn a peck on the cheek accompanied with a quiet "Love you Sis." He did not tease Annie. Jenn reckoned he was not himself and maybe not feeling well. But, she dispelled that thought since he would not have come for his usual Sunday visit if he were sick. Without Bill's stimulus, conversation lagged, and the meal came to silent end. The women excused themselves to tend to the after-dinner chores, leaving Bill and David at the table with coffee.

David spoke first. "Okay, my dear friend, what's in yer craw? as Annie would say. You have been moping around ever since you got here. Are you ill?"

"No I'm not sick! I have a legal problem that I think you can help me with, but I don't know how to approach it with you. Will you hear me out without interruption until I can tell you about it?"

"Since you asked so nicely, you have my full, undivided attention until you announce the completion of your dialogue," answered David seriously but with a smile.

"I got roped in a very old, long-standing black lung case not too long ago. I thought it was going to be a hearing before the Coal Mine Health and Safety Act that usually ends with some form of compensation for the black lung victim, but I was shanghaied into a full-blown lawsuit against a very high-powered legal group with offices all over the country and with very deep-pockets footing the bill. It's just me against them." Bill paused to collect his thoughts.

"Continue, you have my full attention. Your conundrum is intriguing so far."

"Conundrum is an understatement. Choosing whether to have coffee or tea this morning was a conundrum; what I am talking about is a full-blown disaster. How would you like to be the only doctor at mine disaster with only a tongue blade? Please don't minimize my problem!" Bill practically shouted.

"I shall remain silent," Doctor whispered.

"Thank you. Please forgive my rudeness. To continue. Under the workers' compensation law, unforeseen difficulties cropped up involving claims for occupational diseases primarily involving the cause of the disabling or death of a worker, or even whether or not disease was even present, or the identification of the disease itself. Until recently, the compensation of industrial injuries or diseases was under state control. That too, recently changed when the feds passed legislation to provide compensation for black lung. The Feds surmised that coal mining is different than any other kind of work because of the nature of risk involved. Also, its isolation, both geographically and culturally, caused a unique, singular society untouched by the 'outside' world. Neither the union nor mine owners showed concern for safety, occupational health or educational dysfunction of the workers children."

Bill paused and suggested that they warm up their coffee. Doctor agreed that was a fine idea. They arrived in the kitchen to find it empty except for the perpetual fresh pot of coffee with a pitcher of thick cream waiting. They replenished their cups and chose to go to the living room with its stuffed furniture instead of back to the dining room table. They settled in.

"Continue," requested Doctor Cabot.

"Okay. From now on you can interrupt anytime you want since this part is almost all related to medical. I will not reveal the name of the plaintiff in order to be rigidly ethical for both of our sakes. By the way the patient is from Beckley. He might have worked in the mines near here, but I don't know that. Bears looking into. Several years before he applied for benefits he experienced the same symptoms as many before and his peers. It started, as usual, with shortness of breath followed by the coughing up of a black mucus. At this point he finally applied for federal benefits and a U.S. Department of Labor certified doctor gave a diagnosis the most lethal form of black lung, complicated pneumoconiosis. The government ordered his employer, a large coal company, to begin paying him monthly benefits, but, as is almost always the case, the company appealed. The patient now found himself in a world of administrative law judges who must parse through mountains of medical evidence, legal arguments, strange rules, company lawyers who were experts in circumnavigation and procrastination and doctors who seemed to diagnose almost anything but black lung."

"Just a moment, please Bill. Are you intimating that physicians have been making fraudulent diagnoses? Really! That is preposterous! There must be hundreds of physicians involved in the diagnosis and treatment of lung diseases and chance alone would prevent most false claims on either side."

"True, but the big law firms have selected doctors in their pockets and they manipulate the situations to guide the claimant through the system to get a favorable diagnosis for their purposes. You will see an example of that as I continue with the story."

"I will be paying rapt attention," Doctor Cabot said haughtily.

"Okay, the first day of court, I'm told, a bevy of lawyers huddled around the defendants' table with more behind them in the gallery. The patient was there by himself, I guess you would say he was representing himself. He couldn't find a lawyer and that was before he talked me into representing him. This is common. Possible claimants' attorneys have avoided the federal black lung system en masse. Time and money favor the coal companies, because they have the funds to hire all kinds of experts and drag things out until the cows come home. Even worse, if a claimant can find a lawyer, he's legally barred from charging fees, so he must gamble on winnin' an unwinnable verdict."

"Question. Do I understand you correctly that a lawyer for the plaintiff cannot charge for his services?"

"You heard me right."

"Hardly equitable. What is the justification for such a rule?"

"Don't know for sure but some politician must have thought he was defending the plaintiff from exploitation by ambulance-chasing vulture legal beagles. Strangely enough, that rule applies to only coal-mining disability cases."

"Puzzling, to be sure. Okay, continue. You left with the patient at a table by himself with no legal representation. What could he possibly say?"

"All he could do was to read the report from the examination paid for by the Labor Department with a diagnosis of pneumoconiosis and that's what he did. After that it was the coal company's lawyers turn and they bombarded the court with exhibits, medical reports, depositions, and name and credentials of doctors who had reviewed the evidence."

"More important, though, was what was NOT put in the record. Back some time ago, a suspicious mass was removed from the plaintiff's lung and sent to the hospital's pathologist, where the surgery was done, to rule out cancer, and that is exactly—and only—what he did. He didn't mention anything related to black lung, or even that the patient was a miner."

"Sloppy work, indeed," commented Doctor.

"True. But here is where my case may be strengthened. I got an anonymous phone call from someone who said he had evidence that the coal company lawyers had obtained the pathologists' slides and sent them to two of their pathologists whose opinions typically supported the firm's case. This time though, they were snookered. Both pathologists did the ethical thing and said the mass was probably a result of black lung. While this would normally be a final blow to most lawyers, the mining firm's lawyers did not give up. Instead, they withheld the reports of their own consulting physicians thus leaving only the incomplete hospital pathologist's report and its singular diagnosis of 'inflammatory pseudotumor'. The informant told me he would only tell what he knew to just one person…only one person."

"So, what do you want me to do? It appears you may be defeated unless your anonymous benefactor provides a solution. There is nothing I can do about that."

"Not so," retorted Bill, because YOU are the only person the anonymous caller will talk to."

CHAPTER SIXTY-FIVE

SPRING WAS SINGING ITS theme song. Beauty was everywhere, unabated. Birds sang; frogs chirped; trees shouted with pink, white, and red blossoms. David recalled a greeting offered by the pastor at one of the services he and Jenn had attended: "This is a day the Lord has made." At the time he heard the phrase he thought it was trite, but today it was a glorious expression to be shouted to the hilltops. He decided it was a day to explore Bland County. East River Mountain would most certainly be magnificently adorned with a multitude of blooming plants and trees. Fortuitously, he had an intern assigned to him from Welch Hospital, so he determined he was quite capable of attending today's caseload. So, he called Jenn and declared, "We are going for an outing. Go, prepare yourself accordingly," he teased.

"Well, that could mean anything. Do you mean my little black nightgown or clogs and blue jeans?"

"Do not tempt your lord and master, evil woman. Hiking clothes are the dress of the day."

"For real? Where are we going?"

"Rocky Gap, Virginia. We might try to find an antique shop, or an eatery. Or maybe an old army buddy. Who knows?"

Jenn's demeanor changed from jovial to serious in a flash. "You are going to try to find the writer of that mysterious note, aren't you?"

"That might be a side consideration, yes. But mostly I plan to spend the day watching you in your tight blue jeans. I could not handle that glorious sight without the distraction of the Spring foliage."

"You are so full of bull hockey, but Ah will try my best to outshine Springtime just for you."

David loaded up the Jeep with a basket of goodies and a thermos of hot coffee prepared by the loving hands of his mother. Mrs. Cabot had fully integrated into the Appalachian lifestyle to the degree that her son often wondered if she was the same woman. She had shed the two-piece suits with the frilly blouse that had been her uniform while living in Boston. She now wore loose-fitting flowery house dresses, comfortable flat leather oxfords with men's white socks. Except for their hair, from the back, you could not tell Mrs. Cabot from Annie.

Jenn came bouncing out of the kitchen door wearing a M*A*S*H tee shirt, sneakers, and…tight jeans. David might be a Harvard gentleman, but his mouth dropped into a lascivious stare, quickly morphed into a sheepish grin, neither unnoticed by an impish Jenn. After looking her up and down he inquired, "Where did you get the MASH t-shirt?"

"Ah ordered if off the TV show. Did I get it too small?"

"Too Small?" Silence. "Too small?" Uh…no. It's… magnificent," he blurted.

"You said tight and Ah aims to please. Kind of brings out the lecher in you, don't it?" Jenn teased.

"I am not given to lecherousness," David protested.

"Well, if'n you ain't yew orta be 'cause yew air a'lookin' at one sexy woe'mun," Jenn teased in the native mountain dialect.

"Get in the Jeep before I turn you over my knee."

"Promise?" Jenn mocked.

"Now cut that out!" David yelled, mimicking George Burns of radio fame.

The drive down—a definite contradiction since it was mostly uphill—was inspiring, especially Pinnacle Rock. Its base was embroidered as with white lace by dogwood trees. The carefully placed color of rhododendron, redbud, the tantalizing aroma of honeysuckle, and the raucous songs of the many birds combined to create a multidimensional mosaic on the senses. They strolled along the path resplendent with tulips, crocus, daffodils, even dandelions heading to the spot where they had had their first kiss those eons ago. They relived the moment and resumed their trek to the Wolf Creek Valley via the East River Mountains.

Route 52 twisted and turned through South Bluefield where millionaire homes were built during the hey-day of King Coal and were still occupied by 'money'. They were particularly lovely now, ablaze with Springtime foliage. David guided the Jeep up Bland Road to where it dead ends on Cumberland road, then a right turn to where Maryland Avenue ends on Washington Street. A 270-degree switch-back from west to east starts the long upward climb on Route 52 to the top of East River Mountain where they parked the Jeep at the over-look and took in the splendor of the view of the valley below enhanced by an abundance of Spring color.

The descent from the summit was far more curvaceous with many twists and turns causing the drive to be extraordinarily time-consuming. Unlike the ascent, the descent revealed appreciatively more colorful foliage with few distant views. At the foot of the mountain—now on the Virginia side—they were surprised to encounter a massive construction project that turned out to be the beginnings of a tunnel through the mountain. A short stretch of dirt road ended at the town of Rocky Gap situated on Wolf Creek.

They found a small diner across the street from the high school. "Does this look like a decent place to you?" asked David.

"They have a daily blue plate special and, in my experience, they are nearly always good since they are mostly homecooked the old fashion way," opined Jenn.

"The blue-plate special it is then," David complied as he nosed the Jeep into the small parking lot.

The temperature was pleasant and the entry to the eatery was blocked only by a screen door. David held the door for Jenn and she led the way in. A middle-aged woman wearing a lace-trimmed apron greeted them and smilingly led them to one of six tables all covered with spanking white ornate, table cloths. None of the other tables were yet occupied. David decided to use the "shot-in-the-dark" direct approach, and as they were being seated, he inquired. "Does Tom Duggan still work here?"

"Mercy sakes alive! He ain't worked here since before he left for the war in Korea. He's my cousin, you know?"

"He was in my outfit in Korea and I remember him saying that he was from here. Do you know where he is now?"

"Last Ah heard, he had gone up north somewhere to go to school and is now workin' for the gov'ment in some capacity. What kin Ah get ya'll to eat?"

Jenn said, "We'll both have the blue-plate special. You want ice tea, Hon?" She inquired of David and he agreed with her choice, noticing the use of the term of endearment for the first time.

"Lemon?"

"Yes, for both of us."

"Be right back. You kin warsh your hands through that door over there," she pointed.

It wasn't five minutes later that the waitress returned with two large platters featuring a large slab of meatloaf and a mound of hand-mashed potatoes, both smothered with brown gravy, and a side of green beans. They heartily polished-off their plates and sopped up the remainder with home-made light rolls. They reluctantly declined apple pie and asked for the check. The waitress placed the check on the table and commented, "I asked my Mom about Tom and she said he had been seen recently down at the old Jennings Place over at Bastian."

"Bastian? Where is that?"

Gesturing, she indicated a direction and accompanied it with, "Down the road about eight miles. It's got a big fancy sign by the road. You'll see it."

David looked at the check and remarked, "I can't believe we got all of that food for such a pittance." He then placed a tip equal to the total bill and still thought he had gotten a major bargain.

"So, it is my guess that we are going to Bastian to visit the Jennings's Place," said Jenn. It was not a question.

"We will just take a quick look. Nothing more. It's probably a wild-goose-chase anyway."

"You wanna bet?"

"I will take that bet. What are you putting up?"

"A roll in the hay." She said sassily.

"I don't have anything of equal value to match that bet. Tell you what, I'll let you set our wedding date and we will not deviate from your selection. Fair enough?"

"You got a deal. That's the only way Ah'll get that roll in'a hay from you. Then she said quite seriously, "You really mean that about the weddin' date?"

"Yes," he answered.

Just then the sign for the farm came into view. They passed under the arch created by the sign and followed a well-kept dirt road through lovely plush, green grassland. The house just down the road was a two-story Salt Box with a large, inviting front porch. The road ended at the yard that apparently doubled as a parking lot since there was a lone late model station wagon sitting in front of the house. Doctor parked beside the station wagon and started for the house. A man with a shovel came around the house and asked Doctor if he could be of help.

"Yes," answered Doctor. "Is the owner available?"

"You mean the real owner? He ain't here but th' lady who's a'rentin' it is. Jes' go'head and knock on the door. She'll answer."

Doctor started for the porch and Jenn jumped from the Jeep and caught up with him just as he reached the door. He knocked and called out. "Anybody home?"

A voice from within said, "Just a minute. I'll be right there."

They waited as foot falls came closer to the door. The screen door opened and there in front of them was Mrs. Peters, Calvin's Mom. No one spoke. Dead silence prevailed.

Mrs. Peters, finally recognizing her visitors, quickly pushed the screen door open with a big smile and equally large greeting, "Dr. Cabot, Miss Gullion, what a wonderful surprise. Come in, come in, please. I cannot believe this. I'm sorry Tod is not here. He will be so sorry he missed you."

She led them to a comfortable sitting room furnished in early American and bade them to sit.

"Thank you" Jenn and Doctor said in unison. "This is a lovely room," Jenn added.

"May I get you some refreshments? Coffee? Tea? A beer maybe? I am so thrilled to see you. Calvin is doing better here in the country with horses and cows. He has his own dog! An English Setter! They love each other so much. Oh, please forgive my rudeness. Why are you here? Do you have some news for me about Calvin and maybe testing? Tod didn't explain why he canceled the Charlottesville trip, something to do with his work and, also, the company got rid of the plane. Is it possible to still get the evaluation?"

"Yes, it is," Doctor replied as Jenn shot a look in his direction.

"It is not too late. We were apprehensive about losing contact with you after your abrupt cancellation. Finding you today was fortuitous. We were looking for a young man that I had served with in a MASH Unit in Korea who lived in Rocky Gap when he entered the service. I have anticipated seeking him out on several occasions but always encountered an interruption. Upon awakening this morning to such a glorious day, we decided what better occasion could possible present itself for a foray across the mountain?"

"What is the soldier's name? inquired Mrs. Peters.

"Tom Duggan."

"Oh, we know him. They are working on a case together."

"Case together?" Jenn inquired.
"Yes, they both work for the Government."

"Well now, this is another fine mess you've got us in, Stanley," opined Jenn. "Reminds me of being in a dairy barn lot. No matter how careful you are you're gonna' step in cow…"

"Do not say it!"

"Ah was gonna' say 'doo'. You got your mind in the gutter."

"To the contrary, the situation is well in hand and going precisely as I had anticipated."

"Bull…"

"Do…not…say…it!"

"There you go again. Ah was going to say 'hockey'. You just never learn, do you?" Jenn said, laughing at him.

"Enough. Please get serious; we have important matters to consider."

"Like what?"

"Our wedding principally. Then…"

"Whoa. You mean real soon?"

"Yes."

"Well glory be. Ah thought you would never ask. Are you goin' to plan it, or should I?"

David laughed at her and replied, "Neither of us will get the honor. As you are aware, Mom and Annie are just waiting for us to set the date to activate their strategy."

"No joke," Jenn said. "What are you going to do about the Peters' thing? You left her with the expectation of receiving help for her boy. You're not giving her more false hope, are you?"

"The answer is unequivocally, NO! Bill told me just last week that your nephew is still at UVA for an extra semester to take a couple of qualifying courses to better prepare himself for his new job with the State, and to finalize the Autism study, that, by the way, is turning out to be of major significance. He will be glad to schedule us, you'll see," David said, pleadingly.

"Okay, Ah'll yield to your dubious wisdom. Let's head for home so I can get the girls started on a weddin' before you back out again," replied Jenn.

"There you go again. Manipulating the facts to suit your perception of a situation. I did not back out as you say. Unforeseen Circumstances intervened of which you are well aware."

"You backed out. Admit it."

"Aww…dog bite it!" David stuttered in frustration.

CHAPTER SIXTY-SIX

THE HINT SUGGESTING THAT his prime suspect in organized crime activity may be an employee of the Federal Government prompted Doctor Cabot to seek the counsel of the Sheriff, who suggested they meet at Doctor's office around five the next day.

"I will have 'The Girls' set another plate at the supper table and I will not take no for an answer."

"See you tomorr'a then," responded the sheriff.

It was almost six o'clock and Shirley was closing up shop. It had been a heavy day. Jenn had left about half-hour ago leaving Doctor Cabot to turn off the lights and lock the file cabinets. He had previously thought the security of the building was adequate until about a month ago when it appeared the files had been pilfered. One high-profile black lung patient record was taken or misplaced. Since then all black lung cases were placed in a new steel vault with a sophisticated combination lock. It was probably not coincidental that the file disappearance occurred around the same time Bill spoke to David requesting his possible testimony in an ongoing black lung case.

Doctor completed his assigned chores and went to join the women folk. He found them so deep in discussion of wedding plans they didn't even notice his arrival.

He cleared his throat and announced his presence by declaring, "I am an integral part of these nuptials, are you not aware?"

"Only minimally," Mom declared. "Supper's on the stove. Help yourself."

He did as he was told—with pleasure—since that was the first time in his life that his mother had given him such a command and he knew it was because she was part of the same 'whole' as he. She felt secure with her new family—categorically secure.

Sheriff Hare pulled up and parked in back of the house at precisely five P.M. As usual clinic was still going strong so he went straight to the kitchen in search of Miss Annie. He found the 'Bobsy Twins'—his new name for Mom and Annie—joyfully engaged in cooking and conversation.

"It smells plumb heavenly in here," Sheriff declared.

"Well it orta, cause two ang'uls air'a doin' th' cookin'," Annie declared in her loudest voice. "Come on in an' set'ch self down. Supper's almost ready and we'r a'waitin' the clinic crew. Yew want coffee?"

"Now Miss Annie, when did you ever know an officer of the law to refuse coffee? Please and thank you ma'am."

"Yur'welcome. If'n you ain't seen the mornin' paper hit's over thar on the table."

Sheriff had just settled down when the noise of Jenn and David ascending the backsteps to the kitchen reached them. They seemed to be engaged in a friendly argument and as they bounded through the kitchen door, she pushed him along in front of her yelling, "Tell them. Go ahead, tell them, "you chicken poop, mealy mouthed, back-slidin' weaseling quitter."

"I said nothing that deserved such verbal abuse…"

"Shut up and tell'um before Ah get physical, then you'll know what abuse is. Tell'um, NOW!"

"Okay, okay. I simple suggested, suggested mind you, that maybe circumstances dictated the need to postpone the wedding for a week or two."

"Week 'er two? You just said downstairs until the first of th' year. That's uh week er two?"

Mom finally stepped forward and suggested calm. "David," she said, "I have never spanked you before in your life but if what Jenn is saying is factual, then I am about to break a record. There is no way on God's green earth that you are going to…weasel, is that the word, Jenn? out of the plans that we have all been slaving over for…how long? Now you get ready for supper. We have a guest in case you do not recall?"

"I was just teasing, Mom. Gee whiz, you women certainly are serious over a minimalist ceremony…" and that opened a floodgate of feminist angst.

Doctor made a rapid exit yelling and laughing over his shoulder tauntingly.

Table-talk was light and followed a line of mostly fluff. The Ladies baited David with wedding suggestions that he pointedly ignored as he and the sheriff were politely waiting to get to their appointed conversation. Dessert was a deep-dish peach pie with the choice of the cream, plain or whipped, along with the requisite coffee. Sheriff polished off two large servings with about a quart of cream on each. Doctor abstained electing only for Annie's special blend of wild-picked chicory and Chase and Sanborn coffee. Sheriff took the last sip of coffee from his mug and suggested,

"Doctor, let's refill our coffee cups and go into the library. I believe you have something for me?"

Grateful that Sheriff took the initiative, Doctor stood and said, "Let's. Pardon us ladies," and meandered to the library via the coffee pot, followed by Sheriff Hare.

They sat in Queen Anne arm chairs with an ornate baroque table between them for what seemed like an eternity. Finally, Sheriff broke the silence; "Ah believe you have some new information?"

"I do." Silence, as Doctor pondered.

"Well?" inquired the Sheriff.

"We found Tom Duggan."

"Really? Where?"

"Bastian, Virginia. He was recently seen on the Peters farm by a lady who owns a restaurant in Rocky Gap where Duggan worked before he was drafted into the Korean war. We went—"

"Who's We?"

"Jenn and I."

"Does she know the whole story?"

"No. She thinks that I was just looking up an old army buddy."

"Are you sure?"

"No, I am not…sure. We went to the Peters Farm and there we were met at the door by Mrs. Peters whose son is a patient of mine. She was excited to see us and invited us in for refreshments. I asked her if she knew Duggan and she gleefully answered in the affirmative stating that her husband and Tom were 'working a case together' for the Federal Government."

"You gotta be pullin' my leg. That ain't possible."

"Just stating the facts Sheriff. That is exactly what she told us."

"Now ain't that a fine kettle of fish? Workin' for the government. Well, let's consider that she is tellin' the truth as she knows it, and that they are, really, working for the Feds, which agency? And if they are coming into Mercer County, which I suspect they would be, then why haven't they contacted my office?"

"Perhaps, in line with your concerns for the possible involvement of law agencies in the area, they do not trust you either?" asked Doctor.

"Rite'cha are. Good detective thinkin. Now with that in mind, consider the anonymous note found in the drowin' victim's pocket, and the evidence it was placed there after he was apparently drowned and before he was placed in the Bluestone, then somebody is tryin' ta'get a message—to you? No, not you, but through you? He used a dead body as a messenger? It must be Duggan! He's around and knows from the past that you might be in the area, so he chose Bluefield as a likely place. So, did he, or his agency, move the body into Mercer County?"

"A real long shot, don't you think?"

"Not if you consider that along with the fact that Duggan's finger prints wuz on the money found used to make the Company Store purchase. That had to be a real goof or— on purpose and Ah'm uh' bettin' it was deliberate.

"That is most illogical. There is no way that such an isolated incidental clue would find its way to me."

"Wrong. We are being watched. They–whoever they are—tracking just about every move you make which means they know that you are collaboratin' with me. Now if the good guys are tracking each other, then who are the bad guys? We have been assuming Peters to be tied in with the mob somehow when he just might be undercover. Is Duggan teasing you into contacting' him? If he is, he sure ain't givin' you much to work with. Your finding him was pure luck even though that's what you were after. And Peters; what was his motive for getting you on a plane to Charlottesville? Why did he change his mind? We know that the plane was registered to a Cincinnati suspected mob associate. Did he get wise to Peters? Are we bein' suckered inta' somethin'? Questions, questions. That's all we have. The big one, though, is what do we do now?"

"I think I have already addressed that concern," Said Doctor Cabot.

"How? What have you done.?"

"At the bequest of Mrs. Peters, I intend to pursue the evaluation of her son at UVA. Jenn's nephew is involved in a research project directed at identifying unique neural correlates in auditory processing deficits and I cleared the way for her son to be rescheduled for that evaluation. One of the caveats of that opportunity is that each parent must stand for a personal interview."

"What if one of them is not the real parent?"

"No matter. The history is more for parenting than being a parent."

"Well, Ah suppose that makes sense to you; it don't to me."

"Another reason for the interview is to see if Peters even shows up. He seems to have disappeared or made himself quite scarce for some time now. Where is he? Maybe this will bring him to the fore so that we can begin to extrapolate some tangibles related to our enigma. Are we chasing our collective tails? Are we engaged in activity related to the Governor's edict? It appears to me that Mr. Peters is a critical player in those details."

"Doc" puzzled the sheriff, "You plumb lost me there. Just be careful, and lawful, in anything you do, and I am behind you all the way."

CHAPTER SIXTY-SEVEN

Jɪᴍ ʜᴀᴅ ʙᴇᴇɴ ɪɴ school for several weeks now and tonight was family conference time planned to coincide with first progress report. Miss Annie had fixed all his favorite dishes—Jell-O—and Margie was playing hostess—she had made the Jell-O. Everyone was excited, even Doctor who had ordered in a specially decorated cake for the occasion— with Annie's approval, of course.

The table was set and the family began to assemble. Jenn noticed an extra place setting and inquired whom it was for and Annie said, "Fer your brother, Bill. He has uh way of showin' up fer spe'ul o'casions."

They were preparing to be seated when Jim said boldly, "I wish't ever'body wud hol' hands so Ah kin say a blessin' if'n ya'll don't mind, cuz ya'll are my family an' Ah want to tell God how much Ah 'preciate that."

There was no hesitation as hands were willingly reached for. Jim began. "Lord fer u'long time Ah thought yew din't care 'bout me. Now Ah know better. Thank yew. Amen."

A pin dropping would have sounded like thunder. No one spoke. The spell was broken by Bill who stormed through the kitchen door with a hearty cheer, "Hear there's a celebration for our school boy here tonight. Wouldn't miss it for the world."

Doctor whispered, "Annie you ol' con artist. You knew he was coming all along." Annie just grinned and ordered, "Ya'll start eatin'now."

Bill was the first to ask Jim for details of his studies. "What's the first thing you learned of importance, Jim?"

"Well ah guess ah'd hav'ta say Ah ain't supposed to say ain't," said Jim laughing.

"You're joking aren't you, Jim?"

"Ah am, and, yew notice Ah put the D on there? Ah am real proud to say that we are learn'n to talk in'tell'gee'bul? So's we can ku'mu'nu...talk so we can unner'stan' each other. Air teacher says if'n we don't larn to talk rite, he will have trouble teachi' us. He says Ah.m doin' good."

"He is absolutely correct, Jim and I, for one, think you are doing marvelously," said Doctor.

"Hear, hear." said Jenn and Bill enthusiastically

Margie said, "Eat'ch Jell-O, Jim. Ah made it."

Joyful laugher followed. As the party appeared to be ending, Bill turned to David and asked, "Got a minute for me? Ah've got information on the trial. Ah'm scheduled to present my case next week and Ah'm puttin' you on first. Are you ready?"

"I most assuredly am. I don't think there is an iota of doubt that you will win with the irrefutable evidence revealed to me by your anonymous tipster. Let's go to the library where we can talk."

CHAPTER SIXTY-EIGHT

THE BAILIFF CALLED THE court to ordered by announcing the arrival of the Judge.

"All rise. this court is now in session, the honorable Judge Fred Green presiding."

The Judge lumbered to the dais and fell into his chair and mumbled, "Be seated."

He then turned to the jury and asked them if they were ready. He saw nodded heads and heard whispered yeses. Judge then said, "well then, let's get back to it." The Judge turned to Bill and inquired," Mr. Gullion, Ah believe it's your turn. Are you ready?"

Bill, the lone companion of the Plaintiff, was seated with him at one table. Bill glanced over to the defense table where enough occupants sat to field a basketball team with reserves aplenty.

Bill then faced the Judge and said, "Ah am your honor. A'd like to call as my first witness, Dr. David Cabot."

"Objection, your honor," called the Defense. "Dr. Cabot could not possibly have any pertinent information regarding the case since he arrived into the community long after this claim was filed."

"Mr. Gullion?" the Judge questioned.

"To the contrary, Dr. Cabot is in possession of vital information clearly supporting the Plaintiff's position."

"Objection overruled. Continue Mr. Gullion."

Doctor came forward from the gallery and turned toward the Bailiff.

"Please state your name for the court."

"Dr. David Cabot"

"Please raise your right hand."

"Do you solemnly swear that the testimony you are about to give is the truth, the whole truth and nothing but the truth, so help you God?"

"I do."

"Please be seated."

The jury was obviously acquainted with the Doctor and smiled at him as he passed them on his way to the witness chair.

Bill rose from his table and asked, "Dr. Cabot, do you have any experience with black lung."

"Yes, I do. I have a practice in Boston Knob where over fifty percent of my case- load is men dying from black lung."

Several jury members nodded their heads in agreement.

"The Defense violently responded, "Objection, Your honor, prejudicial."

"Sustained."

"Fact," retorted Doctor.

"Doctor, your standin' in the community don't allow you to sass me. Now act rahght."

Bill accepted the free point and asked the next question. "Please continue, Doctor."

"Black lung disease can be surreptitious. Early on, it may be specifically asymptomatic often mistakenly considered to be the result of smoking or other medical problems like heart disease or asthma both of which can be a comorbid with black lung. Too often simple black lung develops into progressive massive fibrosis before a diagnosis is made, usually after about 10 or 20 years of exposure. However, due to more careful diagnosis we are finding that miners are now dying at a much younger age."

"Objection. Calls for a conclusion not in evidence."

"Over ruled."

"Additionally, the cases of progressive massive fibrosis appear to be growing exponentially—"

"Objection."

"Over-ruled."

"— as reported by the National Institutes of Health."

"Thank you, Doctor. Now let's move on to the diagnosis and treatment of progressive massive fibrosis. How is it diagnosed?"

"We usually see the coal miner first experiencing breathing problems or chronic coughing. However, the preponderance of coal miners ignore all signs of black lung until its insidiousness becomes irreversible—"

"Objection. Calls for a con—"

"Over ruled."

"—repeat, irreversible. I do not believe it is ignorance of the disease that causes coal miners to not seek early detection, but rather the inevitability of the results— "Objection"

—the miner is locked into,—"OBJECTION"—a lifestyle where he is doomed to die no matter— "OBJECTION, YOUR HONOR, OBJECTION. IMMATERIAL, LACKS FOUNDATION!"

"Sustained. Doctor you will save your editorializin' for the newspapers."

Bill grabbed onto the presented opportunity by asking, "Doctor, what percentage of progressive massive fibrosis die of the disease?"

"Objection."

"Over ruled."

"Really no one can say. There is no cure so if they acquire it they expire with it. Too often the miner is aware that he has black lung but cannot afford to quit work so death by the disease is a forgone conclusion. If they had the opportunity to leave the mine once the disease is suspicioned and diagnosed, then progression is stopped and even sometimes reversed."

"Now Doctor, so far your testimony has been in terms of generalities. Let me ask you this. Do you recognize the plaintive?"

"No, I do not."

"Have you seen him before today?"

"I don't know. His name appears in my appointment book and a chart with a number was assigned to that name, but no such chart was found in my records. Recently we had a break-in and the files were—"

"Objection."

"—pilfered."

"Move to strike. Irrelevant."

"Sustained. The reference to a break-in will be removed."

Bill continued. "So, what you are saying is that there are no records of the Plaintiff having been seen in your clinic?"

"No, I did not say that. I said no such chart was found in *my* records."

"Oh? There are other records?"

"Yes, in the stored files of my predecessor at the Boston Knob Medical Clinic, Dr. Stan Fields.

"Objection. Those records are inadmissible for lack of evidence as to their origin and verifiability. Anyone could have put anything they wanted to in those unsecured files."

"Tell me, Doctor, where are those files?" Bill innocently asked.

"They are in a secure vault at the Bramwell Bank and have been ever since the death of Dr. Fields."

Have you seen those files?"

"No. I have not."

"Then how do you know the Plaintiff's charts are in those files?" Bill inquired.

"Two reasons. First, the Plaintiff told me he had been a patient of Dr. Fields, and second, in Dr. Fields's papers was a report on his research on black lung. He had carefully documented every black lung patient he had been following for twenty years and placed them in the bank vault several months before his death."

"Objection, Your honor. This is the rankest form of hearsay."

"We'll see about that. Ah think that we need ta'be doin' a bit of vault divin'. Court will adjourn and meet at the Bramwell Bank at nine in the morning."

Bill and David lagged behind and left the courtroom later to avoid good-will wishers. David lounged in a chair and Bill sat on a table. They were silent for long seconds. Finally, Bill mused, "Ah sure hope you are right about the records in the bank vault. If they are as detailed as you expect, this trial should be over in the morning."

"I am confident it will be. I never met Dr. Fields, but I feel that I have known him for many years. The documentation he left behind could have been written by two different men. His clinical notes were simplistic if not naive. He probably wrote them in the same language he used to explain his findings to his patients. On the other hand, when he was writing in his journal, he used precise, articulate and scientific language suitable for the most sophisticated medical journal. I expect to find his black lung notes to fit that protocol. I do not doubt the existence of those records nor do I doubt the release they will offer to your client and others caught in this dishonest trap set by the mine operators and their collaborators."

"I do so hope you are right," Bill whispered.

Morning came, and the Bank was swarming. The word had spread and newsmen as far away as Charleston were on hand. The Judge had ordered the presence of Sheriff Hare and two of his deputies as crowd control and to assure the security of the contents of the vault. The vault was, in fact, a file cabinet-sized safe-deposit box, the rent having been paid by automatic withdrawal from the clinic trust fund established as a part of Dr. Cabot's ten-year commitment. Limited space demanded the reduction in size of the defense contingent to one, Bill, the jury, the Judge and Sheriff Hare. The bank president did the honors of removing the box and carrying it to a table placed in the center of the lobby that was not yet open for business. The bank president inserted his key into the box and turned to the Judge with the question, "Who has the other key?"

Silence. Nobody moved. Then, from the back of the room a voice called out, "I think Ah do."

The entire room turned as if on a puppet's string to see Jenn holding an unopened envelope toward Sheriff Hare. He took it and passed it to the Judge who checked to see that the seal had not been broken and tore off the end. He tilted the envelope into his hand and *the* key fell out. Judge then handed the key to the Bank President who inserted it into the other slot of the box, turned both keys, and the box, stuffed with medical charts, opened. Without a word, the Judge went to the alphabetically ordered files to that of the plaintiff. He extracted the fat folder and dumped its contents on the table for all to see. There were x-rays, lab reports, clinical notes, and before and after pictures of the Plaintiff. The Judge turned to bill and said, "Mr. Gullion, Ah will entertain a motion for a directed verdict."

CHAPTER SIXTY-NINE

THE COURT DECISION WAS received with the same stoic acceptance as just about every other event in the Mountains: "So what? We won't git nothin' out of hit." As Dr. Cabot considered these events he concluded that, to a very large extent, such an attitude was justified. For over a century the coal miner had been at the mercy of scoundrels of one kind or another. If it wasn't the operators with their company stores, it was the Union with their own agendas not necessarily aimed at helping the man under the mountain. Multiple agencies set out with altruistic goals that often created an unwieldy maze of laws, rules, procedures, etc. that too often worked at cross purposes to lead the applicant to an administrative dead-end. Hence, if a claimant had even a slight chance of obtaining any kind of compensation for the disease, early detection was absolutely necessary to allow time for the resistive application process while, at the same time, continued exposure—out of the necessity to earn a living—was further complicating the disease. Ostensibly, under new federal laws, any miner diagnosed with black lung must be assigned a different job so as to be removed from the offending environment. Claims could be filed under some new federal regulations but total disability was required. Surviving spouses and children of miners who died from black lung were also entitled to monthly benefits.

Unfortunately, it was often an uphill battle to qualify for benefits under either the Federal program or State workers' compensation. The mining industry fought these claims vigorously, leading to lengthy legal battles. The laws favored the miner, the enforcement favored the operator.[25]

Doctor had been researching the beginnings of a campaign to have coal miner's pneumoconiosis (black lung) established as a compensated disability that began in the West Virginia coalfields in the late 1960s. He noted that, as the amount of coal mined increased, so did the number of miners with the disease. Still, he was appalled to discover that black lung was generally ignored. His own medical colleagues contended that 'miner's asthma' was a normal condition for mine workers and actually posed no serious problems with claims that the disease did not show on x-rays. It was a fairly common perception that malingering was rampant causing cynicism toward all claims, even the legitimate ones.

Dr. Cabot's own newspaper presented articles about President Tony Boyle, of the United Mine Workers Association (UMWA), pushing for black lung recognition at a time when an explosion at a Consolidation Coal Company mine occurred taking the lives of over one hundred men. A national television audience heard defenders of the company suggest that disasters were an accepted risk in mining. He was pleased to read that social unrest was thriving and the miner's situation was leading 'Poverty War' volunteers to become engaged in multiple civil protests, encouraging

---

[25]   Even today?

299

the formation of the Black Lung Association to guide a compensation bill through the state legislature. Events in West Virginia made black lung a national issue as Congress passed the Coal Mine Health and Safety Act of 1969. The new law placed strict standards on dust levels and provided federally financed compensation for affected miners, and their widows, and children. However, the number of conditions, exceptions, alternatives, substitutes and a multitude of cross-agency conflictions made the application process near impossible. But, that was the easy part; before submitting the application, a doctor's diagnosis was required. Since most of the doctors were employed by the coal companies, it has been claimed that getting a diagnosis was not always forthcoming. This attitude was incomprehensible to Dr. Cabot who maintained the attitude that he was an advocate for his sick patients and the conscience of malingerers. He would tolerate no shenanigans and he became an expert in spotting them in the Army Medical Corps.

CHAPTER SEVENTY

DOCTOR WAS LUXURIATING WITH his feet propped up on an open file drawer with Bo's cushion serving as padding. Bo did not need it as he was comfortably ensconced upon Doctor's lap receiving an ear rub. They were both approaching Level one REM Sleep when Jenn bounced into the room with the inquiry, "What are you two hound-dogs doin? Ya'll are sleepin! Aren't you?"

Neither dog nor man made any effort to move. Jenn moved in front of them and plopped down on David's lap, whereupon, both dog and man applied affectionate kisses to her protesting face.

"Yuck! Stop that. Ah don't know which of you is the worst. Now cut that out!"

Bo decided he had had enough and jumped to the floor and David pulled Jenn closer and said, "Let's set a wedding day, right this instant."

Jenn, showing no reaction replied, "You got a deal." But right now, you have a visitor; we will discuss those plans tonight at the supper table, rest assured."

Dr. Cabot sent Bo upstairs to Annie and he straightened his desk to receive whomever Jenn had called a 'visitor' instead of a 'patient'. Shortly the door opened and Shirley presented an expensively dressed gentleman with the introduction, "Mr. Peters to see you Doctor.

Doctor Cabot stood slowly—so as to appear neutral—and extended his right hand to be shaken and his left as a gesture to be seated. "Mr. Peters, what can I do for you?"

Peters, seating himself replied in a cultured voice, "It is finally good to meet you face-to-face after all of this time, Doctor. We have much to talk about."

"Oh, and what would that be?"

"Don't play coy with me, Doctor. I am not one of your hillbilly coal miners to whom you can play doctor superior."

Doctor bristled and responded with an equivalent tone. "And you, Mr. Peters, are not communicating with one of your…cronies."

"I am truly sorry, Doctor. I deserved that. Let's start over."

"Agreed. You go first."

"I came into this community with less than altruistic purposes. You may have heard that I had connection with… the mob, and that is partially true. Because of my wife, whom I love beyond life itself, I found myself beholden to… the mob. She is totally unaware of that…obligation and that she and her son, I am not his father, are…in danger if I fail to fulfil my obligation to them. My job has been to assess this area as a staging point for a tri-state crime syndicate involved in cigarette, drug—primarily the growth and transporting of marijuana—and the mass production of illegal liquor. I have been slacking in the performance of my duties—intentionally—and we are in danger of reprisals from my employers…"

"Please, an inquiry if you do not mind my interruption. Who is the young man seen working with you, and why did you choose to locate in Bland County so far away from your assigned territory?"

"Obfuscation and security. You see, no one knew we were living there under a different name until you and your nurse blundered in, and as for Tom, he is a government agent of some kind, which one, I don't know and he would not say. It would appear that his interests lie around legal matters related to miner's medical welfare. I did see a letterhead from a West Virginia Senator but it didn't tell me anything. Also, he made frequent trips to Charleston. I had made contact with the West Virginia State police early on but I never received a response. I know Tom had some sort of inside connection because he mentioned your possible involvement in State Law Enforcement. That's one of the reasons I am here."

Doctor Cabot was staggered by this revelation but he thought he had covered adequality and quickly ask Mr. Peters a tactical question. "Do you know who the young man was that was found in Bluestone dam?"

"Yes, unfortunately, I did. He was a bagman for my employers. He brought in the cash that was used to buy the inventory of the craft store your people opened in Freeman. I don't know how it happened but he was found drowned in the swimming pool of the motel down on Interstate 81 where he was staying near the airport. He was dead when we got there and I stayed away from him. Tom went over and knelt down beside him as if to check his coat pocket. He stood up empty handed so I know he didn't take anything off of him."

"Could he have put something in his pocket," inquired Doctor.

"Yes, that's quite possible. Oh, and Tom did take possession of the boy's bag from his room. He had shown the management his credentials so they were willing to get it off of their hands."

"Did he open the bag?"

"Yes, only to check the contents, then he gave the bag to me. Now can I continue why I am here?"

"Oh, sorry. Please go on," said Doctor Cabot.

"Well…first, I know who you are."

"Not news. As a physician there are many people who know who I am," said Doctor Cabot.

"Not what I know. You are a deputized county cop."

Doctor sprung from his chair as if he had received an electric shock. "How did you find…."

"Simple, you met with the State Boys, the State Boys met with the Feds and Tom is a Fed. He was aware of the bind I am in and he advised me to surrender myself to the 'friendly's, namely you, so that I can be charged with a lesser crime than what the Feds would hang on me."

"My good man, I am not 'hanging' anything on anybody. I know of no crime against the State of West Virginia or Mercer County that you have committed that warrants your arrest. Moreover, even if you had, I will not be the one to arrest you. In fact, based on your story today, my reason for being an officer of the law has been satisfied and, as soon as I can get to the Sheriff, I am handing in my badge."

"But, I have information of a conspiracy to commit a crime in the State by a known Crime Organization; Won't that work?"

"Conceivably, yes, but I am not the suitable inquisitor. My suggestion to you is that you go upstairs and have Annie provide you with a cup of coffee and something to eat and I will have a confidential tête-à-tête with the Sheriff. He is a stalwart, honest man whom I have grown to respect and he, I'm sure, will properly advise you. If he says you need to be arrested, I shall comply with your request. I will surrender you and my badge simultaneously. Satisfactory?"

"Yes sir, Officer."

CHAPTER SEVENTY-ONE

DOCTOR CABOT PLACED A call to Sheriff Hare post haste. The Sheriff's office answered after a short wait for a connection. He informed the secretary that the call was a bit urgent and was told the Sheriff was out in the County somewhere. Doctor asked if he was in radio range and was informed that he was. Doctor then requested that the Sheriff be given the following message: "Officer needs assistance, Code 2, Deputy Cabot." Minutes later Shirley informed Doctor that the Sheriff was five minutes out, Code 3. "Lights and siren, hot dog!" responded Doctor. He was beginning to enjoy himself as the Mercer County Crime Wave appeared to be waning.

Sheriff rolled into the clinic parking lot with lights and siren orchestrating a symphony of urgency. He was in the door before the last note faded into pianissimo. Shirley pointed to the back of the facility and said, "He's waitin' fer you back 'air."

Doctor heard the commotion as well as the whining of the siren and met the Sheriff in the hallway. "Come on into my office. I have noteworthy news for you. I believe I have unraveled all of our mysteries as being in a single ball of yarn."

"Your message sounded hopeful. What do you have for me?"

"I have the solution to the mystery in custody upstairs drinking coffee with Annie."

"What? In custody? Who…in custody? You don't have arrest powers! I told you, you wouldn't have to. Didn't I?"

"Yes, that is what you said. But you did not say I could not, correct?"

"Okay, forget that. Tell me what you have."

"Sit down and I will lead you through the solution. Here is a tablet and pencil if you want to diagram it as we go along. First, you had a mysteriously drowned boy, young man really, in The Bluestone Lake. Next, he was found to have chlorinated water in his lungs rather than the lake water where he was found. He had a cryptic note in his pocket, in French that directs the finder to a 'Capt. Cabot in Bluefield'. I remembered a word that led me to recall an incident in Korea where, and by whom, that unique word was used and it provided a clue as to the possible writer of the note found on the drowning victim. You found a fingerprint on the note belonging to a Tom Duggan who had served in the US Army and that triggered a memory as to how I knew him and how he had served in the same unit as I. Duggan's prints were found on the money used to buy the inventory of the store our ladies have established to sell their art work. Now, my informant can put all of this together for you. Let's go see him."

Sheriff Hare followed Doctor Cabot up the private stairs to the kitchen. Just as they reached the top Doctor stopped and whispered to the sheriff, "Wait, they appear to be having an intense conversation. Annie has a way of gleaning information from reluctant sources. Let's see what they are talking about."

Annie was talking. "Then why'did'cha tell folks ya'll wuz mair'ed if'n yew ain't?' she inquired.

"Because she is the source of my conundrum," answered Mr. Peters.

"Wh'tha heck air a conum'brum?" asked Miss Annie.

"Problem, puzzle? I found her and her little boy huddled in the entry way of my office one morning on my way to work. I confronted her more with aggravation than anything else since she was blocking my door. Then she looked up at me; her face was a mess. She had been beaten. The child just had a blank look on his face and never spoke. There is a doctor in our building and I asked him to take a cursory look at them to see if they needed to go to an emergency room. He checked her over and said she was just bruised and nothing appeared to be broken. Whoever had beaten her knew what they were doing. He said that the boy appeared to be severely retarded."

"Ah got'uh retarded dotter, so Ah know all'uh'bout that. She is uh Mongol'un idjit. Doctor Cabot says Ah ort to call her a Down Sym'drom. Wha'cha do with them?"

"I am an accountant so I don't need a big office, so there was not room to bring them in there. So, I took them to my apartment. I'm single so I have plenty of room for them. I really did not have the time to search for a home for abused women but I did call the police and the welfare department there in Cincinnati and they told me there was little they could do unless the woman would come forward and file a complaint, which Angie would not do. Therefore, I was forced into the role of caretaker for them."

"Did'cha mind doin' that?" asked Annie.

"Not at all. We were doing quite well until one day I came home from work and found a rough looking man there and Angie had been worked-over again. She made the mistake of going back to where she had been working to pick up her belongings, when she encountered the man who claimed she was indebted to him and owed him a lot of money to be 'worked off' at his establishment. He asked Angie what her 'new man' did that he could afford her and she told him that I was an accountant. The man brightened and said I could work off Angie's debt by providing services for a company in which he was part owner that turned out to be a crime syndicate looking into moving into Appalachia. At first all they wanted me to do, they said, was go in and see if moving into the state could be profitable, and if the people were conducive to mob control. I did that and that's where I am now."

Doctor decided he had heard enough and he and the Sheriff entered the room. He addressed Annie. "Well Miss Annie, how are you doing with my guest?"

Annie spotted the Sheriff and greeted him. "Howdy, Sonny. Yew doin' al'rite?"

"Fine Miss Annie. Me and the Doctor want to talk with Mr. Peters here. You can stay if you want'a but it would probably be borin' for you."

"Ah got work'ta do anyhow. Ya'll go right ahead. I'll be over in the cookin' part of'th house if'n yew need me."

"|Thank you, Miss Annie, for entertaining Mr. Peters for me. I am sure you did a commendable job."

He then turned to the sheriff and said, "In the interest of time I am going to provide an abridged version of what Mr. Peters elucidated for me earlier that prompted my call to you, Sheriff. Is that amenable to the both of you?"

Both indicated the affirmative.

"Okay. This is the way I perceive the scenario developing.

"One: Tom Duggan had given the note to Peters to give to me, reason unknown. Peters put the note in his coat pocket. He was wearing that same coat when they found the drowning victim. Peters covered the dead man's body, out of pity or respect, with his jacket. He left the scene without retrieving his coat. Someone put that coat on the victim, perhaps to clear the possible crime scene, before he was thrown into the lake, most likely by someone with the syndicate that moved the body, but not Peters, because he was with Duggan. At the scene of the actual drowning, the motel manager handed over the victim's bag to Duggan who opened it, checked its contents, closed it and gave it to Peters leaving his finger prints when it was submitted as payment for the crafts store's inventory.

Two: Sheriff's Office extracted the body from the lake, found the note bearing the title and name 'Capt. Cabot', and location, Bluefield; this appears to be more than coincidence. Why it was in French remains a puzzle. Autopsy revealed that water in the man's lungs was not lake water but chlorinated, confirming that the victim had died somewhere else. I surmised that the reason for the note had to do with Duggan's concern for Peters' predicament thinking that I might be in Bluefield practicing and could help him with a solution.

Three: Sheriff questioned why I had my lawyer investigating Peters and informed me that his office was also curious. This brought about my involvement in the mystery causing me to search my memory for the identity of the note writer. As often happens, a totally unrelated event prompted the recollection of an exchange I had experienced with a Sargent Duggan on my final day at the MASH Unit in Korea and completed the circle of evidence except for his position as a Federal Agent. This knowledge came when Jenn and I were directed to the residence of Peters in Bland County, Virginia by a restaurateur who is a relative of

Duggan before his military service and thought her mother had seen him at a home nearby. We went to that home and was greeted at the door by Mrs. Peters who informed us that Duggan and her husband were both Federal Agents.

Four brings us up to where we are right at this moment. Do you have anything to add Mr. Peters? Sheriff? Questions?" tossing the initiative to the Sheriff allowing him to broach the overheard conversation between Annie and Peters.

Sheriff Hare pondered the question for several seconds and appeared hesitant when he spoke. "Mr. Peters, Doctor and I overheard a portion of your conversation with Miss Annie. Sorry about eavesdroppin' but right now we are beyond bein' polite about this whole mess. You seemed very honest with her. Were you?"

"Yes sir, I was and I'll expand on that statement if you want."

"Later. You said you are single. Is that correct?"

"Yes."

"And you had never seen the woman and child before you found them at your door?"

There was a long pause before Peters answered. "Well... no, that's not exactly true. I had seen her at the lounge where she worked a time or two."

"So, she had not randomly selected your doorway?"

"No. She had been there before."

"Is there a reason you are unwillin' to tell us about your relationship? Were ya'll close? Datin'? What?"

"I had met her at the lounge where she worked. We talked a little. Her bosses kept a close eye on her. They didn't want her getting too close to the customers."

Sheriff Hare paused thoughtfully before asking, "Were you just another customer?"

Peters looked first at The Sheriff and then at the Doctor. He covered his face with his hands and leaned back in his chair and whispered, "No, I am not just another customer. It's complicated."

That's' what ya'll always say when you are backed in ta 'a corner. The best I can tell, so far, you ain't done nothin' that will buy you any real hard jail time. Why don't you quit beatin' about th'bush and tell us the whole story? Just what in the tarnation are you doin' in our part of the country? It's obvious you ain't here handin' out *Watchtower* Tracts or sellin' Fuller Brushes. You are knee deep in this mob stuff, ain't'cha?"

Doctor Cabot interrupted saying, "Sheriff, I think that is what he has been trying to undo for the past couple of years. If he was enthusiastic about his assignment I think we would have seen major criminal activity occurring. I think he is frightened because of his lackadaisical efforts towards gaining a criminal foothold hereabouts. Am I not correct Mr. Peters?"

"Maybe, maybe not." Interjected the Sheriff. "Nobody stays that clean that long and lives to tell about it. That business down at that motel was a hit gone wrong wasn't it?" Sheriff aimed at Peters. "You were the target of an unhappy mob action. Somehow you escaped without a scratch and that young man took the brunt of that action. Why did Duggan give you that bag of money? If he's a Fed why did he allow more criminal activity? As far as Ah am concerned you are just another slick Yankee comin' down here to take advantage of us poor ignorant hillbillies."

"Aren't you being a bit harsh?" asked Doctor Cabot.

"Heck no. Think about it. Would the head guy of a big-time mob turn over, even a minor questionably legal job, to an unseasoned outsider? There's more to it than that. What do they hold over you that is an iron clad guarantee? They's gotta' be something more than you have told us. If you don't open up with the truth, Ah'm gonna just turn you over to the State Police and let things take its course, mainly cause this ain't no local matter. On the other hand, we can make it a local matter if you explain, in full, how you really got in this mess. Maybe we can straighten it out, real quiet like, among ourselves if you will just open up."

Peters sat silently looking at the floor for several moments. Finally, he spoke. "I do have an accounting practice in Cincinnati. My office, if you can call it that, was in the same block as the nightclub that was the...uh... headquarters of a southern Ohio Don. They...gambled there and I got into them for big bucks with no way out. They had use for me as a legitimate accountant and I thought that would work off the obligation, instead it got worse. As a part of my 'job' I got in deeper and deeper to where I was as trusted as any member of crime organization can be, I suppose."

"How did the woman become enmeshed in the situation?" asked Doctor.

"Pretty much like I described it to Miss Annie. That part was true."

"She worked at the nightclub?" Asked Sheriff.

"Yes. She was...is...very pretty and she worked as a barmaid and sometimes sang. She had studied music at the University of Cincinnati. She was very good. Wanted to go on Broadway. Having that idiot baby ended that dream, so she worked in nightclubs to make a living. Watching out for her was the only good thing I have ever done. What's going to happen to her now?"

"Not my problem," uncharacteristically mumbled the sheriff. "What I need now is for you to quit beatin' 'bout th' bush and tell me just what the heck you been doin' here in my county for the past two years. Whatever it is it ain't been legal. Just how illegal it's been is to be determined. We can probably convict you of somethin' local so you can serve your time in my jail if you just come clean. Doctor seems to be on your side. How about justifyin' his faith in you?"

Peters paused for a long time and finally sighed deeply and started. "Mainly I have been trying to set up marijuana farms and coordinating with the Mexican growers to grow a hybrid plant that has the hardiness of the West Virginia natural growing plant with the potency of the Mexican less hardy plant. There is an abundance of growing areas on the periphery of abandoned strip mines that looked like a possibility for unobtrusive growing area and also, abandoned mines that were thought by the Mob to be good places to make meth. I used several ways to explore both options and sent my recommendations to the Boss. He took it from there."

"Did any money change hands beside the Craft Store purchase?" Asked the Sheriff.

"No. All I did was find the sites and explore them."

"Did you have permission or were you accompanied by the owner or owners or an approved agent of the same?"

"No."

The Sheriff sat thoughtfully for a very long time. He stood and walked around the room. He then declared that he had to speak with the County DA before he could make a decision. He asked Doctor Cabot to accompany him as he left the room to make a phone call. The Sheriff had a plan that he wanted to propose to Miss Annie and the Doctor. The three engaged in a very serious discussion and came to a suitable agreement after which the plan was presented to Peters by the Sheriff: "Okay, here's what we're gonna' do.

The DA is goin' to endite you on two charges: First, criminal trespass with intent to commit a crime, and Second, Criminal activity with intent. You plead guilty to these charges and the DA will reduce the charges to Misdemeanors with one-year in the Mercer County Jail. If you have any assets they will be liquidated and used to provide for the rehabilitation of Mrs. Peters. You will also be sentenced to 2080 hours of community service, to be served concurrently with the jail time at the discretion of the County Sheriff who needs an accountant. Are you Agreeable to this?"

"What about Angie and her boy? I can't just abandon them."

"You really have no choice. As they say 'you did the crime, you gotta' serve the time'. But Doctor thought about that. "Miss Annie to going to take on Angie as an apprentice paid for out of your impounded funds. The child will be home-schooled by a therapist for one year giving Angie time to get her life together. She is free to stay, but not obligated, for up to a year. At that time, she will be without a criminal record to take over if the two of you want."

"I don't deserve it." responded Peters.

"Indubitably," said Doctor.

CHAPTER SEVENTY-TWO

Dr. Cabot had badgered Jenn's brother into sitting with Tod Peters to satisfy possible doubts concerning his rights. Bill had agreed. The two were seated at the defense table. The District Attorney sat at a table by himself and Dr. Cabot and Sheriff Hare sat in the gallery behind the rail.

The Judge came through the door from his chambers as said, "remain seated. Mr. DA what have you for me today.?"

"Your honor we have Mr. Tod Peters who chooses to plead guilty. He is charged with Criminal Trespass and the intent to introduce hybrid Cannabis in the State. Since the laws on Cannabis are grossly unclear in most states we agreed to drop the Criminal intent charge and agree to a Misdemeanor charge on all counts. We suggest one year in the county jail and 1080 hours of community service."

"How do you plead, Mr. Peters?"

"Guilty, your Honor."

"Counsel, you discussed these conditions with your client?"

"Mr. Peters, do you understand that by pleading guilty you lose the right to a jury trial?"

"Yes, your Honor."

"Do you give up that right?"

"Yes, Your Honor."

"Do you understand that you are waiving your privilege against self-incrimination?"

"Yes sir."

"Were you in any way forced into accepting this settlement?"

"No, Your Honor."

"Are you pleading guilty because you did, in fact, engage in the charges against you?"

"Yes."

"Mr. Peters you are hereby sentenced to one year in the county jail, and 1080 hours of Community Service to be determined on a day-by-day basis by the County Sheriff. Court adjourned. Dr. Cabot, will you remain for a moment?"

Doctor moaned and whispered to the Sheriff. "Now what have you gotten me into?"

The DA walked up to Doctor and the Sheriff and put his hand on the Sheriff's shoulder with a happy smile on his face. "What do you think the Judge has in mind for our own personal Sherlock? Let's go with him and find out," he said tugging on the Sheriff's sleeve.

Sheriff said, "Yeah, let's."

The Judge turned from hanging up his robe when the Doctor and his tag-alongs walked into his chambers. "Why the entourage, Doctor, am I so intimidating that you need a defense team?" the Judge joked.

"Your Honor, I have been shanghaied so many times recently that I do not require an engraved invitation to see another one in the offing."

"Evidence of your intuitive skills in play and that is exactly why *we* have invited you here."

"The emphasis on the 'we' is ominous, Judge," noted Dr. Cabot. "Just what has this inter-legal conclave conjured up to disrupt my efforts got to do to effectively practice medicine in your County?"

"Humor aside, Doctor, we were quite impressed with your intuitive skills in deciphering the puzzle initiated by the drowning at Bluestone. But more importantly you triggered an awareness of the diversity of a more sophisticated crime element in our County; indeed, in our State. We have been wearing blinders regarding the view of crime but this recent event points to a multifaceted new-wave of activities that function outside of intentions such as the new black lung legislation. The laws are there but unethical methods are circumventing their intent. You might say that thwarting the reception of a benefit created by industrial malfeasance cannot be equated to the manufacture and distribution of an illegal drug but, you would be wrong. In each, a beneficial law has been broken, resulting in the suffering of some citizens for the profit of others. Ordinary police departments do not possess the expertise to investigate such crimes. You have demonstrated that you have those skills and we are, therefore, opening up an opportunity for you to continue in your role as a deputy Sheriff or some other designee of official law officer where your authority goes beyond county lines…"

"Judge," interrupted Cabot. "I am immensely honored by your confidence in me but, truly, I am not indoctrinated in the legalities, foundations and nuances of the task you are suggesting for me. I…"

"We are well ahead of you on that concern. You will function as a team member so that you will not work in a vacuum. Just as you collect data as a physician and submit it to laboratories and specialists, you will also collect data related to your skill set and submit it to those who support you. One, for example is Captain Blake, Commander of the Governor's Taskforce on Organized Crime."

"I know him," said Dr. Cabot.

"There will be others like him. He has suggested that you attend the Department of Justice's upcoming training session on criminal investigation to be held in Washington followed up by a shorter session at Quantico. The State will pay your expenses. The Health Department will help by providing residents to fill your practice while you are away."

"You have presented me with far more than I can assimilate off-handed. Right now, the entire scenario is so convoluted it will require careful consideration. Even though you say the Health Department will provide supplemental medical assistance, I cannot give up my practice for a number of reasons, the most limiting being my agreement with Dr. Fields' estate. I have not yet met my obligation under that contract and I intend to stay on if for no other reason than my extensive involvement in black lung. I will not surrender that to anyone, much less a neophyte wet-behind-the-ears doctor. Furthermore. I have promised my new bride to be that I will not postpone our wedding still another time."

Sheriff Hare broke in excitedly, "Hey, why don't you use the training trips for a honeymoon? Ah bet Jenn would love that."

"If you were just married would you want to sit in a hotel room while you mate was involved in training?" asked the DA. "Heck, I know I wouldn't."

"Just a thought," said the Sheriff apologetically.

"I think we are through here today. Doctor, take time to mull it over, discuss it with your new bride and we can discuss it further later. Let's all go home."

CHAPTER SEVENTY-THREE

DAVID APPROACHED JENN WITH the new offer with extreme trepidation. Jenn was a direct approach person; she was leery of subterfuge or contrived scenes. So, the direct approach it was, with one exception. He went to the company store and acquired a pint of her favorite ice-cream. He invited her to the library after supper whereupon he presented her with a heaping bowl. She willing accepted it, took a generous bite and asked him, "Alright, what have you done now?"

He feigned wounded and piteously pleaded, "Now why would you assume ill of my offering you your favorite sweet-stuff?"

"Because you don't have a deceitful bone in your body and I can see through you like a window glass. You know I would follow you into the depths of evil if you just ask me," Jenn said almost pleadingly.

"Then you see the purest of heart with intentions free of decent or ruse," David responded, relieved.

"Okay, get on with it. Am'm listenin' with breathless anticipation," Jenn whispered.

Now assured, David continued, "I have been asked to take on the role of a special investigator for medico-legal crime in the State. I would not give up my practice, particularly my black-lung research that Dr. Fields initiated. Judge Shaffer, the Sheriff, and the DA approached me after the Peters trial. They had previously discussed the nature of my unique acuity in the differentiation of factual evidence and decided that the skill would be most helpful in the new-wave crime armada, particularly those medically and legally entwined."

Jenn interrupted Doctor. "Hey, it's me you are a'talkin' To. Talk Plain English."

"Yes, my hillbilly articulator. What I am elucidating to you is employment that has a fluid job description that allows for a position…."

"Whoa, whoa, whoa…What did I just ask you to do?" Jenn implored.

"Alright! I am talking about a brand-new position that I would make up as I go along. Simple enough for you?"

"More like it. Go on."

"Fraud and crime are moving into our every-day lives in many ways. Here and in our surrounding counties, we see a conspiracy amongst certain practitioners, legal, medical, etc., and coal companies, for example, to defraud workers out of legal entitlements. Legal channels are being used to funnel prescription drugs, i.e. opioids, for nonmedical purposes, through criminal brokers. Funds appropriated for education are siphoned off for non-essential administration salaries and expensive travel. One we just recently halted, albeit temporarily, is the manufacture of meth around here. The data need to prepare indictments on these perpetrators are generally above the skill levels of the average sheriff's department; therefore, being instituted is an experimental position that would fill in on a trial basis. The decision to employ me in the position is because of my involvement in the Peters' case and the testimony in the black lung trial, in which you held the key, pun intended. I will reduce my time at the Clinic to black lung only and hire two new residents to handle routine activities."

"Sounds good," Jenn said with doubt in her voice, "But you just turned our house, if I am permitted to call it that, into a small hotel with all of the required chores. Is that goin' to be my responsibility? For sure Annie can't do it. And the Clinic; who's gonna run it? ME? Back up here ol' future mate, uh, mine, and face reality."

"I have given considerable thought to just those concerns; you are right that Annie cannot manage such an additional load. She should retire, but she would vehemently rebel, so we would promote her to the equivalent of "chef" and hire two additional persons to do the housekeeping as well as kitchen helper. I think Jim would gladly come back as maintenance "chief." We hire a nurse to accomplish the tasks that you have been managing in the Clinic and, as for you, you will be general manager of the whole operation. That way, you can manage by delegation after we are married."

"My goodness you have been a busy li'l bee, haven't you? But ah think you have forgot one tiny little issue. Who's gonna pay for all of these new people? Our out-go is already mor'n our in-come the way it is and you're talkin' about hirin' more people? Dream on my love!" Jenn noted.

"That too has been solved," David countered. "I checked with the bank regarding the position of the Trust Fund, and it is in excellent position having been collecting interest at 6% compounded daily for a very over 20 years. Therefore, according to the trustee, I am allowed to spend the interest anytime irrespective of my ten-year obligation, so long as it relates to the welfare and care of our patient population. That changes if and when I fulfill my obligation at which time I become co-trustee and principal manager of the account. In reality I now function as a co-trustee with the interest reserves and can spend them as I chose. We have far more than we need in the short run and by the time those funds run short I will have assembled a self-sustaining organization from grants and contracts."

"What? A what of what? A self what? What on earth are you a'talkin' about?" Jenn implored.

Given the benefits to the State and Federal Government, one or more of them would probably provide resident-level doctors to cover the Clinic side of our activities. All we would have to do is provide room and board for them. I believe, based on existing black lung funding, that we can get funds from that source. One more thing, since the Federal Government is involved in most of the regulations that I would be dealing with, I should take a two-week administrative indoctrination course at the Justice Department in Washington DC. However, that is not a requirement since my work will be for the State. My thinking is that we could get married now, go on a honeymoon, and then possibly you go along for the training. It would give us a great opportunity to see all of the sites in the Capitol."

"That would work. Let's get busy gettin' married," Jenn bubbled.

Without their noticing, Annie had appeared at the doorway to the library. She was crying as she said, "David, I think my Lonnie's dyin,' will you check on him?"

"Lonnie?" Ask Doctor

"Annie's Husband, silly; you know that," Answered Jenn.

"Oh, how thoughtless of me. Of course."

Jenn reached the door first with Doctor close behind. Jenn called out to Doctor,

"You go on with Annie. I'll get your bag and follow."

By the time Jenn reached Annie's house out back, Doctor was checking for a pulse.

As Jenn entered the cottage, Doctor looked up and said, "Annie was right."

"About what?'

"He WAS dying."

CHAPTER SEVENTY-FOUR

WEDDINGS TRANSPOSE REALITY INTO a fairyland for women and dragons and dungeons for men. Women charge forward with great passion while men cower in bewilderment. The mansion was in absolute chaos. The wedding date had been cast in stone by Annie and Mrs. Cabot, and nothing short of a volcanic eruption of a local mountain would stop those plans. The ceremony was in the Bluewell Union Church, childhood church-home of Jenn and all of her brothers and sisters, lovingly constructed by their father and other men of the congregation during the Great Depression.

The church was a bland as the interior of a building could be. Yet, every conjunction met with a crispness hard to achieve by the most accomplished of craftsmen. All surfaces were of stained wood including the floors and gabled ceiling. The windows were of straight cathedral with plain opaque glass. A simple embellishment-free box-like pulpit stood centered on a single-step ten-foot-deep platform that extended the full width of the "nave." Double doors entered directly into a single aisle down the center into the interior, dead-ending at the pulpit with straight backed wooden benches lining each side. Annie and Mrs. Cabot

Leslie W. Dalton, Jr.

had taken a very practical approach to decorating such a simple building: live trees and shrubs, as tall as eight feet and in full bloom, right out of the local hills. The effect was a wooded grotto requiring no other enhancement.

All was ready. Mrs. Cabot had assisted Annie in the selection of a dress for this most special occasion from her favorite catalog, Montgomery Ward. She chose a navy-blue dotted-swiss coat-dress with white lace trim and a single seam pocket. Accessories included a white cloche hat and low heel white pumps.

The Boston Knob community was there en masse wearing their Sunday-go-to- meeting best. A sea of artificial flowers flowed wildly on top of the heads of the women. The men were in their nondescript usual resplendent in 1930s vintage well-worn hand-me-down wool suits and hair slicked down with great care.

The first four rows of both sides were reserved for family filled with all of the bride's living brothers and sisters, their spouses as well as a large contingent of nieces and nephews. Cars, pickup trucks, and even a couple of horse-drawn buggies lined the road outside the church. The Delph school playground was filled as was parking spaces at Frankie's, and the Sunny South Market.

From behind a pair of large rhododendrons came the mournful sound of a Dobro playing Pachelbel's Canon. The Bride, escorted by her father, entered the wide-open double doors. She wore a white off-the-shoulder A-line satin appliqued dress with tulle overlay that revealed titillating cleavage a bit bold for the time and place. She carried a wedding spray of locally-grown small white carnations. The Groom was handsome in a grey two-button jacket and straight pants. He wore a single white carnation in his lapel.

They met at the pulpit, turned to face The Reverend Doctor Stenson, and were wed.

The party walked the short distance to the La Saluda behind the church moving like a herd of Wildebeest. There they found tubs of iced RC Cola, a selection of Nehi fruit-flavored drinks. An assortment of food was available including hotdogs.

The wedding cake was a very large home-baked double-layer sheet cake adorned with a border of small red carnations.

The dance floor was open, and a band played an assortment of music suited to the heterogeneity of the crowd. David and Jenn broke the ice by dancing the first dance to Sentimental Journey, after which they said their farewells and departed for venues undisclosed in the faithful ol' Packard.

Given no problems they would return, after a short honeymoon, ready to embrace a new lifestyle and a new mission devoted to the log-standing plight of the perpetually downtrodden people of Appalachia.

Lightning Source UK Ltd.
Milton Keynes UK
UKHW010714120821
388748UK00001B/207